# Savor

## Isabel Jolie

*"It always pays to dwell slowly on the beautiful things—the more beautiful the more slowly." – Atticus*

# PROLOGUE



"Give it to me straight."

The bright lights hurt. Hell, my whole body fucking aches. Low-level nausea surfaces. An IV is inserted in my arm, and there's a catheter linked to a place I'd rather not acknowledge. My recall is hazy. I am uncertain how long I've been here. The screen to my right shows a steady heartbeat and emits regular beeps.

The surgeon before me has a clipboard in hand, saggy skin below his droopy eyes, pale, thin lips in a solid frown, and unkempt, bushy eyebrows with white strands going every which way.

"Tell me. Whatever it is." Jesus, I can handle it. Anything he throws my way, I'll be fine. One foot in front of the other. I'm a fighter, not a quitter.

He stops staring at his clipboard. "You are one lucky man. We almost lost you, but you pulled through."

"Don't look so happy about it." If he thinks almost dying will get me down, he's got another think coming.

His gaze falls on me, and his lips turn up into a semblance of a smile. "Do you have any family we can call?"

A female voice interrupts. "I've asked. There's no family to call, but his friends will be back."

My friends. My business partners. My memory produces a flash of faces. Sitting in the guest chair. Bent over phones and laptops. They've been here.

I twist my head on the pillow. Near the back wall there's a Black woman in bright-colored scrubs.

"Okay. Well, how are you feeling?"

"Like I got shot." This man's bedside manner sucks. He doesn't need to pussyfoot. "My arm is still attached. Right?" He nods. At the moment, my right arm is strapped to me, and I haven't attempted to move it. "Is it going to work okay?"

"There's no reason to suspect you won't regain full mobility."

*Then why the fuck are you so glum?*

"Three bullets. You're lucky." His eyes scan the monitor as he repeats my assessment. It's like he has dismissed me. "My last patient, not so lucky. Be grateful."

That little addition hits me hard in the chest. Harder than you'd think, given I served in Afghanistan and lost most of my team in an ambush.

The doctor moves over me and lifts bandages. I presume checking his handiwork.

"How's the pain?"

"Manageable. No more pain meds." The bushy eyebrows lift. "Please."

"You don't mean that."

"Yes. I do."

"Do you have an addiction?" He flips through papers.

"No. But I don't like the way these drugs are making me feel."

"How do you feel?"

"Hazy. Can't remember…" I trail off. I don't know exactly what I can't remember, but I have flashes, not succinct recall.

"That's from the surgery."

"I'd rather not—"

"Mr. Thompson." He waits until my gaze meets his to continue. "You essentially had three surgeries. You need the pain medication."

He drones on about the medication he's giving me, about my expected recovery, what's normal to experience and what's not. I listen, but my eyelids are heavy, and the room grows dark.

When I wake, the television at the end of the room is on, but it's silent. The chair creaks, and I slowly turn my head. Wolf.

They asked about family, and this guy is mine. He's the only person listed in my will. He leans over, elbows on his knees, phone in hand. Aryan Wolfgang, Wolf for short. If Wolf's here, then that means…

"All good?" I ask.

Surprised, he lifts his head. He looks tired, about as tired as that surgeon who was here earlier. But he smiles.

"We stopped it?"

"No. It happened. To a limited degree. We stopped the bulk of it." My eyes widen, and the green graph quickens, visually reflecting what's going on inside my chest. "It's over. Markets are rebounding."

"Damn." I process this bit of news for what is probably not the first time.

We'd been hearing whispers about an attack on the US electrical grid. A flash of the men in the basement hits me. Men dressed like utility workers. Gunfire.

"Spectre took responsibility. Kane couldn't resist building his notoriety. Now he's on the FBI's most wanted list."

Wolf crosses his arms over his chest and grins. I understand why. We're going to get that fucker.

# THE ONE WHERE
# STELLA GOES OUT



"I can't believe I let you talk me into coming here."

The bartender slides our fancy martini glasses filled to the rim with sugary sweet blue. He doesn't spare us a glance, but I can't help staring at him. I thought you had to be twenty-one to serve alcohol in California, but I swear the guy looks like he's one of my son's friends. And my son is fifteen.

"What's wrong with this place?" Jenn searches the crowd, her posture articulating that this place is fantastic and I have issues. She might be right. "We can go someplace else after we finish these drinks. I think the place across the street has a good wine list."

So does the Hotel Californian, our first stop of the night. We're in the touristy area of Santa Barbara, near the beach.

"I'm sure all the overpriced bars in the area have an extensive wine list. Doesn't change the fact I would need to order the least expensive bottle, which is probably headache inducing. Especially after these." I pointedly clink Jenn's glass.

"Not tonight, sweetheart. I'm buying." She throws a manicured finger in the air to squelch my protest. "We are celebrating your new job. Six figures, baby! I am so proud of you."

"Well, I don't have that paycheck yet."

"Which is why it's on me." I usually fight her when she wants to pay, but since she chose this pricey place and she wants to celebrate, I suppose I'll let her.

I smile and sip more of my drink. I'm still reeling from my change of luck. I've taken the I'll-believe-it-when-I-get-the-paycheck approach. It's not every day someone offers to double your salary.

"My girl has gone from secretary to director of human resources. And what's the company do?"

"It's a security firm."

"Like home alarm systems?"

"No. It's more than that." My face heats because I don't completely understand everything they do. But I will. Once I start, I'll be handling things like health insurance. I'll need to get the elevator pitch down. I signed a confidentiality agreement, so there are some things I can't share with Jenn. Working for an accountant was easier. No one ever asks what an accountant does. "I'm HR." I shrug.

"With a six-figure salary!" she squeals.

Jenn is an elementary school teacher, so she's especially enthused by the six-figure status. She's been my best friend since our kids were in Kindermusik together as non-crawling infants. She's the one friend who stood by me during my divorce. And even though her husband's career took off and they now live in a swanky house in the hills with a fantastic view of the Pacific Ocean, she's remained my friend. Even though her husband is still friends with my asshole ex, she's kept me around. I love her. It's a deep, eternal love. The kind that can overlook her refusal to sit at my house tonight, drink wine, and binge Netflix.

"Now that you're making the money, are you going to be moving it on up?"

"That's laughable." I grab a menu and scan it. None of these eighteen-dollar appetizers are particularly appealing, but I don't drink often enough to skip food.

"Why is it laughable?" She sounds serious.

I look up from the menu, and it hits me how clueless she really is. It's not her fault. She hasn't had to budget off of a teacher's salary in, well, forever.

"First, I have credit card debt to pay down. Second, my automobile is eighteen years old. Third, Ethan leaves for college in three years." I squeal this last part because the notion increases my anxiety.

"It burns me up every single time I think of the twat asking you to pay half of Ethan's tuition. What an asshole. He makes as much money as Terrell."

"Preacher, meet the choir." It's our common refrain. "Nevertheless, our divorce agreement doesn't stipulate who pays for college. And every chance he gets, he tells Ethan he'd better stay on me about saving money for his college unless he wants to be taking out student loans. Like I have all this extra each month. Like Santa Barbara isn't expensive as all get out. But it's fine. This is the break I needed. If I can just do well at this job… in a few years I might be able to save money for retirement."

"Retirement? How old do you think you are?"

My mouth drops in disbelief at her unwitting question.

"I'm going to be forty." Do I really need to remind her?

"When? Someday." She laughs at her crackpot *Harry Met Sally* joke, but I slap her hand down.

"Not someday." I shake my head, mouth half-open. "Next. Week."

"Still. You have it in your head you'll be single until you die."

"I do not." The denial is automatic, but she's not far off. My brutal, soul-shattering divorce dispelled any notion a man is a reliable solution for anything. I learned the hard way a man is not an acceptable retirement plan. With my new job, I will make enough I could tell Jason to take his child support and shove it. But I won't do that, because he should pay child support.

This conversation has all my muscles tightening. I lift the martini glass and chug.

"If I didn't drag you out, what color would your hair be tomorrow?" She lifts a strand of my hair.

"You don't like my auburn?" I jut my chin out, pretending to be affronted. But I decided yesterday it's a little too red. She rolls her eyes, but this is a topic I would appreciate her input on. "I was thinking about trying warmer brown."

"You're not supposed to dye your hair every Saturday night."

"I'm going gray. What the hell else am I supposed to do?"

"You change your hair color more frequently than I change my nail color."

"So?"

"So, your hair is going to fall out."

"Who says?"

"The box. The box says. Read it sometime." As if Jenn has ever read the box. She goes to a salon that's so fancy I get nervous walking in front of the doors. It's the same sensation I get when I stare at dessert and my thighs expand. Only with the salon, the AC blasts through the open glass doors and my credit card balance grows.

I excuse myself to the restroom, and when I return, the place has filled up. Every barstool at the U-shaped bar is occupied, and nicely dressed patrons hover in the areas that are open behind the stools. Two freshly poured blue martinis sit in front of my partially emptied glass.

"Another round?" I ask.

"Drink up," Jenn says.

"Did you pick an app?"

"Order what you want," she tells me while twiddling her fingers at someone across the bar. There's a man in a black t-shirt across the way. He nods at her and smiles. Then he returns to the conversation with his companions. He's a good-looking guy. Reminds me a bit of Chris Hemsworth. We are in California… Could it be? I lean forward and study the man. No, it's not. Recognizing celebrities isn't my strength, but it's definitely not Chris Hemsworth. The tattoos spanning his finely shaped bicep aren't in any of the *Us Weekly* photos.

"See something you like?" Jenn asks.

I read the menu and point at the tuna nachos. "Okay with you?"

"I wasn't talking about food."

"Huh?" I ask. Because I really need food. My stomach is on the verge of queasy, and I'm getting lightheaded. She tilts her head in the direction of the Chris Hemsworth knock-off.

Her phone lights up on the bar with Terrell's name and a small circle with their wedding photo. His call saves me from having to respond. It's odd she's flirting with anyone here. She's as married as married gets. Terrell would tear apart any man who approached her—limb by limb. And I am definitely not here to flirt. I wave the bartender down so I can put in my order for nachos. He attempts to take the menu, and I grip it.

"We might order something else." Jenn plans to toast my new job by getting toasted. My worst hangovers are all due to Jenn, and one thing age has delivered is the wisdom to know when one must eat. A Jenn night is one such occasion.

"Well, I'm out with Stella." Her whine catches my attention. "Stella has something to celebrate, too." I sense her exasperation. There's color in her cheeks. She looks pissed.

I mouth the words, "What's wrong?"

She tilts her head and frowns. She glares at the phone and then disconnects without a word.

"What's going on?" It's not like Jenn to hang up on Terrell.

"Our babysitter vomited, and one of us needs to go home to relieve her. Carol knew I had plans. That's why she called Terrell, not me."

"What about Sierra? She's old enough to look after Darius by herself now, right?" Sierra is her fifteen-year-old daughter. I like her a lot. She's growing up fast, but she's sweet, dependable, and good friends with my son. Darius is eight years younger than his older sister, and as Jenn will tell anyone, the only reason he's here is thanks to IVF.

"Are you kidding? Ever since some of her friends got driver's licenses, she's lost all interest in babysitting."

"That'll change once she needs to pay for gasoline," I say, but it hits me that it's quite possible Terrell and Jenn won't make their daughter pay for her own gas. And that's just one more conversation Jason and I have yet to have. I'd like to make Ethan, my son, pay for his car insurance and gas when he turns sixteen, but it won't work unless Jason is on board.

"Honey, I'm sorry, but I've got to go." She waves down the bartender with a credit card between her fingers.

"Oh, it's no—"

"Yes, it is a problem," she blurts. "I planned this night out with you over a week ago. Terrell knew I had this planned, yet he's off with the boys and he says he can't leave."

I don't ask, but I know he's with Jason. They work together for West Coast Pharmaceuticals.

"He says they're out celebrating, too. Some new big account." She purses her lips so tightly a hundred tiny lines form above and below her lips.

"Seriously, don't worry about it." My stomach sinks. "Terrell didn't tell Jason about my new job, did he?"

"Oh, no, he knows better than that." She averts her gaze, and my stomach is putty on the floor. Of course he did. Lovely.

I get off the stool and straighten my dress. The cotton is thin and clings a bit too tight for my taste. Her hand wraps around my arm.

"What are you doing? Get back on that stool. We've got food coming."

"Let's get it to go."

"And you need to finish your drink." She waves that hand, and it's not until I realize the bartender is nowhere to be seen that I snatch her arm down.

"What are you doing?" I hiss.

"I'm going to make sure you still celebrate tonight. And you are going to have fun. And in the morning, you are going to call me and tell me all about it. And thank me. Because let me tell you something… that man over there has been checking you out. And he's hot. And you haven't had sex since circa 2016." The accuracy in her estimate is both surprising and mortifying. "Nothing on Netflix is going to be better than this." She wags her finger in my face. "Do not let me down. Live it up."

The man who has been flirting with her approaches, and he looks good enough to lick. He's unshaven. It's a look I don't normally go for, but when a man has biceps and pecs shaped like his, who really cares about the rough around the edges bit? His sandy blond hair is cut short on the sides and longer on the top. The lighter highlights along his crown give him the look of someone who spends a lot of time outside. I'm not generally around men with firm, well-defined pecs like his, and I sort of want to reach out and squeeze them, which is clearly a sign I need to eat food. Alcohol loosens inhibitions and leads to dirty thoughts. Not that I am having dirty thoughts.

He thrusts his hand out, and Jenn pushes my elbow, urging me to take his hand. I glare. She laughs.

"He said his name is Trevor. And I told him your name is Stella." She's speaking to me like I'm one of her kindergarteners. *Shit.*

"Hi. I'm sorry." I have no idea what they said while I was staring at his chest. Judging by his smirk, he's not offended. "My mind can go…" I flutter my fingers to fill in. "Especially when I'm drinking." He full-on smiles, and my queasy stomach twists. "Blue drinks."

I don't know why I add that. What I really want is to throw in a Phoebe and say something like, "So, Trevor, take off your shirt and tell us all about yourself."

Jenn signs her check, and my internal alarm blares when she says, "Well, you two have fun. And Trevor, don't let her go home. This girl is due for a good time. Honey, I am so sorry I have to bail on your celebration. I will make it up to you."

And with a small wave and an air kiss, she leaves. Inside, I am screaming for her not to leave. *What the hell, Jenn?*

"I promise I won't bite." His breath flickers over my ear, and I jump. I'm in massive platform heels, and he still has to bend down to speak into my ear. The music is rather loud, but we're in an upscale place, so he didn't have to lean into my ear. No, he's teasing me. He sees me panicking.

"What are we celebrating tonight?" He lifts his beer to his lips.

"It's nothing. New job. You don't have to stay out with me." I reach for my clutch on the bar. His hand falls on my wrist. The touch is light and electric and startling.

"Hey, I promised your friend. She said you hardly ever go out. I'm the same way. Let me at least buy you dinner."

"Oh, but…" I search for the woman I saw him with earlier across the bar.

"You're saving me from being third wheel."

"Where'd your friends go?"

"Probably back up to their room. We're all staying here."

"Oh. At the hotel?"

He nods and pulls out a stool. The bartender delivers the nachos I ordered and also delivers an enormous cheeseburger and a family serving of fries to Trevor. He unrolls the silverware and puts the cloth napkin on his lap.

"Sit. Would you like some fries?"

Fries to go with my nachos. That's some celebrating right there. But I'm starving, and thin, salty french fries are my Achilles' heel. So, I do what any girl one and a half cocktails in would do next to a younger Chris Hemsworth lookalike. I sit and alternate ogling the fries, his arms, and his chest.

"You really don't mind?" I ask as my fingers deliver a captured fry to my mouth.

"Not at all. Help yourself. We can order more."

"You can have some of my nachos," I offer. The raw tuna is delicious, but there's not as much of it as I might like sprinkled over the fried chips. A plentiful supply of guacamole and fresh salsa are on the side.

He cuts his burger in half, and the muscles in his bare forearm flex from the movement. I should ask him where he's from. Or how long he'll be in Santa Barbara. I should say something, but I'm so busy stuffing fries in my mouth and watching his muscles twitch and flex that I don't.

This is what happens when you go almost ten years without a semblance of a date. And here I am, staring down the barrel at forty, and I can't form a coherent sentence when a good-looking man sits down beside me at a bar. Jenn is right. I need to get back out there.

If she hadn't forced me out tonight, my hair would now be colored a warmer, softer brunette, I'd have on new toenail polish, and I'd be on the sixth episode of one of the *Friends* seasons, or I'd be watching something naughty like *Sex Life*. Now, that woman lived. Billie, the star of *Sex Life*, put it out there. In her twenties, no less. When I was knee deep in dirty diapers, she was having the sex of her life with a gorgeous billionaire. And I have devoted my thirties to paying bills and raising said child while enduring the world's longest divorce from the biggest A-hole.

Trevor wipes his lips with his napkin. His burger is no longer on his plate. We've made small talk, but I'm so in my head I can only hope my end of the conversation made sense.

"Do you live near here?" he asks.

"Not really. Goleta?" I say. I doubt he's heard of it.

"Did you get enough to eat?" It's only then that I notice half the nachos are missing, as are almost all of his fries and my second blue martini.

"Yeah, I'd say so." I'll definitely be going for a long walk tomorrow. A woman my age should not be eating a platter of fries. But hey, I'm celebrating, right? In less than a week, I'll be forty. What an ugly word.

"I have a great view from my hotel room. Any chance you'd like to come up and share a glass of wine?"

Holy smokes. Is he asking me up? He's asking me up. This gorgeous guy with a body from a superhero movie is asking me up to his room. He's not from here. I'll never see him again. Ethan's at his dad's until tomorrow afternoon. It's been ten years. Ten years of battery-operated devices and my fingers and television and books.

*What would Billie do?*

# One Night Engagement

Trevor

She's nervous. I read the situation wrong. We're not near a military base. She's not a woman who simply wants to score with a man in uniform. And, for better or worse, I am no longer a man in uniform. I should pay the bill and call it a night.

She tilts her head, and her front teeth sink into her lower lip. One hand is on her hip, one on the bar. Wheels are turning behind those dark eyes. She's debating.

The soft blush on her cheeks hints that this is not normal for her. Her gaze darts around the crowded bar area, to our empty plates, to the bartender who is working up a sweat mixing drinks and popping tops. There's a mirror on the far wall, and our gazes meet in the reflective surface. She sees me grinning. I can't help myself.

"No pressure." It's an admittedly weak attempt at persuasion. "We don't have to do anything. But upstairs, it's not crowded, and we can talk more easily." I stretch my arm out against the bar and flex my bicep a tad. Her eyes follow the movement.

"Just one drink won't hurt, I guess." She reaches for her clutch and bumps her empty martini glass. "Oh, but I've had two drinks. A third..."

"I'll get you an Uber. Or, if you like, you can drink water and let some time pass before driving home."

She smiles and nods, and I assume this scenario is acceptable to her sensibilities. She's a gorgeous woman. Her hair is reddish brown. When the overhead lights hit certain strands right, there's a pink hue. She has long fingers with rounded, polished nails. I estimate her height without heels to be about five foot seven or eight. She's got full lips, and her dress accentuates luscious tits and curvy hips.

I can tell by the way she answers my questions, and the questions she doesn't ask, that she's out of her element. And of course, that blush. When the light catches just right, she looks almost overheated. Not that I hold it against her. I'm feeling it, too. The attraction hums between us, and I'd like nothing more than to get her up to my room. To roam those curves and to fan that blush to a flame.

My fingers lightly coax her lower back, guiding her out of the bar and down the hall. She wraps her arms around herself. Visible goosebumps line her upper arms. One finger taps against her skin. The brighter overhead lights reflect off a silver ring on her ring finger. It's enormous and covers from her knuckle to the base of her finger. It wouldn't be like any wedding band I've ever seen, but still. I will not take another man's wife to my room, so how to knock out that one percent chance before I hit the elevator button?

"You're not married, are you?"

"No. No." She tucks a strand of hair behind her ear, looks down to the ground, then jerks her head up. "Are you?"

"Nope. How on Earth is a woman as gorgeous as you single?" It's an overused, cheesy pickup line, but I am picking her up, so it fits.

"Ah, well. Luck, I guess." I sense there's more there, but she's not up for spilling her sordid history. And I am one hundred percent okay with that.

"My good luck," I tell her. She beams.

When the elevator doors open, there's another couple to one side. I stand in the back corner and pull her up against me. Her ass rubs my crotch, and it's like raising a racing flag with a man screaming start your engines. My dick obeys.

Unaware of my predicament, she continues fidgeting, and from the mirrored panel I watch her gaze flit from the floor to the buttons on the panel to the couple standing in front of us.

The elevator dings, and the other couple exits. The doors close, and the elevator rises, taking us one floor higher.

"I don't normally do this."

Instinctively, I reach for her hand.

"Nor do I," I say. It's not entirely true, given over the years I've had my share of one-night stands. But I haven't been with anyone since the shooting. Recovering from bullet wounds is a bitch and a half. But judging from the uncomfortable erection that needs adjusting in my jeans, it appears my body has fully recovered.

The elevator door opens, and a man is waiting to enter. I nod in greeting as we step around him and, with her hand in mine, lead Stella toward my room.

I press the key against the pad and push the door open with my arm.

"Here we are." I hold my breath, waiting. It's her choice. She could turn back, but I hope she doesn't. Although what she's doing is dumb as fuck, since she doesn't know me at all. I could be a crazed lunatic.

She steps past me, cheeks blazing. Dumb or not, I am grateful she enters. It's a spacious room with a king-sized bed. Artsy black and white photos adorn the walls. The comforter is bright white. There are sliding glass doors that open onto a balcony and overlook the Pacific Ocean. It's far away, though, as we're at least two blocks from the ocean. If one glances down to the street, you can see the avenue and cars and people.

Her fingers glide over the comforter. She canvases the room in a circle, mouth slightly open. It's a nice room. Pricey. But it's not a suite.

"This place is nice," she says.

"Thanks." I could tell her that one of my business partners, Kairi, picked the hotel, but there's no need. "Let's see what wine we have. I may need to order something from room service." A wine bottle and two glasses rest on the counter, above the mini refrigerator. She reaches for my arm.

"I don't need any more alcohol." I won't argue with her on that point.

"Well, you are celebrating." I step closer and pull her hips up against mine in one smooth swoop. I angle my head, readying to take this up a notch. I want to taste those plump lips. "How can I help you celebrate?"

"Can we just screw?" There's hope in her eyes, and I belt out a laugh.

"Yeah. Yeah. We can do that." I back up because I need some space to gather myself.

"It's not that… it's just that…" She's stammering, and her cheeks are flaming red now. Seduction is definitely not her game. "I haven't been with anyone since my ex. It's been like ten years. I need to rip the Band-Aid. Pop the divorce cherry. Get it done. Jenn is right. Can you help me?"

*Whoa. That's an info dump.*

"Jenn is the friend from the bar?" She nods. "Well, let's see." I pull her back up against my chest and caress her hips. There's no music playing, but I sway as if there is. "I'd say the fact I have you in my hotel room is a pretty good sign I'm game."

"Shit. I know, but you're all talkety-talk." Her arms rise over my shoulders, and her nails scrape the back of my scalp. "And I'm nervous, and it would just be better if—"

I shut her up with my lips. I get it. She's nervous, and she wants to do the deed. I can oblige. Ten years? The woman needs this. And I am a helpful man.

Her soft lips press against mine. My tongue probes, and she opens. She tastes sweet. There's a hint of pineapple and coconut. Her breasts press against my chest, and I squeeze her full, round ass. If she has any doubt about how turned on I am, she won't after this. Fuck. She feels good. Soft. Her thigh rocks into my crotch, and the pressure is perfection.

She lets out a breathy moan, and her nails scrape along my ears and my throat. It's a soft touch that lights goosebumps along my skin and drives me fucking crazy. I maneuver her backward until her legs bump against the end of the bed.

My fingers inch the bottom of her dress upward. She breaks our kiss, and I suck in air, prepared to stop everything.

"Can you turn off the lights?"

I swallow and regain my bearings. The overhead lights are on. Come to think of it, the curtains are wide open. I don't think anyone from across the street can see in, but just in case, I pull the drapes closed and head down the hall searching for the light switch. I find it, and the room darkens. The only light source comes from a motion-activated light in the bathroom.

"Is this better?" As my eyes adjust, all I can see is the outline of her shape. She's standing next to the bed, exactly where I left her. Immobile. "Still want to do this?"

"Mmm mm." It's an affirmative noise, but my gut tells me to slow down.

"Would you like that glass of wine?"

"No." Her high-pitched answer rings with uncertainty.

Her mixed signals give me some of my own. My brain says, *Back this one up, soldier,* while my cock screams, *Boots on the ground, go, go, go.*

She tugs on my shirt, and I obediently raise my arms. The cool air circles over my fresh scars. It's good she asked for the lights off. It's been months since the shooting, but the wounds remain red and raised. The entry point near my shoulder will leave a nasty mark.

Her fingers explore my chest. Her nails glide over my nipples as she caresses my pecs. Her head bows down. I can't tell if she's watching her fingers roam or if she's embarrassed.

"What happened?" she asks. Her light touch tickles.

"Accident." I stand still, letting her fingers explore. She's not looking up at me. I can't easily kiss her, given she's looking down.

"We'll only do what you want," I remind her in a gentle tone.

The light touch of fingers over my abs tickles. Her fingers clasp my belt, and she works it loose. She unbuttons the top button on my jeans, and I swallow.

She tilts her head up, and I cover her lips with mine. Our tongues resume a slow dance. My hands are at my sides, giving her every chance to change her mind.

She reaches inside my jeans, and those long, cool fingers wrap around my erection. Holy hell, that feels good. I break the kiss and whimper as the metal from her ring presses against my shaft. It's a mix of warmth and cold and pressure. And I'm not sure how much longer I can take this slow. I want to slide into this woman, to feel her around me, to pulse my release.

"Can I take off your dress?" It's been a long time for me, too. Judging from my reaction at her hand on me, if she's going to get much out of tonight, I need to take charge.

Her hand abandons my cock. He's sticking out from the top of my pants, whimpering in his own right. Her breath is heavy. She pulls her dress up, over her hips and over her breasts. I assist, tugging it over her head and outstretched arms. Her bra has thick straps, and it glows a soft white. Her panties are a darker color. The mismatched lingerie tells me she didn't set out tonight planning for a hook-up. It's completely hypocritical, but I like that.

Her breasts are large, her waist narrow, and her hips full. The perfect hourglass. She lowers her gaze and bows her head. Embarrassed? Unsure?

"You're gorgeous," I whisper. I reach behind her and unclasp the bra strap. The bra falls to the floor. And then I blink her in. Her breasts are perfection. The nipples are large and round. Hard with desire. There's a thin white scar on the bottom of each, barely discernible, but in this dim light, the scar stands out against the darker areola. My hand squeezes the soft globe, and she closes her eyelids. Her breast fills my hand. Soft and full. I can't wait to taste.

I edge her farther onto the bed, against the pillows. I remove my pants and lay them across the foot of the bed for access, all the while watching her watch me. The air is heavy, weighted. I kiss my way up her thigh and press my nose to her panties. I inhale her musky scent. The lining is damp.

Leaning back on my feet, my dick in a full salute, I slide her panties down her thighs. The fabric stretches tight when I reach her knees. She pulls her legs to her and raises up to assist, pulling the panties over one foot. I place her legs back on each side of me, leaving the cotton panties dangling on the other ankle.

Trimmed, black pubic hair crowns her glistening pussy. She's wet. So wet. She wants this. Or at least her body does. Her hesitancy in meeting my gaze tells me her mind is uncertain. Ten years.

I bow before her and press my lips to her. Her hips rise, and my hands slide beneath her, assisting her movement and bringing her closer to my mouth. My back stretches, and an uncomfortable pain permeates my side where I'm still healing. Still gripping her ass, I move off the bed, feet on the floor. The muscular pain subsides, and I kiss then graze my teeth over her inner thigh. Her fingers fall to my hair, and she mewls, practically panting, asking me for this.

My tongue dips in. I like the way she tastes. I lick her, spreading her vulva. As I approach her clit, her thighs press on my ears.

She pulls on my hair and directs me, whimpering and uttering nonsensical words. I smile against her, loving how turned on she is, how desperate and needy. I slide a finger inside, and she clamps around it then loosens. Her noises increase in frequency as I focus, letting her tugs on my hair guide me. I graze my lower teeth over her sensitive area, and her thighs clasp my head hard, her hips thrust up, and she screams out. Liquid spews on my chin, and I pull back, startled.

Holy fuck. She's a squirter. A mystical, magical squirter. The kind you see in porn or read about.

She's chanting, and the words finally form into a disjointed version of *oh, my god.*

"Did you like that?" I wipe my hands on the comforter before collapsing beside her.

"Oh, yes. Thank you." She covers her eyelids with one hand. "I think I needed that."

"Yeah, I'd say. Do you always squirt when you come?" I am genuinely curious.

"What do you mean?" She lifts her hand, and her eyes crinkle for a brief second, but then her gaze falls down my body. Cum drips from the tip of my cock, because she's sexy as fuck. He's begging for attention.

Those long fingers, now heated, wrap around me, and it's my turn to groan and lift my hips. Jesus. Those three bullets really knocked me off my game. The tightening on the base of my spine tells me I'm so close, just from her touch. She presses her lips along my chest, making her way down to my cock, much the way I journeyed up her thighs. But I stop her. I can't handle those lips. If her fingers have me on edge, her mouth will push me over.

"If you do that, I'm going to come."

She lifts on one elbow, one hand still clasped around me, stroking.

"Would you rather have my mouth or my pussy?"

My dick throbs in response to her question.

"Your call." I should explain more so she understands, but her hands are on my cock, and I need to concentrate so I don't blow my load on my chest.

"I've come this far. I'm popping that damn divorce cherry. Do you have a condom?"

I rise on my elbow to reach for my jeans. She releases my cock, and I gasp for air. She fumbles with my jeans, locates my wallet and the condoms.

"Huh, you have a lot of cash," she mumbles.

"Did you find the condom?" *Who cares about cash?*

She tosses the plastic square to me, and I rip it open with my teeth and sheathe myself in record time. She throws her leg across me, positions herself over me, and begins to sink down.

She's warm. Tight. So fucking tight. She's slow. Very slow. Too slow.

"Do you mind if we do missionary? It's a little... You're wider and bigger than..." I think she's about to use another man's name in my bed, and I don't give her a chance. I flip her over onto her back, lift one of her legs onto my shoulder, and nip at her calf.

"Please. Do it." I drag my thumb along her center, and she whimpers. "Please."

I position my tip at her entrance. She locks her gaze on the ceiling above, and from the position of her chin, I wonder…

"Does it hurt?"

"No. Just do it." My back muscles tremble. I'm poised at her entrance. I want her so badly, but this isn't the way. She removes her leg from my shoulder. Her nails claw my back as she pulls me lower. Her hips rise up, and she grabs my cock and positions me at her entrance. She raises her hips, and warmth surrounds my tip. I push down, entering her. Just a few inches, but I'm deeper than when she climbed on me. I gasp for air, pausing. She's still refusing to look at me, but her hands fall to my ass, and she tugs.

"Fuck me," she mutters. There's determination in her tone, and I am helpless to do anything but obey. She's tight and warm and feels like heaven.

My hips gyrate into her, and I grit out, "This okay? You okay?"

A garbled, "Yes," is shortly followed by, "Harder."

That's all I need. My control slips, and my hips thrust hard, just like she asked. The headboard bangs against the wall.

*Bang. Bang.*

My arm's muscles quiver from the strain of holding my weight over her, but I can't help but watch the movement. And then those nails cover her center and massage, and I'm done. I explode with a shout.

I collapse over her. She squirms, and I shift onto my side. I'm sweaty, and my chest expands and contracts as my lungs beg for air.

"Did you—"

She rolls off the other side of the bed. It's as if my words pushed her away. She's at the end of the bed, gathering her clothes.

"That was fantastic. Thank you for giving me the best birthday present ever."

Okay. So, she enjoyed it. There's that. The bathroom door closes behind her, and I gather my wits. The condom is still on. I need to take care of that.

I hear the toilet flush, the sink turn on, and then she's back in the room. Naked, I step past her, pausing briefly to brush a kiss across her cheek. The back of her head is a rat's nest, and yeah, that brings on a smug smile as I enter the bathroom.

I'm leaning over the toilet, taking a whiz, when the door slams. My stomach sinks. I wasn't expecting her to stay the night or anything, but I thought she'd at least say goodbye.

When I open the bathroom door, sure enough, she's gone. There's no note, nothing. No goodbye. It's the kind of encounter I once dreamed of, but instead, I can't shake the feeling I just got screwed.

# The One with the Morning After

Stella

Jenn: *How was last night? I am SO sorry I had to go home.*

Jenn's text awaits an answer, but first I need coffee. I stumble into the kitchen, turning on a light here and there as I go. Within minutes, Mr. Coffee comes alive, and the drip of life begins. As I wait for sustenance, the quiet of the house unnerves me. And I can't stop my brain from rewinding last night.

I can't believe what I did. I haven't had a one-night stand since college. And then, I was drunk. If I'm honest with myself, I wasn't drunk last night. Two cocktails doesn't disqualify rational thought.

No, a gorgeous guy hit on me for the first time in ages, and I jumped on the merry-go-round. Joy rode the roller coaster. Threw my hands in the air like I didn't have a care.

And this morning? I both hate and love myself. I hate myself because that's not me. It's not who I am. I don't go up to strange men's hotel rooms and bang them. How stupid was I? He could have been a mass murderer. He could have bludgeoned me to death with a lamp. We could have had sex and then he could have passed over papers confirming he's HIV positive. That shit happens. Thank god he used a condom. I had some wits about me. Not many. But some.

But I also love myself a little. Because when he went down on me, that was the best orgasm of my life. Every muscle in my body, from my little toe to my scalp, synergized. And holy shit, after that, everything he did, every touch tingled. I will replay last night during my late-night forays with the rabbit and its compadres for years.

My phone vibrates, and Jenn's smiling face appears on-screen. She insists on FaceTime. I leave the phone flat on the table, offering her a view of my ceiling.

"Soooooo? Did you talk to him?" Her chirpiness elicits my loud groan. "Wait. What was that? Are you hungover? Did my little harmonica get hammered?"

I position my middle finger over the camera lens, then walk away to pour my coffee. Jenn loves to watch *Friends* re-runs as much as I do, and while I normally love her references, this morning it's not cutting it for me.

"Holy shit! You got drunk! That's awesome."

"No. I didn't get drunk. He invited me up to his hotel room for wine." I cross my arms on the counter and lay my head down on them. Saying it out loud does a number on my stomach.

"Oh my god. Oh my god. Oh my god." Her high-pitched chanting would be painful to my ears, except the phone remains on the kitchen table. "Terrell, you've got to take—"

The noises end. She hung up. I lift my head, straighten, and chug my coffee. It's bitter, and that's when I realize I forgot to add sweetener and milk. How is one supposed to feel after a one-night stand? Giddy? That's not the emotion rocking my body this morning.

But, on the bright side, I can finally look Jason in the eye and know he's not the last man I had sex with. Lord knows he's had sex with half the single women in Cali. And I know for a fact he hangs out at bars with some of the very young UCSB students. So I shouldn't feel guilty at all. I should feel like high-fiving my refrigerator. But instead, I'm a little dull inside. Not dead, exactly, but maybe a little shell-shocked.

I'll never see Trevor again. We never exchanged last names, much less numbers. If he's not on a plane to wherever he's from today, he'll probably be on one tomorrow. He was really good looking. I wish I had taken photos. As proof. Proof that I, Stella Johnson, did *that*. Like, there should be some diploma service. You take photos, mail it in, then you get an award in the mail that says, "You boned the best-looking guy in California for the month of February" award. Or a trophy. A trophy that's a replica of the penis… for memories' sake. Come to think of it, if I had taken a photo of that bad boy, it would show up in my feed, "A look back ten years ago."

Ah, and shit, that would be when I'd be on the verge of fifty. I really should've taken a photo. I'd like for Google to email me a photo of my one wild night. My last hoorah before turning forty. My first hoorah post-divorce. God, I am such a loser. My divorce was finalized nine and half years ago.

*Bang. Bang. Bang.*

"Open up." The brass doorknob rattles as I approach. I brace myself, because behind my flimsy front door stands one zealous Jenn. "I know you're in there."

"Morning." She holds up a clear plastic container of muffins and pushes past me. "Ethan still at Jason's?"

I nod, close the door, and head to the kitchen to pour her coffee. Our downstairs is essentially one room with a bar and overhead cabinets separating the kitchen area from the rest of the living area. Stairs line one wall leading to the two bedrooms. The nice thing about this rental is that both bedrooms have their own private bath, a luxury that cannot be underrated when sharing a house with a teenage son.

"Is that a new curtain?" Jenn points at the blue curtain hanging over the square window over the sink. The curtain is significantly larger than the window, but I like it like that. It gives the illusion of a good-sized window beneath, and it prevents my neighbors, who have a similar kitchen window all of six feet away, from watching our every move.

"You like it?" I ask as I hand her the coffee. She takes a seat at the kitchen table, grinning. Her knees are bouncing. "Why are you so excited?"

"Because you hooked up." Her hands clap together. "And I want to hear all about it."

I want to be annoyed at her, but a smile cracks. I take a seat.

"I never told you I hooked up."

"No. But you groaned. And he asked you up. To his hotel room. And he was hot as fuck. So you went. I know you went. You had to… You went, right?" Now she's gripping my knee. I cover my face with my hand.

"Yes."

She squeals. "How was it?"

"Good. Really good." Yes, that's not the part I have any complaints about. It's this morning aftereffect I could do without. But I tell her about it. Not an exact play-by-play, but she gets the picture.

"What's wrong? Are you expecting him to have called by now?"

"No. Not at all. We didn't even exchange numbers." I add that part so I don't get bombarded with *did he call* texts for the next several days.

"That's okay. He was staying at the hotel. An out-of-towner. You both wanted a little action, and you went for it. There is no shame in that. I am so proud of you."

"Proud?" I could barf on the word.

"Yes! You got some action. You've been using Ethan as an excuse for too long."

"He's my son. He's not an excuse." She knows this.

"Honey, I have two kids, and I get out ten times more than you do."

She also has money. I bite back my response. I don't want to make her feel guilty. I never want to make her feel guilty. But the reality is a night on the sofa with reruns is free. There's very little one can do out and about that doesn't run up my credit card balance.

"Honey, I know Jason did a number on you. And you've been locking away that heart of yours, but you can't spend your whole life holed up in this house."

"That's not…" I blink away a tremor of frustration. "This isn't about Jason. I just… Listen, I don't regret last night, but I don't feel great about it, either. Like if I ever ran into him again, I would be so mortified. That's not who I am."

Jenn narrows her eyes and crosses her arms over her chest.

"Are you slut-shaming yourself?" Am I? "I will have none of that. Look at me, girlfriend. That man was hot with a capital H. And you deserved his attention. You hear me? Not every sexual encounter has to lead to a ring on a finger. Sometimes it's just about moving forward in life. Sometimes it's about physical needs. Touch is important to our psyche. Nuh-uh, girlfriend. I am not having you feel bad. One free hookup does not a slut make. And who the fuck should judge, anyway? Do we judge men? No one ever does. Did you enjoy it?" I stop staring into my coffee cup. "Did you?"

"Yeah."

"Did he treat you right?" I think about how he kept asking if I was sure. And I remember the orgasm that flipped my world.

"Yeah."

"Did you use a condom?"

"Yes."

"Hell, yeah, sister, you did. Because you are smart. And you are ready to get out there. You ripped that Band-Aid off. And now you are ready to play. I bet you meet some fine men at that new job of yours. And when they ask you out on a date, what you are going to say?"

"No. I need this job."

"You are going to say yes. Well, find out the whole HR policy, but when you get asked out, and you will, the answer is yes. I don't want to hear about any other response."

"I think I'm going to be the one to write the HR policy."

"Hellz to the yeah. Didn't you say it's a security company? You are going to be around some fine men. Last night marks the start of a new era."

She continues her pep talk until she gets a call from Terrell that Darius really wants her to attend her soccer game. I tell her they should go as a family. And it's true, they should. I never miss one of Ethan's games. But the best ones were when he was younger, like Darius. When he'd look over at me and wave.

Upstairs, I shower and set out my outfit for my first day at my new high-paying job. Then I set about cleaning the entire house. It's one of my Sunday rituals. Since Ethan isn't home, the house feels too quiet, so I set out my phone and play a Sunday morning playlist. The melancholy strains of "Blackbird" by The Beatles blasts through my speaker.

It's uncanny. On any weekend morning, the sound level would be the same. Ethan doesn't wake until close to noon. Yet he's not in the house, I know it, and the whole place reeks of emptiness.

The front door opens as I'm kneeling before the vacuum cleaner, wrapping the cord in place so I can put the machine away for another week.

"Ethan? You're home early." It's not even noon. Technically, according to our court agreement, he's supposed to stay at Jason's until six p.m. But we haven't followed that agreement closely in years. Still, when he stays over, Jason rarely brings him home so early.

"Yeah. I have a school project." He lumbers up the stairs, his weekend bag slung over his shoulder.

"Did you have a good time?" I call after him.

"Yeah," he mumbles.

"He's a talker." The deep timber hits me in all the wrong places. I hate that voice. I rest my hand on the top of the vacuum cleaner and face the doorway.

"Do you need something?" Jason pushes the door fully open and steps into the den. He surveys the space with clear judgment. I'm glad I just cleaned. Nothing is out of place. The carpet displays orderly vacuum lines. Lemon scent fills the air.

"Is anyone else here?" The intrusive question raises my hackles. I grit my teeth. Count to three.

"No."

"Heard you got a big pay raise. That's good. You shouldn't have a problem paying your half of Ethan's college tuition. He also bought a guitar this weekend. I'll deduct your half out of the child support."

"Nice try. Child support doesn't work that way, and you know it."

He grins. He likes to push my buttons. I don't have any idea why. In those first few years, I would lose all rational thought and scream like a banshee. Until one day Ethan entered the room with teary eyes.

Inside my body, I rage. But Ethan is upstairs, and I will not raise my voice. I will be professional. I have less than three years and I am done with this man other than possibly running into him at graduation ceremonies and Ethan's wedding.

"Did you need anything else?"

He runs his index finger over the top shelf. He used to do that when we were married, too. Checking for dust. I walk to the door and rest my hand on the knob.

"No." He leans his shoulder against the wall. "Did you have fun last night?"

There's no way he knows what I did last night. Jenn wouldn't share details with Terrell. But he knows he interrupted my night, because he was out with Terrell. He kept Terrell out, so I couldn't have Jenn. And he wants me to know it. Jason is a transparent ass.

"I had a fantastic time last night. Thanks for asking. I need to leave to pick my suit up from the dry cleaners, so if you don't mind." That last bit isn't true at all, but I am victorious when his jaw flexes. Yes, that's right. I now have a respectable job that you can't disparage.

I watch him head out the door to his BMW parked on the curb. A woman sits in the passenger seat. She looks up from her phone, and our eyes meet. She's new. When Ethan was younger, it used to bother me that Jason rotated through girlfriends like a photo carousel, but my lawyer told me there was nothing I could do about it. And Ethan didn't seem affected. He never spoke about Jason's girlfriends to me. I shut the front door and lock it.

Jason's BMW reverses out of the driveway, and I head upstairs. The door to Ethan's bedroom is closed. I rap my knuckle against the panel door and wait.

"Yeah?" he calls out. I push the door open. He's sitting on his bed, a laptop open on one side, an iPad on the other. His overnight back sits in the middle of the floor. His window shade is closed. Our cat stretches across the bottom of his bed, head lifted, watching me, the end of his tail flicking up and down.

"So, the weekend was okay?"

"Yeah."

"What do you think you want for dinner?"

"Whatever." He gives me the standard Ethan shrug. I read it as he'd like for me to close the door and leave his room.

"Do you have any laundry I need to do before school tomorrow?"

Now he grins, because he's supposed to do his own laundry, and I'm basically offering to do the chore he hates.

"I think I'm outta clean boxers." I slide open his closet door. His laundry basket takes up half the floor space, and it's overflowing. There's a smelly sock aroma that is all Ethan.

"Okay. I'll take this down. If you'll promise to do something with me after dinner."

"Like what?"

"I don't know." It's my turn to shrug. "Watch a TV show? Play a game? Your pick."

"Deal." He returns his focus to his laptop. I think he's texting someone.

"Do you want me to take the clothes in your bag too?"

"Sure."

I unzip the bag and pull out all the clothes. They're thrown in with no semblance of order, so I assume they're all dirty.

"Hey, Mom?" I am pulling the door closed but open it wide to hear him. "I'd like your chicken and rice casserole tonight, if you don't mind. And biscuits."

"You got it." We smile at each other, and warmth fills every particle of my being. It's ridiculous, but whenever he requests a specific dish, I am absurdly pleased.

The problem with Ethan being fifteen is that now the countdown to him no longer living with me has taken on a sharp-edged reality. The next three years are going to fly by, and I'm going to blink and I'll be unloading him at college. All his one-word answers will be delivered via phone. Or worse, text. And then what?

Life was easier when Ethan was younger, and he needed me. Of course, I didn't see it. When every moment he wanted me to be right there, I craved a moment alone. It's funny. Fast-forward ten years, and I have an endless supply of time to myself, and I'm the one begging my son for interaction.

"People Need a Melody" by The Head and The Heart greets me as I enter the kitchen and slide open the laundry closet door. I begin my affirmations. I have a new job. I doubled my salary. Mr. Wolfgang respects my skills and believes his company needs me. I have a son and a best friend I would give my life for. I am strong. Oh, and I also let loose last night and had the orgasm of my life. I am strong. Did I already say that? I will repeat it. I deserve to because I kept my cool with the asshat. I am strong.

# Inside the Wire

Trevor

My shoulder muscle aches where they dug the bullet out. I fumble through my overnight tote until I find the muscle cream. I've been doing physical therapy for months now. I might have overextended it swimming. It's February, and the Pacific is on the chilly side. The cold water probably didn't help.

I can almost hear my old sergeant. "The only easy day is yesterday." It's the favorite refrain of every SEAL trainer ever. I lean back onto the pillow, remembering the damn bell. My next tattoo might be that bell, simply because when I think about it, I always smile.

"You tired? Need a break? Want a massage? Some hot chocolate? Go ring the bell." You ring the bell, you quit. I never quit. I made it.

BUD/S training. It's what every SEAL goes through. The best time of my life I never want to repeat.

The bathroom door is open because I'm alone in my new condo. But glancing out into my sparsely furnished bedroom, I'm reminded once again of my hook-up who flew out of the room while I took a whiz. I shake it off and finish getting ready.

It's just as well she skedaddled. I had to be up early in the morning to sign papers with the Realtor and to move into my new place.

Down here, I'm going to be in charge of training our agents. I plan to pull from the BUD/S training program to ensure our agents are the best. Hell, it's not a contest. There are no medals in our new line of work. But I am a big believer that training keeps you alive. More sweat, less blood.

Arrow Security is a high-tech security organization. Physical security, surveillance, training, and tactical operations like K&R, or kidnapping and ransom. Most of our work is international, in countries that US diplomatic policy requires the US remain uninvolved. For our government clients, we mostly do black ops.

We've been building our team by leveraging our military connections. Wolf and I oversee the physical security and tactical missions. Erik and Kairi oversee the IT division, or what I think of as all the computer shit.

Erik and Kairi plan to remain up in Napa Valley. Erik's wife, Vivi, has family up there, as does Kairi's boyfriend, David. Soon,

David will get a title promotion from boyfriend. They already live together.

Kairi and David drove down with me to help me move. They were at the bar with me when I met the redhead. David's newish to me, but not to her, given they were high school lovebirds. They're only staying down here a few days.

Yesterday was move day, and today will be a busy one in the office. Intelligence sources provided a windfall of critical information on the head of Spectre, a man who now graces the FBI's Most Wanted list. Today we get briefed.

Taking down Spectre, the organization responsible for last November's West Coast Blackout, is our highest priority. We are working with the NSA, FBI, and CIA, and we're closer than we've ever been to dismantling the cybercrime organization.

Years ago, Erik and Kairi worked within the organization. When they saw how the hacker collective had taken a decidedly greedy trajectory, they strove to dismantle it. Those efforts carried a high price tag, and Erik hired Wolf and me for security. We eventually returned to the US, and the four of us began building Arrow Security, significantly aided by government contracts.

One thing my near death proved to all of us is that there's no need to fly under the radar. No, we have adopted an offensive war strategy. We spent too long laying low, but now we're going after the fucker responsible for my scars. And for that matter, Kairi's internal scars. Kane, the head of Spectre, didn't physically harm Kairi, but he hired an assassin to kill her partner.

Finally, we're on a mission to take down the fucker. And I, for one, can't wait.

When I exit the condo, I rap my knuckle against Wolf's door. Cars on the street below crawl by and slow to a stop at the stoplight. A surfboard covers the top of one Jeep, and an ankle strap flaps in the breeze. One cyclist weaves around the stalled automobiles with a messenger bag strapped across his shoulder.

I'm not necessarily a city guy, but I have to say, movement and humans underfoot sit better with my psyche than the rows of grapevines where we spent the last year. Back when we were on the run. Hiding out in a vineyard. And then I got shot. The men who shot me did not survive. All thanks to top-notch training and grueling workouts.

Someone's radio plays on a nearby apartment balcony. I can't quite make out the words, but the melody is reminiscent of Jack Johnson. Bright blue, clear skies and a light chill in the air combine to forecast a good day.

Santa Barbara's small-town vibe can't be beat. Palm trees line the streets, it hardly ever rains, the temperatures are always mild, and the Pacific Ocean and a wide, sandy beach are blocks away. It's not really a small town. The ideal conditions attract anyone who can find a living here, and it's now technically a sprawling small city. But in the little part Wolf has claimed for us, it's one hundred percent fantastic.

Wolf's clearly not home, so I hustle down the stairs to the street, round the corner, and nearly collide with him. Our fists bump in greeting.

Our condos are one story above the street. Before I made the offer, Wolf told me about the location. Promised the street traffic dies down early in the evening. We share a roof deck, and our front door balconies butt up to each other. He under-sold the area. There are bars and restaurants on every single block. We've got a mountain view to the east and deep blue ocean to the west.

"You need coffee?" he asks. He slides his phone into his pants pocket and heads in the direction of our office, conveniently located two blocks away.

"Nah. Had a protein shake."

"How many miles did you do?"

"Just five. My knee's giving me some trouble." It'll be good to have a flat, sandy beach to do my morning runs. The rocky dirt trails in Napa were good for the quads and glutes, but my damn achy knees could benefit from some cushion. "Were you waiting for me?"

"Eh, I figured I'd hang out and welcome you into the office. Didn't think you'd get a late start."

It's five after eight. Since I moved in yesterday, I debated meeting up with Kairi and David for breakfast this morning. But David has big plans, and I didn't want to risk screwing up his surprise. Plus, Santa Barbara rocks a vacation vibe, but we're here for work.

"What time do you get into the office?" I ask Wolf. He's been working from here for months on his own.

"Seven thirty."

My mouth drops. "You waited thirty-five minutes for me?" *Damn, he must've missed me more than I realized.*

"Nah, more like five. I maxed out a few extra sets at the gym this morning. Figured you'd aim for eight."

We pass the side of a brick building with a beach scene mural that covers the entire side of the building. On the mural, there's a sign dug into sand, and it reads, "Santa Barbara. Wish you were here."

One door opens into a shoe store. There's another glass door beside it, and Wolf pulls it back, opening it for me. The walls are painted black, and the floor is a shiny black tile. It might be black marble. A couple of black leather chairs with shiny silver legs are against one wall. There's a reception desk, and a woman sits behind a glass front. I remember Wolf telling me the glass is bulletproof. There are cameras in the corners of the room. We agreed to keep some cameras visible. Other cameras remain hidden in the walls.

I don't want to judge, but it feels that Erik, our other partner, and Wolf were like two kids in a candy store designing this new space. You'd think we were expecting Afghan rebels to storm the building. Erik and Wolf both love gadgets. Funny thing is both men don't require gadgets. Erik is a jiu-jitsu master. He's lean and quick. He's a fierce opponent on the mat. And Wolf is a beast. The guy is six foot seven and all muscle. I've seen expert fighters back away and run when stared down by those ice-blue eyes. My brother can be a scary motherfucker. But he's also strategic. And who am I kidding? I love weapons and gadgets as much as any soldier.

The woman behind the counter smiles in recognition. Wolf waves to her and says, "Morning."

An indiscernible black door opens in the wall, and she exits. She's wearing jeans, Doc Martens, and a professional blazer and top. From behind the glass, it appeared she wore a business suit.

She extends her hand, and I shake it.

"Tabitha Patel," she says, but I know her name already. I read her profile before we hired her. She's highly trained in hand-to-hand combat and is also a skilled marksman. She's former Army, fluent in Hindi, Bengali, and English. I'm not sure how long she'll be happy on reception desk duty, but she has twin toddlers at home, and my hunch is this is a dream job, at least for now. As I understand it, she helps us with projects from behind the desk. And, obviously, she serves as first line of defense.

"Trevor Thompson. Nice to meet you."

She returns to her desk and leans down. A black glass elevator door slides open.

When the door slides closed, I comment to Wolf, "She's definitely a good hire."

"She is. And she can hear you, as can several others."

*Right.* He grins. Within seconds, the doors open again. We have the entire top two floors of this converted warehouse, plus a roof which I've been told has ocean views. We're at least eight blocks from the ocean, but it's always nice to lay eyes on that mass of blue.

Every piece of furniture in the space is black leather. Each desk boasts an ergonomic office chair. Wolf stops at a corner office.

"This one's yours."

"Nice." The corner office has never been my aspiration. Desk duty in the military isn't a good thing. Or at least, it wasn't on my personal radar. But times change.

"Smith will be by in a bit to get you set up on your computer." I nod and take in my view of squat buildings and a small swatch of ocean off to the left.

"No welcome packet?" I tease.

"HR starts today. You think we should ask her to create an employee welcome packet?"

"Joke," I say. Although not really. We probably should have an employee welcome packet. But, as is clear by the mostly vacant space, most of our employees work virtually. "An electronic welcome packet might not be a bad idea. Is there a coffee machine?"

"Come this way." We pass a conference room with a glass interior wall and video screens on the two opposing walls. Closed doors line up on the far wall, and I assume those doors open into offices.

Wolf points at the next corner office and says, "That's me."

His desk and office are as empty as mine, except for two enormous monitors. Finally, we enter a small room that's set up like a kitchen. Well, a kitchen without an oven. There's a full-size refrigerator, three small round tables with chairs, and a long counter. On the counter is a coffee machine with an array of photo images of different drinks. I snag a mug from an open shelf and select the Americano.

"Thanks, by the way, for the hookup with the designer. She did a phenomenal job." She instructed the movers with the furniture delivery, oversaw art installation, and offered to stay behind and unpack me. Since all I had were clothes, electronics, and weapons, I declined her services.

"How'd you like that hotel?" Once again, I get a full-on flash of the woman from the bar. A second later, my ego takes another hit.

"No complaints. How was San Diego?" I am never clear if his trips to San Diego are pleasure or work. Out of habit, I never ask many questions unless we are face to face.

"Good. Interviewed two more candidates. Went on a nice dive. Spearfishing. Didn't get anything. What do you need to get settled? Your cars are here, right?"

"Yep. I drove the Jeep, and Kairi and David drove the Tesla."

"Any chance they'll move down here?"

"Ah, I think they like the area. Kairi would be down for it, but I get the sense David's reluctant to leave his mother behind. And he's never answered me straight when I ask about the difficulty in finding a pediatric clinic down here. The house they bought back in Napa...it's cute." Kairi is one of our own. Unlike us, she's not former military, but she's been with us for years. Our little team has been through hell and back. When you hear about people having adopted families, well, Kairi, Wolf, and

Erik are mine. David is Kairi's old high school boyfriend, soon to be more. If the pediatrician proves himself, I'll adopt him too. He's helped to bring Kairi back from a dark place, so I'm already indebted to the guy.

Lights flicker on, and I move to the doorway, peering out, while Wolf waits for the machine to spit out his coffee.

"I figure today will be a lot of meet and greet?"

"Actually, we've got a call with Erik in five. He's got a team pouring through the Phantom update. We'll take the call in my office."

The chair across from Wolf's desk is comfortable. His view is like mine, only the snippet of ocean is to his right.

"Shit. Let's move to the conference room," Wolf says.

"Okay." There's annoyance in his tone. I've spent the last year working from a sofa, so in this situation, I can go with the flow without any hackles rising. "There's a good speaker phone."

When he closes the door, he hits a button and the glass frosts.

"We can see out, they can't see in," he tells me.

"We need that level of security in our own offices?" Jesus, I thought we were thoroughly vetting our hires. Or, no, who am I kidding? It's one of his toys.

I pull out a chair and sit. The coffee isn't half bad.

"Erik asked me to take the call in here and to kill the monitoring. Not sure why." He presses on his phone, and the far monitor flicks to life. Erik's face fills the screen. I recognize the room he's in. It's his home office. He and his wife, Vivi Rossi, recently moved into a swank hilltop house that is as much of a security compound as this warehouse office Wolf created.

I'd rather invest my time and money in weapons. Since we moved back to the States, though, I've spent more time investigating surveillance equipment. I also had to recuperate and did so from Erik and Vivi's home.

"What's up?" Wolf asks. He pulls out the chair across from me but angles it so he can see out into the common area. My chair fully faces the inner office. I see one or two additional employees, but the desks remain mostly empty.

"Still downloading the Phantom update. Confirmed the numbers are to both Kane and two other Spectre executives. They swapped out numbers, so the leads are dead, but we're using the information to inform our plans." Phantom is a government program that offers no-click tracking. Meaning you can feed it a phone number, and it can download everything on someone's iPhone or Android.

Three months ago, Spectre became enemy number one when they attacked the United States power grid. We've been examining links between a CIA double agent and Spectre, and it eventually led us to some valuable phone numbers.

"We'll keep monitoring leads and see if we can pick up any more active numbers. If we can get a location, obviously, that's end game," Erik says.

Wolf and I are skeptical. Over the past few months, we've picked up live numbers. Chased one down to a dumpster. Phantom is a powerful cyberweapon, but it still has limitations.

One, a tracker only works if the person keeps the device. Two, there's always a risk information is planted for a setup.

"In the meantime, we're watching wine auctions. His buying habits show he's been hitting them regularly." The guy is an egotistical prick, so I'm not at all surprised he's gotten into the overpriced wine game.

Erik continues with a topline of Kane's favorite digital apps. There's not much we can do with any of that information.

"Santa Barbara Wine Festival," Erik says, seemingly out of nowhere. "Vivi and I are coming down for it."

"Cool. What are the dates? You need a place to stay?" I have three bedrooms, but even as I offer my place, my gut says he'll stay at one of the swank hotels.

"No." His response is clipped. "We got an in to put a proposal together for the security at the event. The festival will include multiple events, including a worldwide auction. Our proposal will include digital and on-site security. A man by the name of Mark Miller is going to be contacting you, and you'll need to do site visits. We are one of three security firms invited to submit our credentials."

He continues debriefing us with information on this international auction and on the key players he's expecting will attend. Governors, senators, CEOs, and billionaires. He's uploaded a complete VIP invitation list for the three-day event onto our Intranet. Tickets will be available to purchase by the general public. We won't have a complete list of festival attendees, as tickets will be sold on site, but we will have a final list of auction attendees three days before the ball. The auction committee will regularly update the attendee list, and it is conceivable the President of the United States might attend. We'll need to present our expertise in coordinating with alternate groups, like the Secret Service.

As he gives us the details, energy suffuses the room. It's a similar energy derived from planning missions. Thinking through all the ins and outs is scintillating. And these prestigious attendees will bring on advanced adversaries. I crack my knuckles. I like thinking about facing off with said criminals.

Wolf taps on his phone.

"I've got to go in under five," he tells Erik. "Thompson can stay on if needed."

Wolf flips back and forth between calling me by my last name and my first. During the workday, he's all last name, as if we're back in the military. It's fine. His last name is Wolfgang, which earned him so much crap it took a millisecond before he shortened it to Wolf. His first name is Aryan. And yeah, we never use that, either. It just doesn't fit. But everyone knows me as Trevor. It's not a hoity-toity name. It's a good, solid name. I'll give that one to Mom. She did a decent job with the name game. Not much else, but that's fine.

"We've got two new ransomware cases. And you and Trevor will get a call later about a security detail needed in Syria."

There's movement across the room. Erik and Wolf continue speaking, running down a complex project status sheet. But my focus centers on the woman who entered the main area outside the conference room. It can't be. But no, it sure as fuck is.

Her hair is pulled back tight and smooth. She's wearing a knee-length skirt and a button-down blouse with knee-high boots. Clasped to her chest is a notebook. Long gone is the mini dress from Saturday night. But her professional attire retains attitude and personality. Her reddish hair shines darker in this space, or maybe it's because it's pulled back, but even without bouncy waves, I would recognize her anywhere. That's Stella, the woman from Saturday night. The woman who left the room while I was taking a whiz. Wham, bam, thank you, sir. *Who is she? How did she track me down?*

My hand instinctively falls to my waist, but I'm not carrying. Both her hands are in sight. She's scanning the room. One of our agents, Hayes, is at her side, fawning over her.

"Erik, I gotta go. Our new HR director arrived. We done?" Wolf's abruptness signals the end of the briefing.

*Holy fuck.* Stella mentioned she was starting a new job. That's why she was out. Celebrating. Her new job is with Arrow? Something tells me she will not be pleased. But I am.

"Trevor, all good?" He's asking me if I am clear on what I need to do.

"Oh, yeah, all good." I throw Erik a wink for kicks. It's hard to see through the glare from his glasses, but I am fairly certain he rolled his eyes. The screen goes black.

Wolf is already out the door and shaking hands with Stella. And oh, do I have questions.

# THE ONE WHERE STELLA STARTS A NEW JOB



The cubicles are as empty as the day I interviewed. This is not a good sign. The unease in my gut threatens to evolve into unwieldy cramps.

Thank the gods I didn't increase my spending level before receiving my new paycheck. If this doesn't pan out, I can return to Mr. Martinez and plead for my old job. Muriel, the junior accountant in my old office, mentioned last week she culled a stack of resumes from responses to the job post, but he has yet to review them. I feel her pain. Reviewing resumes will be a low priority for him. It's Muriel who will do two jobs until a stressful disaster forces him to hire.

"Can I get you a coffee?" Hayes, the Arrow employee who greeted me at reception, is a friendly young man. I'd guess he's in his early twenties. There are no lines around his eyes, no hints of gray, and he has the healthy glow of someone who spends time outdoors. If I were a bartender, I'd definitely card him. Hayes assures me Mr. Wolfgang is in a meeting and will be right out.

"No problem."

The space is eerily quiet. There are no phones ringing. There's no music overhead. Even in the elevator—silence. There's a fresh paint scent lingering in the air. But it's not just paint. I inhale deeply. It's a new car smell. New carpet, new upholstery, new everything. Jenn gets a new car every three years. The first thing I do when she drives me somewhere in her new car is breathe it in. I love that smell. But should a place of reliable employment emit a new car smell?

Hayes leads me to an enormous coffee machine. The apparatus intimidates. In Mr. Martinez's small office, I managed the kitchen. I ordered the supplies, cleaned the coffee machine and the refrigerator. If anything broke, I fixed it or replaced it. If they expect me to handle this machine, I will sorely disappoint them. A device like this must need daily cleaning, but how would one do that?

"You just press the button for the coffee you want. Cappuccino is my favorite." My stomach is quite unruly, and while coffee is my lifeblood, my knees risk knocking together. "Sweetener is on that shelf. See these options here? You can choose if you want nonfat, regular, or cream."

Oh, Sweet Jesus, I bet the dairy gets added each day somewhere within that machine.

"Does this machine come with an instruction booklet?"

"It's really not that difficult. See, watch." He lifts a black mug down from the shelf and pushes a button. The machine sputters to life, and brown steaming liquid squirts out. "See?"

"Am I going to be in charge of running this machine?" Does the receptionist downstairs manage this machine? She introduced herself as Tabitha Patel, and we said hello this morning as she verified my identity with my license.

"Huh? No. There's someone else who does it."

"Who?" My gaze runs up and down Hayes. I peg him as the kind of guy who has no idea how things happen. The men in my life have always been that sort. The toilet paper magically appears on the roll. Mystical elves fold the laundry. Abracadabra, and the refrigerator is restocked.

"I'm not sure. I think it's the cleaning crew's job?" Okay. That works. Mr. Martinez hired a cleaning crew, too. They vacuumed, emptied the trash, and cleaned out the bathrooms. Management of the relationship with the cleaning company fell into my purview. I'll believe the kitchen doesn't fall under my domain once I locate my desk and figure out what needs to be done. The fact that I won't be a receptionist is still surprising to me. I served as a receptionist, secretary—or perhaps one says personal assistant these days—bookkeeper, human resources, and office manager for Mr. Martinez. I first met Tabitha Patel on the day I stopped in to meet with Mr. Wolfgang. I wouldn't call it an interview. He recruited me after visiting our offices and he discovered I was his company's bookkeeper. He had some questions about health insurance, which is a complete bear, and I spent time with him answering his questions while he waited for Mr. Martinez to get off a phone call.

Mr. Wolfgang smoothed over everything for me to join him here. He took Mr. Martinez out to lunch, and when he came back, Mr. Martinez said he'd miss me but that he couldn't come close to matching Mr. Wolfgang's offer, and that he was happy I had this opportunity. He said he liked to think he mentored me and helped me move forward in this world. I liked him more in that moment than I did in the prior nine years combined.

"Ms. Johnson, welcome." Mr. Wolfgang fills the doorway to the kitchen. Men that size are the reason I don't want my son playing football. My son is tall and thin, and there are high school boys who match Mr. Wolfgang in girth. Those giants would crush Ethan. Thankfully, despite Jason's best efforts, Ethan didn't go the football route.

"Did you get some coffee?" he asks. Mr. Wolfgang is gracious. I'm sure that as the days go by, assuming this job pans out, I'll see other sides to the boss.

"I'm good, thanks. But I was just asking Hayes… is this something that I will need to manage? Because I'll need an instruction book. I've never seen a machine like this." No, Mr. Martinez had the traditional coffee maker where you pour in grounds at the top each morning and the coffee pot sits on a hot plate.

"No." Mr. Wolfgang angles his body sideways and gestures with his broad shoulder. "Shall we go to your office? I'm sorry I wasn't outside to greet you. We had an unscheduled meeting."

I follow him back out into the cubicle area and add a mental note to ask how he wants me to handle his schedule. I prefer a collaborative Google Calendar format, but if he prefers a different source, I can learn. Most calendars follow a similar user interface.

"You can pick a different office if you like, but I was thinking we'd put you here. You'll have a good view across the cubicles for any additional hires you make on your team and there are vacant spots on each side." We cross the floor, and he opens a door. *A door.*

The office is similar in size to Mr. Martinez's. The back wall is a window with a view across low buildings and the tops of palm trees. Two black leather chairs sit in front of the oversized desk, and in the corner there is a small, round table with two chairs.

"Will this work? We also have a room designated for any storage you might need. Most of our files are electronic, but I assume there are some documents you'll want paper backups for. Jetson will be by to get your laptop set up. We have a couple of options, and he'll go over those with you."

"Jetson?" I ask, making sure I got the name correct. It's probably a last name.

"He's our IT guy. He asked for a code name."

"Is he a big movie buff?"

Trevor gives me a strange look. "We hire a lot of former military here."

Oh. That's right. I guess military guys might have code names. I never really thought about it.

He steps to the side, and I breathe in the moment. This is too much. It's a dream. This office is the most beautiful space I have ever seen.

"You can order artwork. We've been working with a designer. She'll stop by later on this afternoon to take you through some options. You can order plants or whatever. She has some ideas for the space, too. I told her that as our HR director, from here on out, she'll work with you, if that's okay. As I mentioned, if you want to hire an office manager who reports to you, feel free. We'll have to vet any person you interview, since security is our business. We'll discuss the hiring process later. I've been doing it all myself for a while. I'm looking forward to you taking over. If I recall, you said you want to get boots on the ground before determining your hiring needs?"

There's no way I said the phrase "boots on the ground," but I nod because it's the point, not the words, that matter. And yes, I definitely need to get my bearings. Right now, I am reeling and dizzy with all the newness. Maybe I should wear a suit?

"Ready for a tour of the place?"

"Yes."

"You can put your stuff down on the desk." It's only then that I realize I'm clutching a notepad and my left shoulder is weighed down with my pocketbook and an old briefcase I dusted off last night.

"Oh, right. Will I need to take notes?" I ask.

"We won't expect name memorization on day one. We've only got a few people inside the wire at the moment."

"Excuse me?"

"On base." He smiles. "In the office. It's military lingo." The corners of his lips lift. He might be smiling.

"Okay." I swallow and set everything down on the shiny black surface. "Yes, I wondered where everyone was. I mean, I know the business is doing well. At least, based on the accounting I've seen, but it's unnerving seeing an empty office."

"It'll get busier. For the most part, there's no reason to require employees to come into the office. But as you'll see, we have a need for a secure base for operations. Now, you've already met Hayes."

He steps back while I gape at my office. My office. I remain in awe. I have a door.

"Follow me?" he asks. I nod repeatedly, but thankfully, he's not looking at me. He's two feet ahead of me as he leads me past several open doors and unused offices.

The wall of frosted glass is now clear, and inside the room there's a long conference table, and monitors hang on the wall. Natural light fills the once-dark interior room thanks to the sun filtering through the windows. Allowing the light to come through that conference room makes an enormous difference in this interior lair. Clearly, these men love black, but the space needs some lighter touches.

"And here's one of our partners, Trevor Thompson. He'll be working from these offices most days, like me."

I tear my attention from the blue sky view out the conference room windows. Wolf pushes open another black office door, and I am hit with an overwhelming urge to dive under a nearby desk.

*Fuck me sideways into Tuesday.*

Rising from his chair is my Chris Hemsworth knock-off.

"Trevor, this is Stella Johnson, our new HR director. She's going to get our shit straight."

A cocky smile traverses his lips, and my survival instinct kicks in.

"It's nice to meet you, Mr…?" My tone rises, punctuating the question while simultaneously emphasizing that he and I do not know each other. I hope my pleading gaze communicates everything I need it to. *Please don't let on we know each other. Please play along. Please.*

"Thompson," he supplies. "Welcome. And you can call me Trevor."

"Yeah. You can drop the misters. We're not formal around here. Everyone here calls me Wolf." Mr. Wolfgang is already several steps down. "I've only got ten minutes to give you the tour. Sorry. Trevor, we'll talk later?"

"Why don't I give her the tour?"

"You know your way around?" Mr. Wolfgang sounds skeptical.

"It's not that complicated. You go. Then we'll loop back on this morning's meeting?"

"Works."

And with that, it's just me and my one-night stand.

# Private News Network



Trevor

"This is awkward," she says.

I shouldn't grin. But as much as I try to maintain a straight face, I can't. She holds her hands behind her back. She won't look me in the eye. A heated flush spans across her cheeks. She didn't plan this. She's as surprised by this turn of events as I am.

I come around the desk and sit on the edge. From here, my feet are two feet away from hers.

"Is it awkward?" I ask, playing her word choice back at her. I cross my arms and stare her down, mentally urging her to lift those eyes. "Lucky is the word I would choose."

"Lucky?" Now she looks me in the eye. She has dark blue eyes. That's a detail I didn't notice Saturday night. Her mouth forms an "oh." She disagrees. Her lashes flutter. Her breasts rise and fall. "Look, Mr. Thompson—"

"Trevor."

"Ah, Trevor." She pushes her shoulders back, and her chin juts out. There's a mental battle going on, and I'd say she just got control of her forces. "If I had known you worked here, I would have never done," she swallows, "what we did," she swallows again, "Saturday night. That was..."

"I thought it was pretty great."

"Well, yes." Redness descends in splotches across her neck and across the swatch of exposed skin above her breasts. She huffs. I force my lips into a straight line. "Here's the thing." She directs her gaze to the corner of my desk. "I need this job. I have so much riding on this job. It's important to me."

"Whoa, whoa. Who said anything about us impacting your job? Your job here is safe no matter what happens between us." This is not the military. There is no non-fraternization policy.

"There is no us." Steely determined eyes drill into me. "And I would appreciate it if you keep what happened Saturday night between us. I really... I haven't done anything like that... That's not me. And I don't want any of the other men in the office getting that idea. This is very important to me."

I lose the urge to smile. I get where she's coming from. We're a high-testosterone firm. Most of our field agents are men. And no, I don't want them getting that idea about her, either.

"I understand. I won't tell a soul."

"Thank you. I appreciate that." One hand toys with an earring while the other arm crosses below her breasts. She doesn't look comfortable.

"But for the record, we could date without anyone—"

"No. I will not jeopardize this job. This job… it's a dream for me. And for my son."

Son. Whoa. Okay. That little bomb should shut me up, but I have to make my point.

"Stella, for the record, no matter what happened with us, or what might happen between us, your job is not in jeopardy here. I'm one of the founders of this company. We aren't uptight."

"Well, maybe you should be. You open yourself up to considerable legal risk if you allow interpersonal office relationships. You should consult with your general counsel."

I've never been a business guy. But I am a team member, and her statement reminds me I'm not a lone wolf. My actions can impact this company we're working to build.

"Why don't I give you that tour now?" I check the time. We have an FBI briefing in just under an hour.

I follow Stella out of my office, and Hayes hustles up to us.

"There's a vendor downstairs. H&M Food Distributor. Do you have time to meet with him? He's not on the calendar. Patel said I should check with you before I turn him away. She wanted to meet with Wolf, but he says that's under your purview."

"I thought you were HR director." What the hell is Wolf saying she needs to order food for? Stella beams at Hayes like he's a lifesaver.

"Office management will fall under my purview. I will hire an office manager." I could be wrong, but I think this excites her. If that's the case, then it's all good. "I'll be happy to meet with him. Should I go downstairs, or…?"

"I'll bring him upstairs. Patel doesn't allow someone up unless they have a designated meeting."

"I'll give you that tour at a later time," I call out to Stella's retreating back.

Hayes hears, of course, and responds with an ever-so-helpful, "Oh, I can give her a tour of the place."

"Thanks, Hayes," I grumble.

I lose the next thirty minutes with Jetson. His wire-rimmed spectacles and angular chin earned him his code name. But I picture George Jetson with thick blond hair. This guy has thick black hair. Admittedly, it sticks out like George Jetson's, but he's Pakistani. I think we could improve upon our code names. He introduced himself to me as Jetson, so I deduce he either likes this moniker, or his real name isn't dumbass American friendly.

Thanks to Jetson, my office looks like Christmas morning. Jetson wheeled in boxes of electronics. He set up two new enormous wide screen monitors, a new laptop, keyboard, and various additional gadgets and charging pads.

"You know, I do have a laptop."

"You need an upgrade."

I stifle the obvious question. Why do I need an upgrade? I don't care enough to sit through his explanation.

My new laptop has new-age fingerprint recognition. I leave him in my office, happily creating passwords. My hope is that fingerprint recognition means I don't have to remember any of those strong passwords he is gleefully creating.

I'm the first one in the conference room, but it's not long before Wolf joins me. He closes the door behind him, and the frost effect covers the windows. There are, like, three employees on the floor, so it's overkill.

As Wolf goes about bringing screens to life and connecting to a network, I stare out the window and tap the end of my pen on the table. I didn't think I'd see Stella again. And I'd been a bit bummed. Slightly offended she didn't want to hang around or offer the opportunity to exchange numbers. But I can't hold it against her. I've been there. Had the hookup I had no intention of calling. Since I was staying at a hotel, she may have assumed I lived far away. Regardless, being on the no-call end of a hookup sucks.

An unsolicited image of her in my bed comes to mind. Her wild, dark strands against that backdrop of white. Her full, perfect breasts. And that… that's what I've got to block out. She wants professional, she'll get professional. It's just my damn luck she'd end up working here.

"Hi, guys." Kairi's voice wafts through the speaker.

"Where are you?"

"I'm in the hotel."

"Where's David?" Wolf asks in a gruff tone.

"He's up at the pool getting us lounge chairs and ordering champagne." She sounds giddy.

"Does that mean you chose to jump?"

"Yes," she squeals, and her smile somehow floats through the speakers.

"You aren't coming in? Isn't it required for you to come in and show off the ring?"

"There's a rooftop pool."

Wolf taps his pen and stares at the black speaker. I want to kick him under the table. This is big for Kairi. For a long time, I didn't think she'd ever have the courage to put herself out there again. "The moment our meeting ends, I'm going to have a celebratory engagement lunch with an ocean view."

The screen flashes to life, and several heads appear in squares across the monitor. This interagency briefing will go out to teams with different functions across the globe.

A woman in a serious suit with dark skin and hair fills the largest square, and it lights up as she speaks. She introduces herself and welcomes everyone to the Wired Task Force.

These briefings can be annoying because they could easily communicate the entire update in writing. But, because of the nature of sharing information, I can see the benefit in allowing an open forum for feedback, questions, and cooperation. This particular task force is led by the IC3, or the Internet Crime Complaint Center. Normally, Kairi and Erik, or someone on their team, would sit in on these meetings. But I've been sitting in to listen out for leads.

Spectre, the organizational name that typically tops IC3 reports, is noticeably absent from today's updates culled by the Wired Task Force. Their illegal activity has been minimal since the blackout. It doesn't mean some of the crimes we're monitoring aren't caused by Spectre, but they're playing a defensive game at the moment. Their activity lull is frustrating. We're setting traps all over the place. Phishing for a bite. Monitoring wine and art auctions. One way or another, our multi-pronged plan will work, and we will dismantle the organization by chopping off the head of the viper.

The NSA is leading the charge to take Spectre down. By claiming responsibility for the West Coast Blackout, they became known as the world's foremost cybercrime organization, and by doing so, became a prime target for the NSA, FBI, and CIA. And given Erik and Kairi used to work for the bastards, there's bad blood swirling under the bridge. By bad blood, I mean it's personal.

After our briefing with the FBI concludes, Wolf asks if we can sit to discuss our new clients and our hiring needs.

"Don't you think our new HR director should sit in?"

Wolf and I have been hiring employees using military recruitment strategies. Good people from our network. And we've been winging all kinds of minutiae that I suspect is going to bite us in the ass. We're growing, and we need to get things under control and organized. His lower lip protrudes, and his half nod is all the agreement I need to go find Stella Johnson.

# THE ONE WHERE
# JANICE GOES KABLOOEY

STELLA

"Mom, where's my Black Keys shirt?" Ethan bellows his question from somewhere in his room. We have thin walls, so while yelling isn't the most peaceful form of communication in the early morning rush, it works.

"It should be in your drawer. You didn't wear it this week, did you?"

"Where?" he screams.

"Your drawer," I shout.

"Where?" he bellows again. I drop my mascara wand and give myself a once-over in the mirror. My blush is a little too much, and I swipe it with toilet paper, then pound down the hall to

Ethan's room. I swing the door open. He's on the floor, his overnight bag open, filled with clothes.

"What are you doing?" He goes to his dad's every other weekend.

"Packing. Dad got VIP tickets to The Wallows in LA tonight. I want to wear my Black Keys tee."

I step past him, open his t-shirt drawer, thumb through the stack of black folded tees, locate the shirt in question, and pull it out.

"Here you go." He takes it from me and drops it into the bag.

"Have you seen my Nikes?"

"Did you check the bottom of your closet?" He lumbers two steps to his closet, bends down, and picks them up. I check the time on my watch.

"All right, buddy. Five minutes. It's my first week. I don't want to be late."

I rush down the stairs to get my coffee and pop a bagel into the toaster for Ethan. I am loving my new job. They include me in meetings. At first, sitting in a meeting room caused my nerves to go haywire.

All of my career, I've been the one who coordinated meetings and set out the coffee or food. To be the one sitting at the conference room table, contributing and offering ideas... it's completely ridiculous, but it's an absolute high. The fact that I am still on cloud nine with my newfound job is probably why I'm not put out about Ethan going over to Jason's off-schedule.

I'm not even the slightest bit annoyed that once again he's doing something with Ethan that I couldn't remotely afford, and that neither of them bothered to mention it to me.

Actually, can I afford it? This weekend, I need to sit down and go over my new paycheck and do some budget planning. Maybe, just maybe, I'll be able to splurge on Ethan and do fun things that aren't free.

My phone rings, and I answer on speaker.

"*Hola!*" Jenn shouts.

"*Buenos días.*" She gets to school early and has time to gab. I don't, especially on a day I'm running late. "What's up?"

"Well, I was calling to wish someone a happy birthday!"

She sings out the song as I munch on a piece of banana. When she finishes her loud, off-key song, I clap and say, "Thank you, dear friend."

"I'm so bummed I can't take you out tonight. If Terrell didn't have this required work retreat this weekend, you know I'd be with you, right?"

"You already took me out to celebrate." *And trust me, I celebrated.*

"Yes, but this is a big one."

I cringe. "Thanks."

"No, you know what I mean."

"It's another trip around the sun. And it's a number I'd rather not think about." Or apply to me, really. Not that thirty-nine is a fantastic number. That one sucks too because everyone thinks you're lying.

*Boom, boom, boom.*

Ethan's heavy steps down the stairs announce his impending arrival.

"Gotta run. Love ya for the call."

I hand Ethan his OJ, toasted bagel, and banana, and gather up my coffee mug and backpack. On the first day at Arrow, I noticed everyone else carried a backpack, not a briefcase. Life in a security company differs from an accounting firm—and in all the right ways.

My bosses are amazing—even the one I slept with. They treat me with professionalism. When Trevor entered my office an hour after our initial meeting, I'd frozen like a chocolate-covered banana. It could be a bad thing, or so I thought. But no, he'd pulled me into a meeting. My first ever meeting as an attendee with an active role.

Wolf and Trevor have been doing their best on employee benefits. But health insurance is a tricky thing. I think if I dig in, I can improve the policies they offer. Both men told me they aren't concerned about cost—they want to provide their employees the best health insurance they can, and they want to know if someone is injured on the job, they and any dependents are covered. To hear that employee-first philosophy spoken out loud is like a dream come true. Mr. Martinez cared first and foremost about the bottom line because, let's be real, the profit is what he takes home.

"Mom, when are you going to get the AC fixed?" Ethan rolls down his window the moment he hops in the car.

"We live in Santa Barbara. We don't need air conditioning."

"Yeah, right," he grumbles. He takes over the radio. He completes driver's ed soon, and he'll be the one driving Janice. Yes, a few years ago, we named my car Janice after the shrill, annoying character on *Friends*, because around then is when the brake pads gave out and a shrill high-pitched screech accompanied each touch of the brake. Then other engine parts broke in rapid succession on the ancient Honda Accord. Ethan said that because the car is burgundy, it had to be a female name. We agreed to disagree. I believe burgundy can be a male color.

I turn right into the line of cars at the drop off in front of Dos Pueblos High School. Janice trembles when I slow. The vibration is unfamiliar. I lay my hand on the dashboard to confirm that, yes, I haven't felt this before.

"You need to get that checked out."

"Maybe she just needs oil."

"Mom." It's amazing how loaded one word can be, depending on the inflection used.

"I will."

Ethan rolls his eyes. There was a time in the not-too-distant past when the idea of going to the mechanic kneaded my stomach into knots. But today, it's mildly annoying. A suction on my weekend time. Thank you, amazeballs job.

"Dad says if you didn't waste money, you could afford a better car."

"Is that right?" There is a smile planted on my face. It's the expression I have perfected over the years. I refuse to speak badly of his father. I will not do it. Ethan waves to someone passing by on the sidewalk.

"Are you coming back Saturday or Sunday?"

"I think Sunday. We're staying at a cool hotel in Hollywood."

"Is it just you and your dad?" I hate myself for asking. I truly do. I don't care. I don't want to know. But no, that's not true. He's my son. I should ask who he is spending the weekend in LA with.

"Dunno." It's our turn for him to hop out. "Love you, Mom."

"Have a great—" The door slams shut. Ethan catches up with one of his friends I recognize. His friend smiles and waves at me.

"Hey, Mrs. J," he says. He's a good kid. He doesn't come over anymore, but when they were in middle school, I used to see him quite a bit.

I press the accelerator, and Janice jerks forward, then backward, then she settles into a forward roll. Maybe this weekend I'll look into trading her in. Ethan is right. It's overdue.

The only thing is I don't think I ever got the title from Jason. The car is definitely mine. It's a part of the divorce agreement. I remember asking Jason for the title, but I eventually stopped. It didn't matter to me that much. But now it's one more thing I'll have to deal with. I can't imagine any dealer worth his salt will just take my word that the car is mine.

Cars pack the 101. I flick to my traffic app and cringe at the bright red streak along my route. I'm only about ten miles from our office, but ten miles with a wreck on the 101 freeway will be an emotional journey. Both windows are down, and the stink of car exhaust has me coughing.

Janice jerks forward and backward. The vibration intensifies into a tremble on the steering wheel. A warning light flashes. It's the temperature light. Smoke steams out from Janice's hood.

"Janice. What are you doing to me?"

Fanfuckingtastic. One week into the best job I've ever had, and I'm going to be late. The waft of steam thickens, and I hit my right blinker. Fuck. I might even need to call the fire department. Janice's Blue Book value is less than three thousand. My stomach sinks as it hits me. This might be the end of Janice. On the bright side, I might not need that title after all.

# Dust Off

Trevor

Mateo digs his thumb into my shoulder over my inflamed scar. Inside my head, I growl. But I suck it up.

"Doesn't look like it hurts," he says.

"It's getting better," I grumble.

"Keep doing the stretches. These muscles right here," he karate chops my shoulder muscles, "are getting too tight. They're overcompensating. That's not what we want."

"Copy that."

Mateo is the PT guy I found in Santa Barbara. My physical therapist back in Napa sent over the routine he's been doing on me, which includes a lot of muscle work, physical and with various machines.

"Your paperwork said you were shot three months ago. You're doing amazing." *Fuck, yeah.* "How are you sleeping?"

He goes down the emotional trauma symptom list. I negative it all. There have been studies done on SEALs. Statistically, we're not as likely to suffer PTSD. We're hardwired differently. That's not to say I don't have the occasional flashback. I remember all confirmed kills. I especially remember the one tango's face as he held up his Glock and fired. How his pupils enlarged when I kept coming. How his muscles recoiled when I used his dead body as a shield until I could get my fingers wrapped around his Glock and eliminate his compadres.

Three bullets. I'm a lucky motherfucker. But when I stumbled upon the hired goons installing surveillance equipment, all I could think was if I didn't end them, they'd kill Kairi. She was upstairs. And they weren't going to get to her. Not on my watch.

I survived. They didn't.

"In my opinion, you're doing amazing." Mateo slaps his clipboard against his thigh. "You're the first gunshot victim I've worked with, but you're doing better than I would've expected." My body is a weapon, and I maintain it. Being in a superior physical condition aided my recovery. "But you can push yourself too hard, you know."

I squint and study the short, muscular guy. *Is he critiquing me?*

"You're doing good," he continues, "but you can overdo it. An injury will force you to take a few steps back."

"I'm training for an Iron Man."

He smiles, flashing a set of solid white chompers.

"All right. Three times a week. Right here. And if you feel pain, listen to it. Copy that?" he asks, playing my words back to me.

Mateo is going to work out. Which is a good thing because I don't feel like PT shopping. Thirty minutes later, I'm entering the office.

"Morning, Patel."

"Morning, Thompson." Patel grins as she pushes the button behind her desk. I enter the door that goes back behind reception. Gun racks line one wall. The area is fortified.

"Got your coffee. Black. And the morning breakfast sandwich."

"Thanks so much. What do I owe you?"

"Nothing. You'll get me next time." Movement on one monitor catches my attention. It's a skateboarder gliding by outside on the sidewalk.

"Heard you're getting a dog?"

"Well, it's more like my dog is getting delivered to me, but yeah. Who told you?"

"Wolf. He mentioned your running partner would be joining you soon."

"Yep. This dog is amazing. Could've done a tour. Best trained dog I've ever encountered."

"She's welcome to join me here anytime she wants."

"Good to know. You doing okay with this? I mean, is front desk enough for you?"

Her neck cracks when she tilts it sideways in an extreme stretch, but she doesn't flinch.

"I'm doing work down here. It's like having an office set away from everyone else. My husband likes knowing I'm behind bulletproof glass. The hours are reliable, which with kids in daycare works for me. It's good. I'll let you know when I want more."

I'm about to tell her to be sure to do that when a landline rings. Reception is the only desk in the office with a landline. She holds up an index finger, signaling she's going to answer. I lean back against the wall. I want to finish this conversation with Patel before I head up.

"Arrow Security." Patel's professional voice is markedly different from her shooting-the-shit tone. She's got corporate down. "I'll notify the team. Do you need someone to give you a lift?"

Patel flits her dark eyes to me, and her brow wrinkles. "What are those sirens for?" She pauses. "Are you sure you're okay?"

"Your engine is on fire?" There's a hint of incredulity. Wolf is upstairs, so I know she's not talking to him.

"Hey, Stella—" I push off from the wall and hover near Patel's chair. Loud noises emanate from the headset. "Girl, don't worry about being late. Listen to the firemen."

"What the—" Patel's hand shoots up, silencing me.

"Okay. Bye." Patel sets the headset down. "Stella's car is on the side of the 101. Fire truck just arrived. Engine fire. Can you believe that?"

"But she's okay?"

"She said she's fine. Worried about being late for work. She'll take a cab once she deals with the fire department and calls a tow truck."

"Call her and find out where she is. I'll head over. She doesn't need to take a cab."

"How will you get through traffic? The 101 has to be backed up for miles."

"Just find out where she is. I'll get to her."

"You've got one of those emergency vehicle lights, don't you? You know they're illegal?" She shouts the question as I'm pushing the door open onto the sidewalk.

"Call me when you get her mile marker."

Things between Stella Johnson and me have been completely professional this week. In meetings, her pen is in constant motion. I bet she's filled a notebook. She will ask questions if it pertains to employee benefits or expense, but if a topic doesn't pertain to her job, she's silent.

My speed hits ninety. I weave in and out of cars, scanning my rear and side view for cops. She's not in danger. The fire department is at the scene. Yet, a sense of urgency fuels me. The energy is reminiscent of the high from a rescue. My senses are on full alert. My skin tingles. My vision sharpens. Noises intensify.

It's nonsensical. But is it? I've always craved action. In high school, I trained as a lifeguard. The Navy gave rescue new meaning. I've toyed with the idea of pursuing a volunteer fire department gig. There's nothing like a good adrenaline-pumping rescue. Yet here I am, building a security company and sitting on a base assignment. My thumb finds the dial on my steering wheel and pumps up the volume.

Traffic isn't as backed up on the southbound track as expected. I turn off the nearest exit, loop under the overpass, and head toward my colleague. My teammate. I flip off my dashboard siren and line up on the shoulder, pulling in behind a big-ass red fire truck.

A couple of firefighters are hanging out on the end of the truck, one with a cigarette in his hand, and they nod.

"That your wife?" one of them asks.

"No." I smile to let him know I'm a friendly but don't slow my steps.

Stella is about twenty feet ahead. A damsel in distress, she is not. She's got a phone to her ear, and she's letting someone have it. She's pulled her reddish-brown hair up into a ponytail, and she's waving her finger in the air. The hood to her car is open, but there's no smoke. I step closer and see they have hosed it down. She's driving an older model Accord. I'm not a car guy, but my hunch is this one is totaled.

"A&W Tow offered twenty-five less." Her chin dips, and frown lines punctuate her lips. Someone is pissing her off. "I will call them." She sees me and says, "Asshole."

I halt in my tracks. *What did I do?*

"Not you. That fucker. All these places are fuckers. A woman calls, and they jack their rates."

I've got the good sense to remain quiet. She jabs her phone with her index finger.

"Where are you getting it towed?" The dump is where it needs to go. I'm pretty sure she could take her tags off and leave it on the side of the road. I've seen other cars do exactly that. It's probably not legal, but eventually the state will haul it off to the dump.

"I don't know." She paces the ground. One fireman comes up to her and hands her a card.

"This guy is my cousin. Call him. He'll tow it. Might take him a few hours to get your car, but he's good for it. I just spoke to him. He owns a small garage past Ellwood Pier. If he can't fix up your car, he'll sell the parts and work something out with you."

She narrows her eyes at the man. "He won't try to hose me?"

"No. And if he does, you let me know, and I'll take care of him. But he's given me his word. He'll do you right."

"Thank you…" There's a lilt in her tone that asks his name. It's a flirtatious tone I haven't heard since last Saturday night.

"Ben. Ben Ryder. I wrote it down, along with the name of the garage and their number."

I step closer to her and rest a hand on her shoulder. "You sure you're okay?" I ask.

I can see she's okay. But that man needs to back off. The fireman who's currently trying to make sure she gets treated right gives me a quick nod and steps back to join his team. *Yeah, that's right. She's got someone to help her out, Ben.*

"I'm fine. I'm just pissed. I always get pissed when people try to take advantage of me." She's a spitfire. She crosses her arms and spins on her heel to face her car. She looks like she wants to tear into it.

"Let me give you a ride to the office." Those blue eyes glimmer. Shit. I think she's going to cry. She's gone on what no doubt was an emotional high, and she's about to crash. But no tears fall. She blinks a few times, turns, and wraps up with the fire department.

I stand back and bide my time. I'm here if she needs me, but I'm not about to get in the way. Her back is to me, and that's when I see the magenta streaks of color coursing up in thick chunks to her ponytail. I don't remember seeing those colors before. It's a punk look. The kids take one thick chunk of hair and dye it an offbeat color. It would fit on the kid skateboarding by this morning.

Stella chose magenta. She's gutsy. Strong-willed. She's got fight.

She wraps up with the lead fireman and heads my way. I'm not sure, but I think that damn fireman put his number on that card too. That's fine. She doesn't want to date me. She knocked me out of the running when she found out we worked together. What did she say? We'd be stupid to allow fraternization? Or something like that?

I get her point. They heavily frowned on fraternization in the military.

"We can go now. I don't have to wait for the tow truck."

Traffic whizzes by, so I'm careful to position her away from the highway edge. I do not push ahead to open her door for her. There's a negative energy emanating from her body. My gut tells me that, at this moment, Stella needs to open her own door.

"Looks like you need to go car shopping," I say after our doors both slam shut. I'm in my Jeep. I don't always drive it, but today I did because I knew it would look less suspicious with a red light on the dash than my Tesla. Turns out I didn't even get to use my red light.

"Yeah. We'll see what the garage says, but yeah…" Her defeated sigh speaks volumes.

My mom was a single mom. I know that look. She's holding it together through sheer will.

"The company has a vehicle you can use while you get everything straightened out."

"I don't remember any company vehicles." Ah, shit. I'm lying to the wrong person. She's our benefits manager.

"Yeah, well, maybe we didn't allocate everything correctly." Wolf and I have been learning about a lot of things we didn't do correctly over the last week, so it's a believable statement. I check the side view and speed up onto the freeway.

"Thanks." She leans her head back against the headrest and closes her eyes. Wind whips her hair, creating a flurry of reddish brown and magenta.

"What color would you say your hair is?"

"Auburn?" She sounds unsure. "Oh, you're talking about this." She points to the thick streak stemming from the base of her neck. "The box says fuchsia passion. Supposed to be brighter. I didn't bleach before doing it, so the color's a little off."

She stares out the window, and I take the hint and leave her alone.

If she's going to take my Tesla, I'll need to get a charger installed in her house. I can have that done this afternoon while she's at the office. Or I can look into a different car option for her. I'll talk to Wolf. She's on our team. We take care of our own. I like the Tesla, though. It's safe. I'm not a soft-hearted whackadoodle, but I do like that it's good for the environment. And I have the Jeep and don't need to drive to work, so loaning her my Tesla makes the most sense.

"You didn't need to come and get me, you know." She draws me out of my thoughts.

"You're on our team." I glance at her. Those dark blue eyes are something else. "Colleagues, remember?" I toss the words at her. Not because I believe them, but because it buys me space.

Takes the heat off. "How's your son get home from school? You need to pick him up?"

"No. He's staying at his dad's. Even if he wasn't, he'd catch a ride with a friend." She crosses her legs and gazes out to her right. Far off in the distance, over the patchwork grid of neighborhoods, the Pacific shimmers under the rising sun. "Soon he'll be driving my car." She smiles, and those white teeth blind me. "Learner's permit," she adds.

I do the math in my head. She must've been young when she had him.

"I suppose I should weigh that in when I go car shopping."

"What kind of car are you thinking?"

"I have no idea. I guess I know what I'll be doing this weekend."

"Let's go out to dinner. We can do some online car shopping. I'll help get you set up with the company car in the meantime."

"Trevor..." She's shaking her head. My interpretation of that shake is she's telling me it's a no.

"Colleagues, remember? Besides, I have nothing else to do. I don't know anyone else in town except Wolf, and he's off to San Diego. You're on our team."

"And you take care of your own." She says it to me like I say that a lot. Maybe I do.

A text comes in from Wolf.

*Where are you? There's a situation in Brazil.*

. . .

My Jeep is old school, so it's not wired with voice-activated messaging. The wind is too loud for Siri to interpret anything I say, anyway. I hand my phone to Stella and ask her, "Will you respond and tell him I'm ten minutes out?"

"What's going on in Brazil?"

"I'll find out in eleven minutes." I'm not positive, but I suspect she rolled her eyes at me. "My guess would be it's another ransom. It's pretty common in Sao Paulo."

"Like ransomware? What Kairi and Erik deal with?" She's been studying up on what we do at Arrow. For someone with a nonmilitary background, she's taken it all in stride.

"Nah. In Brazil, it's kidnapping."

"Shit."

"It's not a big deal. It's bullshit, really. There're a slew of different outfits that figured out decades ago they can target corporate expat businessmen and their families. Insurance companies pay the ransom. They don't really intend to do harm. It's become a business in its own right."

"What does Arrow do?"

"Eh, sometimes the business hires a private group to rescue. If it's their kid, they don't wanna wait for the insurance company to pull it together. So, we'll go in and rescue. Sometimes it's more complicated. If it's diplomats or some VIP. Each case is different."

"That's why you care so much about employee benefits? Because what you guys do is dangerous?"

"Can be. But if we train right, we put the odds in our favor."

"So, it's not like mall security?"

"No, Stella. It's not like mall security."

"I knew that. I know that." She tilts her head back on the headrest. "Do you go rescue people?"

"Sometimes. It's been a while since I've gone on a mission. I've been more strategic of late."

"That's good." I'm not sure I agree with her. I never aspired to a desk job. "So, you stay safe."

This time, I'm the one looking any direction but at her. I am not prepared for my physical response to her innocuous statement. She didn't mean anything by it. It shouldn't feel good to hear it.

# The One Where
# Stella Finds Out

STELLA

"All right. You ready?"

I can't take my eyes off the charging station that has magically appeared next to my carport. It sports the fancy Tesla logo, and there's a hose thing hanging around the base like at a gas station. Except instead of gas, it pumps electricity.

My instinct is to put up a fight. I don't take handouts. I don't need a handout. But Arrow management has an anything goes policy with employee benefits, at least based on what I can tell. Pretty much every expense seems to go on the business, but they are founders. Mr. Martinez was the same way to an extent with his own benefits, but those benefits did not extend to a single employee below him.

And then there's the car. It's gorgeous. It's a steel gray with white seats. I want to decline the car because of the white seats. Who the hell puts white seats in a car? Did Trevor not notice the inside of Janice?

"Stella? We've got to get going?"

My across-the-street neighbor exits his house with his wife. He waves, but I see him do a double take before getting in his truck.

"Do you think this car will be safe here?" I would really hate for a company car to be stolen from my property.

"It's not going to get stolen. Besides, this isn't one of the high-end models. It's an X."

That means nothing to me, but okay. I'm really not a car person, so I'll have to take his word for it. He is my boss, and he has insisted I use this car while I figure my car situation out.

"Is your neighborhood not safe?"

Trevor steps into the six feet of grass that is my front yard. The grass is weedy and sparse. Yet there's enough of it to require mowing, much to Ethan's chagrin. I've thought about digging it up and doing a desertscape, which is common in this area, but it's a rental, so I don't see the point in spending the money. But I pay the water bill, and there are months when I think I would save money if I ripped the grass out. Water gets more expensive every year.

"You've got a gated entrance, right?"

"Gated?" I choke on a laugh. "There are two entrance columns. Those gates don't function. It's a low-crime area. But this is a nice car." That said, there are some high-end cars parked in the driveways. I'm being me… too nervous and worried. "I'm sure your car will be fine. I hope. I'd just feel so bad if—"

"I'm not worried about the car. I'm worried about you."

"Oh. No. It's safe. I wouldn't live here with my son if it wasn't. We're in a good school district." When you've got a public school kid, that's the only thing that matters. "I've lived in this house for, well, ten years. I didn't mean to give you the wrong impression."

He casts one last frowning glance down my street.

"Seriously, it's safe. I promise." I hope it's safe for the company car. Maybe I shouldn't do this.

"You want to drive, or you want me to?"

I drove the Tesla home. Trevor had been here waiting for me as he oversaw the installation of this electrical pump. Patel helped me figure out the Tesla. Thank goodness. I would have never in a million years figured out the television screen in that car without a guiding hand.

"You?" I suggest. Trevor has on cargo shorts and a gray t-shirt. The sleeves of a black thermal wrap around his trim waist. And he's wearing running shoes. Some days at the office he's worn jeans, but he's always casual. And he always looks mouth-wateringly delicious.

The temperature has begun to drop, and he unleashes the black thermal from his waist. When he slips it on over his head, his t-shirt rises, exposing a sliver of a certain eight-pack I remember a little too well. God, that man is fit. What am I doing going to dinner with him? He's my boss.

"Are you okay?"

"Yeah, why?"

"You're just…" His words trail, and it hits me. I'm staring like a nincompoop.

"No, I'm sorry. I'm fine. Let's go. You drive."

*Do you mind if I change?* is on the tip of my tongue. The pads of my feet are throbbing. I'm wearing heels because I always wear heels in the office. It's just a thing I do. But it's better if I keep my entire office outfit on for this dinner. It'll help me remember I am an employee and he is my boss. One of my bosses. Even so, my boss. Yes, he's gorgeous. And the best sex I've had in my life… even if it was a little awkward afterward.

"You know, you don't have to take me to dinner."

The turn signal on his Jeep clicks loudly as he turns out of my neighborhood.

"You've said that a few times. And I've explained that I want to. Arrow is a small company. We go out to dinner with colleagues all the time."

I have a feeling once I dig into expense reports I will indeed see that is true, but it's just the two of us, and is that really a good idea between two colleagues who shared a hotel room? But we agreed to forget about that. It's behind us. Never to be mentioned again. The event that shall not be named.

The wind picks up as he gains speed. The doors are on his Jeep, thank god, but the top is off. My ponytail whips around wildly, the ends battering my face. The sun is setting over the horizon and the dull glow of brake lights and headlights portend nightfall. We speed along the 101, headed back toward Santa Barbara without speaking. It's an easy silence, because we'd have to shout to be heard over the wind and his blaring radio.

The noise diminishes as he turns into the parking lot for The Boathouse on Hendry's Beach. It's a restaurant I'm familiar with. You have to be willing to wait forever to get a table. There's a crowd, and the parking lot is full. He drives up to the valet.

"You know there's going to be a long wait, right?" It's Friday night at sunset. The Boathouse has amazing beach views and excellent food. You don't get that combination and no wait. Plus, they don't take reservations. He's new here, though. It's not his fault. He just doesn't know.

He gives me a cocky grin. The same sexy-as-fuck cocky grin he gave me a week ago. The cocky grin that had me agreeing to go up to his room.

He slaps the valet on his back and says something I can't hear. Then he's at my door, opening it for me.

"My lady?" he says as he offers his hand.

"Colleague?" I counter. Colleagues can go out for dinner. Lord knows Jason goes out to dinner with his colleagues all the time. I can do this. I just need to keep our situation front of mind.

We wait behind a couple at the hostess stand. My stomach grumbles. I'm not a late eater. After years of life with a son, I am used to eating at a reasonable hour. Maybe there will be room at the bar, and we can order appetizers.

"Hi, Samantha?" The hostess blushes in response and smiles. I don't think she knows him, but she's smitten. I get it. Completely. Although I can't help but think this hostess is closer to Ethan's age. I'd guess she's a UCSB student. "We're a table for two. My buddy said you'd hook us up?"

"Wolf." Now she really grins when she says his name. "Come right this way."

We weave through the restaurant, then outside onto the coveted outdoor patio, then right up to the glass panel that blocks the ocean breeze.

"Will this do?" she asks. Trevor nods and carries on with her, but I am in shock. I have never, in all my years of being in Santa Barbara, gotten one of these coveted tables. We have an uninterrupted view of a golden pink sunset. Immediately, I'm taking out my phone and snapping photos. Jenn needs to see this.

Once, she and I got up ridiculously early to get brunch here. You have to or you wait, like, two hours. Even then, we were seated near the parking lot.

"Is Wolf dating her?" I ask after she departs. I overheard her asking Trevor to be sure to have Wolf call her. I didn't like how she sounded a little desperate. I'd like to take her aside and coach her a little. Give her a few pointers on men and let her know that if they make you feel desperate, then they so aren't worth it.

"I don't know." He's reading the menu, but when he glances up at me, he laughs. "I really don't. I asked him about dinner locations, and he sent me here. Wolf and I go way back. He makes friends everywhere he goes."

"Really?" The oversized man doesn't strike me as the happy-go-lucky kind of guy at all. He's quite serious in the office.

Trevor's lips curl up, and he returns his gaze to the menu. Something is amusing to him, and there's nothing comical on the menu. If I knew him better, I'd push. My guess would be there's a backstory about Wolf and the hostess. But I'm a colleague, and he should not spill about one of my other bosses. That would be highly unprofessional.

The waitress approaches and gives us the specials. After she leaves, Trevor asks what I'm going to have.

"Oh, the boathouse seafood pasta." In the back of my head, I can hear Jason saying the word pasta in a questioning tone. "I know I probably shouldn't, but I hardly ever get to come here, and it's my favorite dish." I've only had it twice. I'll walk a few extra miles tomorrow. Ethan isn't home, so I can do that.

"Why shouldn't you?" His gaze falls to my thighs, and a patio heater somewhere nearby kicks on. "You should eat what you want. What do you think about a chardonnay to go with dinner?" I can only nod. Damn, those words are food for the soul. He's already gorgeous, but the man skyrocketed to earth-shattering perfection with that statement. He's my boss, though. My boss. He continues, asking me about appetizers.

We end up with a dozen oysters and a couple of oyster shots.

"So, Stella, tell me about your son." The question is the best question he could ask. Because it reminds me I have a son who needs me to keep my job. And he's my son. There's really nothing that I like to talk about more.

"His name is Ethan. He's a freshman at Dos Pueblos High. He's a really good kid." I know parents always say that about their kids, but Ethan really is. "Do you have kids?"

He shakes his head, and his lower lip puckers out ever so slightly. I suspect he's trying not to grin.

"Well, if you don't have kids, you don't want to hear about mine." I fiddle with the napkin in my lap and take in the setting sun. It's truly spectacular tonight. It's a mix of golden yellows, oranges, and pinks.

"I actually would. What's he into? Sports? Band?"

"He does like music. He plays guitar. I guess he's learning saxophone. He's listening to a band in LA tonight." That's a part of his life I haven't been able to contribute to as much as Jason. Until now, I haven't been able to afford pricey concert tickets. "Ethan has a million Spotify playlists. We listen a lot together at home."

"So, he's a music guy?"

"And he likes some sports. He's a runner. He can surf." He outgrew his wetsuit, though. I've been combing resale sites for used wetsuits. Haven't found one yet that has met his approval. "He plays lacrosse, soccer. When he was little, he played basketball and baseball, but they kind of fell to the wayside."

"No football?"

"Funny you should ask. His father would love for him to play, but he's never gotten into it. Are you a big football guy?"

"No. Just curious. Trying to get a sense of what kind of son you've raised."

"Why?"

"Because I want to get to know you." That comment forces my legs to cross. If he wasn't sitting right here, I'd fan myself. "So, his father? He's around?"

"He is." I wish the fucker wasn't, but he is.

"Were you married?" His back hits his seat.

"Yes. I've been divorced for over ten years. If you count the years we were separated, more like twelve or thirteen. Our divorce took… it was…" I wave my hand. No one wants to hear about drawn-out divorce drama. And I don't want to relive it.

"How old were you?" Now he's leaning forward, concern etched around the corners of his eyes.

"Let's see. I was twenty-four when I had Ethan. Jason and I met in college. We were separated by the time I was twenty-six." Yep, I've been on my own for a while now.

He scratches his jaw. He's wearing a thoughtful expression.

"Are you wondering how old I am?" I don't know why I ask him that. If he knew how to access employee documents, which I'm fairly certain he doesn't, he'd have the answer.

"Thirty-nine?" he asks, one eyebrow raised.

"Yeah." There's a sinking from my throat down to my stomach. I'd so much prefer he guessed younger. I can't force the word *forty* out of my throat, and besides, there is zero reason to tell him today is my birthday.

"You gave me enough numbers. I could do the math."

"Oh, yeah. I did, right?" He smirks. "How old are you?"

I, too, could look at his file, but I've had enough to do getting my feet on the ground this week. I haven't gone snooping.

He hesitates. I lift my glass of chardonnay and sip. He flashes that sexy smirk. It's seriously the sexiest. If he ever tires of the security business, he could model.

"I'm almost twenty-nine."

Wine splatters across his thermal. Not for real, but in my head, his shirt is ruined.

# About Face

Trevor

Sunday is my long run day. Long runs test both mental and physical stamina. The best long runs are mapped out and planned.

Today is not my best day. My pace is down. The sand seeped into one sock, so I cleaned it out and headed onto asphalt streets. I mapped this route, but it's my first time running it. Sweat beads across my brow, a healthy burn coats my lungs, my knees bear a mild, familiar ache. Fifteen-point-five miles. My aim had been for sixteen. I may overshoot it. Maybe I'll swing by the Gold's Gym, hit some weights, stretch, carb up, then go for a second run.

After checking my stats, I click to a text from Wolf.

. . .

Wolf: *Stop by. We'll patch E in.*

There's no need to respond. He's my next-door neighbor. I'll see him in a bit. I drop the phone back into my pack and resume a brisk pace. Our offensive strategy is moving, but it's slow. Kairi has dozens of fake profiles on various boards monitoring Spectre. We've set traps right and left, hoping Spectre will bite. It's a lot like hunting deer. You gotta stay quiet and hidden and bide your time.

A stacked pillar comes into view. An identical one stands sentry on the opposite side of the road. Stella Johnson's neighborhood.

A lawnmower engine and a loud blower are the only sounds as I turn left onto Stella's street. It's a peaceful neighborhood scene. Most everyone is inside, or at least they aren't hanging out in the postage stamp front yards. A faint melody spills from an open window.

Three houses away, and my pace slows to a walk. My shirt is drenched. When I lift the hem of the shirt to swipe my face, it smears the sweat droplets. There's a young man pushing a lawnmower in Stella's yard. He has hair down to his shoulders, split down the middle and tucked behind each ear. He's wearing an oversized t-shirt, loose, droopy board shorts, and flip-flops. This must be her son. His hair is a chocolate brown. I don't see any similarity between this boy and Stella. Or young man. What do you call someone who is right on the edge? A teen?

He's tall. I'd guess around six feet. The t-shirt hangs off his thin frame. He bobs his head, and that's when I notice the glint of white in each ear. He's jamming to tunes while he takes the five minutes to shave the weeds in Stella's front yard.

The Tesla is parked in the carport and charging. And just behind the Tesla, bending by the fence, is Stella. My feet halt as I do a doubletake. Her hair is back in a ponytail, she's on her knees, and my sight sets on her fine ass in very short cutoffs.

When I set out, I aimed to double-check the safety of Stella's neighborhood. See if the car was there. If she was out and about on a Sunday or sitting inside. Curious about her.

I hadn't expected her son would be outside in the postage stamp–sized yard. Nor did I expect her to be. Yet here she is, doing yard work. I pause at the juncture where her driveway and her neighbor's driveway merge. She lifts her head.

"Trevor?"

*Ah, shit.*

She's wearing sunglasses, and I can't get a read on what she's thinking as she approaches. Her brow is smooth. Her loose cut-off denim shorts are shorter than the minidress she wore the night we met. The tattered V-neck tee fits tight around her breasts. Her Sunday outfit is mouthwatering.

"Hi." I wave as I force my gaze upward from her full, shapely breasts to her face. The movement must catch her son's attention because the engine halts.

"What are you doing here?" One thing about Stella, she doesn't mince words.

"Went for a run."

"From Santa Barbara?" Her mouth drops open. "Do you need water?"

There's a platypus filled with water strapped to my back and energy packs in the side pocket.

"I'm good. Thanks. Is Sunday yard work day?"

"Mom?" Ethan interjects.

She gives him her attention.

"I'm done. Anything else?"

"No. Thank you."

I step forward, prepared to introduce myself. Ethan sees me, I swear he does, but he turns and heads to the door.

Stella shouts, "Ethan."

He turns and she points.

"Mower. You've got to put it up."

He nods, returns to the mower, and pushes it down the driveway. The kid has zero interest in meeting me. And he doesn't seem to think twice about leaving a stranger alone with his mother. Was I like that at his age? Would I have walked away when a strange man approached my mom? Probably.

Once he's out of earshot, she turns to me.

"Have you had a good weekend?"

"Yep. You?"

"Lightened my hair." She points an index finger.

"Looks good." Honestly, she'd look good with blue hair. Purple hair. Any color under the sun. But I'm partial to the reddish-brown hair, what she calls auburn, from The Hotel Californian. I don't see much of a difference in her color today, but there's no need to cop to that.

The gate clicks, and it's only the two of us in the driveway. She rocks back on her heels. There's a cloudless blue sky overhead. One vehicle drives by on the street.

"Your son's back home." Like a dipshit, I state the obvious.

"He got back yesterday. It wasn't really his dad's weekend."

"You on an every other weekend arrangement?" I know a few divorced families. The divorced men I know are military men, and while they'd love to have fifty-fifty timeshare, their careers don't allow it.

"We are, although we kind of leave it up to Ethan. His dad doesn't live far away."

"That's good." I'm not sure what else to say, but seeing her at this moment, in the driveway, I'm drawn to her. "So, this coming weekend?"

Her attention is back on the house. Her hand shields the sun from her eyes. She's searching the yard, presumably hunting for her son. But he's inside. I heard the door close and saw his shadow move near the front windows.

"Will he be at his dad's this weekend or here?"

She exhales loudly to convey exasperation. "Who knows?" She gives me a soft Stella smile. "I'll probably find out Friday. And even if I do have Ethan, he'll want to spend it in his room."

"So, you'll be lonely? That's a shame." I grin, and she smiles back, knowing what I'm about to say. "Do you—"

"No."

"You haven't heard the rest of my question."

"I don't need to. I'm not interested," she says as she pretends to busy herself with lawn tools.

"You were pretty interested the night we met." She drops her jaw, but I can still see that hint of a smile.

"Look." I follow her as she starts pottering around the lawn, pretending she has things to do. "All I'm saying is I really enjoyed Friday night. Did you?"

"It was… fine." She tries not to smirk.

"Fine?" I dart in front of her and take the box of tools from her hands. "Well, if it was only fine, then you clearly need to take me out. Show me how it's done."

"Oh, do I?" She pulls the box back. We're closer, maybe ten inches apart. The rise and fall of her chest quickens.

"Trevor…"

"Okay, okay, since that doesn't make you happy, I guess that settles it. I'll take you out. Next weekend. Dinner. Not as colleagues." I tug on the box so she stumbles closer. "Just think about it. That's all I'm asking."

I can see her internal struggle, but I can feel the energy between us, and so can she.

"I'll think about it."

"Fantastic. So, next weekend?"

She shakes her head, but those plush pink lips curve into a teasing smile.

"Think about it." And yes, I'm not above flexing my sweaty bicep as I lift the bottom of my t-shirt to wipe my face once more. I would give her the smile that usually works on the ladies, but there's no need, as her gaze locks on my abs.

"I'll think about it," she says.

I am not a brilliant man. But I am smart enough to avoid pushing my luck. I give her a quick salute, toss in my smile that sometimes works on women in bars, and take off to resume my run and meet up with Wolf.

We've got two dozen irons in the fire. And our number one client, the NSA, is breathing down our necks for a progress report on Spectre. I understand the need to report back up the chain, but there are some things you can't rush.

# The One with The Rules

Stella

"Hi, Mr. Cohen. Thank you so much for coming in to meet with me."

"No problem at all." He holds his tie close to his chest as he extends his hand. His salt-and-pepper beard is heavily salted, and he's more or less bald.

We both take seats at the small table in the corner of my office. I've set out notepads and water bottles. A cloudless blue sky shines through my office window. It's a normal day in Santa Barbara.

Wolf agreed for me to meet with Mr. Cohen after he did an extensive background check and had him sign nondisclosure agreements. I could tell he didn't necessarily believe this was a path I needed to explore. I hope I'm not wasting my new company's time, but I've been reading business books and taking advice from thought leaders like Stacy Abrams and Adam Grant courtesy of my library card. I tend to shy away from the books that are a call to become the next company CEO, but I do love the books that talk about Plan B and perseverance.

Mr. Cohen lifts a folder from a briefcase. Unlike everyone in the Arrow offices, Mr. Cohen uses an actual briefcase. The brown leather is weathered and worn on the edges and has aged to a rich brown.

"You mentioned you wanted to discuss employment agreements and contracts. I brought some samples for you to consider. Standard boilerplate. I do agree employment agreements are a good idea. It's not uncommon for businesses starting out to overlook this, but now that you've exceeded ten employees, it's a step you should implement. Especially given the work some of your employees perform."

"And many of them are virtual. There are some aspects to that, steps we expect our virtual employees to take to ensure security, that I don't completely understand. But I'd like for that to be documented in the employment agreement as well."

"You emailed me those expectations, correct?"

"Yes." Erik provided about three pages of detailed requirements. The convoluted language made me happy I had an office and would work in person.

"Employees can be a company's weakest security link. The most important thing is that you provide the training and equipment so your employees can be compliant. These employee agreements protect you to some degree, and lay out expectations, but the fact is, once you've got an agreement over one page in length, most people won't read it. Executives will pass it to another lawyer to read. So, you can't rely on the employee agreement to be your training document."

"Oh, I understand. And completely agree."

My heart stutters as I plan to bring up a very rehearsed question. My eyes flicker to the clock on the wall. Wolf and Trevor will join us in less than ten minutes… I'm running out of time to ask it. Oh, hell, it's now or never. I pretend to nonchalantly jot notes as I ask, "I'd like to hear your opinion about fraternization policies. At this point in time, Arrow doesn't have one."

Was my tone innocent enough? I dare to look up from my pad and keep a neutral face as I stare at Cohen, praying he thinks this is just an innocent question, and that I'm not, in fact, imagining being fucked so hard by my boss this very moment and getting wet just thinking about it. I cross my legs.

We don't have policies, period. The men have only hired those they trust. I am the first hire that doesn't have a military background or a prior business connection. Wolf trusted me. But I suppose, if you take a step back and think about it, I worked with him indirectly for over half a year as his bookkeeper and the woman answering the phone at his accountant's office. He and Trevor both believe they excel at reading people. And they are probably good at it. But based on my nighttime readings, the company requires additional protections. That's part of the reason they hired me, to figure this stuff out.

"You can set whatever fraternization policy you want." The pen in his hand hovers over the notepad, prepared to take notes and then I presume whip it into legal language.

"I'd like your personal recommendation. I don't have experience in this matter. But I believe that while we are creating the company policies for Arrow, it's something that should be considered."

"Absolutely." He scratches his beard, and his eyebrows lift slightly. "My personal opinion is you are better off to recognize it's going to happen. Especially in a company with hires in their twenties. You've got singles who are working long hours, traveling together, eating meals together. My wife and I met at work." He shrugs. "I think you'll have more problems down the road if you deny human nature and declare a strict non-fraternization policy. Another way to do it is to request that if any employees are dating, to disclose it to the company. Projects and lines of reporting would need to take that relationship into consideration. Both parties would need to declare the relationship is consensual." He pauses. "In a place like this, working on security, I would recommend you think more about your policies regarding mental health and addictions. With more men than women employees, I'd also pay careful attention to the corporate environment. I'm assuming your ultimate worry is legal risk, and from my brief observations, I'd say that's where your greater legal risks lie."

Right. I devoured the entire first season of *The Morning Show* in one weekend, so that's where my head has been. But he makes a good point to this television junkie. We hire former military, many who went on tours. What are we doing to ensure they are mentally well? I've never dealt with this before. I feel out of my depth, lost with no idea where to start. What would we do if we determined an employee suffered from PTSD? From an earlier experience or from on the job? And if an employee is injured on the job, what would our policy be if they became addicted to painkillers? I stare at my notepad which is filling up with more questions but no solutions.

In terms of women, I'm not so worried about Patel and me, as the only two women, choosing to sue, but should we hire more women? We're a diverse group, but are there diversity goals I should target? There's so much to do my head is swirling.

There's a rap on the door, and it hits me. I'm nowhere near ready to have my bosses join us for this meeting. I have more research to do. I should deliver a recommendation after I've done due diligence.

Trevor and Wolf enter, and the room shrinks tenfold. Wolf has met Mr. Cohen, but Trevor hasn't, and there's a shuffling of shaking hands and introductions between Trevor and Mr. Cohen.

"Ahm, I'm realizing I might have set this meeting up prematurely. Maybe I should continue meeting with Mr. Cohen, and I'll come back to you with my recommendations." Wolf's eyes flash a warning that sends my insides plummeting. "Or questions. I can send you questions."

"The meeting is to discuss corporate policy, correct?" Trevor is the only one in the room wearing shorts and running shoes, but those broad shoulders and perfect posture command respect. Today he's wearing a collared shirt, but it's short sleeved and fits snugly around his biceps and pecs. His black shorts hang low. His hair is damp, and he smells like Irish Spring. I stock the showers on the second floor, so I know exactly what I'm smelling. I bought it on a Costco run, which I've been told isn't necessary in the future, because I am authorized to order all office supplies online.

Mr. Cohen and I exchange a glance. He doesn't speak. He's leaving this entirely on my shoulders, as he should, because I am his business contact.

I refuse to look at Trevor. The last thing I need is to blush. *I'm a forty-year-old professional woman. Act like it. Don't look at him. Look at Mr. Cohen.*

"This meeting? It's to discuss corporate policy?" Trevor's repeated question pushes any mild blush over the top into bright red territory.

"It is. I thought—"

"Let's go to the conference room." Trevor holds an arm out against the door.

I don't appreciate being cut-off mid-sentence. Yes, I was probably about to stumble all over myself as I gathered my thoughts, but when I lead the way into the conference room, every single man insisting I walk before him, internal frustration stomps out any insecurities. *Get it together, Stella.*

"I don't want to waste anyone's time, so I'll get to the point. I asked Mr. Cohen here to help advise us on employment agreements, which we need." I direct my attention to both Wolf and Trevor, but mainly Wolf because I can't be caught staring at

Trevor. They silently acquiesce by blinking. "Mr. Cohen has brought up some additional areas of concern to the company. I'd like to do more research and come back to you with recommendations. I assume the original expectation that Wolf relayed stands."

Blank faces convey confusion.

"We are to do what is right by the employees. Offer the best benefits available in the industry," I clarify.

"The best benefits available," Trevor corrects. "Our employees risk their lives for us."

"Exactly. I haven't yet explored mental health or addiction policies, and I need to do that." I leave diversity off the table. I'm not touching that without a lot more research.

Wolf and Trevor exchange a silent glance, their lips in straight lines.

"Fine," Wolf says.

"Erik provided expectations for online security. I realize now that will require training too. Are there any expectations that either of you want to be incorporated into company policy or the employee agreement?"

"There are physical training requirements," Trevor says. "I'll get them to you. And I'll oversee all training. I already noticed a couple of our recent hires aren't fit." Wolf raises one eyebrow. "Enough," Trevor adds. "More training in peace means less blood in war."

Mr. Cohen visibly swallows, and my pen slows. I tend to write every word down in meetings, but I choose to leave that last phrase undocumented.

"Is that all from a company policy perspective? Is there anything else you wanted to discuss?" Trevor raises an eyebrow and taps his index finger on the table.

My exposed skin burns, which fuels the frustration from earlier. I am too old to be acting like an insecure schoolgirl. But I know exactly what he's referring to, and I also know why he's bringing it up. Wolf must have taken him aside and given him a heads up when he invited him to this meeting.

"Mr. Cohen and I discussed his recommendations regarding the company fraternization policy."

"And why would we be asking him what our company policy should be? Shouldn't we decide that?" He directs his question to me, and it hits like a punch to the stomach. Years ago, Ethan hit me close range with a Nerf gun. It's an identical oxygen deprivation experience.

"Oh, absolutely, Mr. Thompson. She simply asked for my professional recommendation, but I will write the policy exactly as you specify." Silently, I thank Mr. Cohen for fielding a question I should have had no problem answering.

"And what was your professional recommendation?" Wolf asks of the lawyer in the room, but his gaze falls squarely on Trevor. If I were to guess, he is silently telling him to stand down.

"My recommendation is you allow fraternization but ask that couples document if they are in a relationship."

Trevor narrows his eyes, and his lips offer the slightest hint of a smirk. "Document?" he asks.

"When assigning projects, clients, promotions, teams. It's just good information to have so you can ensure—"

"Got it." Trevor smiles. Full-on smiles. "Makes sense to me."

Within minutes, Wolf and Trevor exit the conference room. My meeting with Mr. Cohen lasts much longer, but he proves his worth by offering to send me a lot of the information and resources I need.

Back in my office, I close my door and scroll through my phone. I want to call Jenn, but she's a teacher. She can't talk to me during the day. The issue I have with the fraternization policy being lifted is I just lost my cover. Now, I have to tell Trevor I don't want to date him. And I can't blame company policy. I can tell him I don't think it's a good idea. It's not. And I can also mention the age. He's in his twenties, for god's sake. He's a child. Of course, Jenn would tell me I'm being crazy. As she pointed out with a touch of callousness, Jason certainly doesn't let age difference impede who he dates. But he's a guy. He's supposed to date women who are half his age plus seven. By that formula, I should be looking at men who are what... sixty-six? Who the hell came up with that formula?

*Knock. Knock.*

"Yes. Come in." No one ever knocks on my door.

Trevor enters, and the knob clicks closed.

"Did you finish everything you needed with Mr. Cohen?"

There's a long list of empty check boxes on my notepad. The meeting is finished, but my project list is far from done.

"Stella?" The concern in his tone brings me back to my desk.

"Yes, sorry. Just… there's a lot to be done. How can I help you?"

He places his palms on the edge of my desk and leans, lording that Irish Spring scent over my work area. His gaze runs over my pad, possibly reading my list.

"You can't do it all in one day."

"I know that." My defensiveness is justified. Of course I can't knock out everything on the list in one day. But I plan to tackle as much as I can each day. My salary doubled when I joined Arrow. I will earn my salary.

He stands. He runs his fingers through his now dry hair. The blond streaks stand out when it's dry. Those turquoise eyes get me. He's truly a gorgeous specimen. A beautiful young man. *Young* being the operative word.

"I won't take up much of your time." That smirk crosses his lips again, and I am conscious that I use that phrase quite a bit myself. "But one of my check boxes for the day is to confirm a day for our date. Is Ethan with you this coming weekend?"

Ethan's photos fill the corner of my desk. One recent, one of him as a toddler, and one in his baseball uniform because it's so stinking cute it makes me smile every time I look at it. I focus on those photos and answer the gorgeous young man.

"Trevor, I am completely flattered you would like to go out with me, but it's not a good idea."

"Might I ask why?"

"Because. You should date women your own age." He could date models. Gorgeous, skinny women without a single stretch mark who look fantastic in string bikinis. Truly, this should be a no-brainer for him.

"Age is relative." He comes around behind my desk and blocks my view of Ethan's photos with his toned, chiseled chest. With purpose, I focus on his pecs, because if I look into those eyes, I'm done. "Haven't you ever heard of the phrase 'an old soul'?"

"I have, but…"

"My soul is ancient. I have lived multiple lifetimes. Been through hell and back. I don't need a dreamy-eyed giggler. And as I recall, you and I have chemistry. Have you forgotten?"

He is inches away. Those pecs rise and fall. Thick blood vessels traverse his forearms and biceps. The man has no extra body fat.

"Stella?"

My name on his lips, in this proximity, elicits a whimper. With great reluctance, I tip my chin upward, and damn, those eyes.

His lips fall to mine. Soft, warm, secure, tender. He cups the back of my head in his palm, and I open for him. Our kiss deepens, and my brain shuts off. The world goes black. Frissons of heat and electric tendrils crisscross my skin.

Footsteps sound in the hall. *Holy shit. We're at work.* My palm flattens against his chest, and I push.

He steps back, breaking the kiss, and I gasp for air as my surroundings come back into focus. I stumble back, my fingers over my lips. I shouldn't have. That should not have happened.

Trevor seems unaffected. Until I notice the protrusion in his shorts. His teeth dig into his lower lip, and he lays out a sexy-as-fuck half-smile.

"I think you'd like to go out on a date with me." *Well, of course I would!*

"That's not the question."

"Please," he says.

In my inner ear, Jenn screams, "Don't be a pearl-clutching moron!"

*Live a little.* I exhale.

"Okay. But we play by my rules."

"I'm always down for that."

"This," I wag my finger between us, "can't happen in the office. And we don't tell anyone."

"I thought the good lawyer recommended full disclosure?"

"If the two are in a relationship. But we're going to keep it casual. So, no need for disclosure." He narrows his eyes, calling bullshit. "I don't want other men here seeing me that way. I need respect."

That's a language he comprehends. He only needed a reminder.

Moonbeam

Trevor

Wolfgang: *Skydiving?*

Wolf's text came through after my morning run, bike, and swim. Water droplets drip from my hair onto the phone screen. A couple of swipes with a towel eliminate the water issue.

Me: *Can't. Have plans.*

Within seconds, the phone vibrates.

"Going on a day date?" The mockery in his tone has me grinning. *Yes, dipshit.*

"What's it to you?"

"Well, like I told you, I don't want her quitting after Casanova breaks her heart."

"There will be no heart breaking." Truth, if I hadn't already been with her, I wouldn't be pushing this. But I have been with Stella. I sit in that office every day knowing how she fits me like a glove, how she tastes. Imagining her lips around my cock. And we're both consenting adults.

"All right, Casa. What about tomorrow?" My muscles involuntarily flinch from his continued use of my old codename. It's bullshit. The overused name could have been handed out to anyone on our team. Even some of the married members played the field from time to time. As the youngest on our team, I received the blunt end of the stick on shit like that.

"Tomorrow?"

"Skydiving?"

"Oh, sure."

"Want to head out early?"

"Let's play it by ear." If the date goes well, I plan on waking up at Stella's.

"Winds should pick up by noon. Afternoon's not looking good."

"I'll call you." I end the call before he can say more.

When I arrive at Stella's front door, it's a little after one. I have a list of date ideas. It's not like me to plan dates, but I'm in a new town, so a little reconnaissance is needed.

And there's something about Stella. She's a hard worker. Independent. She's been at the office for less than a month, and she's made it her mission to take care of every office need. My gut tells me she's overdue for someone to take care of her. Not forever, but for a date.

I grew up with a single mom. Couldn't stand most of my mom's dates, but I saw how much it meant to her when one of them treated her right. The little smiles she'd have as she dusted or vacuumed. That dreamy look she'd get. She didn't think I noticed, but I totally did. I rolled my eyes and pointedly looked the other way, but I noticed.

I knock. And wait. A car drives past at a fast clip. Then another speeds by, going the opposite direction. The distant hum of a lawnmower mixes with music flowing through an open window, but I don't see the mower or the open window.

The door flings open, and Stella appears, breathing heavily.

"You're early." She sounds affronted. I check my watch.

"Ten minutes." That's on time in my world. "I'm always early." Being late is unacceptable.

"Well, it's just as well. I wasn't sure what to wear. What are we doing?"

"I have a list of possibilities."

She gestures for me to enter. "Let's hear them. Anything involving a wetsuit is out."

Her comment has me chuckling. She must visit the office showers, as that's where I hang my wetsuits. I don't always use them, but it's March, and the water is cold, even for me.

"All right. How do you feel about jumping out of a plane?"

"Next." She doesn't even turn around, just charges into the kitchen. "Do you want anything to drink?"

"I'll take a glass of water." She's barefoot. Leopard spots cover her loose-fitting pajama pants. A bright pink silk robe partially conceals a tight-fitting tank top. I like how her tank top dips low. She has fantastic breasts, and that top really shows them off. I also like how it flattens against her stomach and accentuates the curve of her hips. Those pants are far too loose, but I imagine they pull down easily. Her toenails are bright pink, too, like her robe.

"Am I killing all of your ideas?"

"I told you, I've got a list." There's a counter between us, and I rest my elbows on it. She slides a glass my way.

"I hate to say it, but I should really go car shopping. Not that I want to."

"There's no rush, Stella. Really."

"Well…I suppose I should wait to hear from the insurance company. Although I'm not optimistic they'll give me much." Neither am I. That car was a POS.

"How do you feel about going on an urban wine tour?" I'll be happy to take her car shopping, but it's not how I want to spend our date.

"It's a beautiful day. That sounds nice. Better than talking to car dealers. You think we can get tables outside?"

"We'll start in the Presidio. Maybe wrap up with dinner near the beach." They call it the Funk Zone, the area where I live that I am envisioning for dinner. I don't use the phrase because it's obnoxious.

"So, maybe jeans and a top with a sweater in case we're seated in the shade?"

It takes a second to realize she's waiting for me to answer her.

"Sounds good. And comfortable shoes."

She heads up the stairs, and I check her place out. It's neat and clean. The furniture is worn, but there are no holes in the upholstery. Brown stains mar the tan carpet in spots. Framed photos of her son fill some shelves below a window. On the wall, a couple of photos hang. One is of Stella and her son when he was a baby. She's spinning him in the air, laughing. It's a black-and-white photo, and her hair looks black. She looks young and carefree. Happy. Beautiful.

I return to the kitchen and resume leaning against the counter. There's a box on the counter with an image of a woman with neon blue hair. I pick it up, and I'm reading the box when Stella returns.

"You dyeing your hair blue?"

"Considering it. It's semi-permanent. Low commitment. I might do a streak. Like the pink chunk? Right here?" She lifts her hair and shows me the general area.

I nod.

"It's my Saturday night ritual."

"You dye your hair every Saturday night?" That sounds like a god-awful tradition.

"On Monday, you can see what I come up with," she says with a wink.

She's cute. Spunky. I drop the subject as we leave the house and climb into my Jeep. If my mission succeeds, she will not be dyeing her hair tonight.

* * *

"So, is the military where you got your injuries?" Her question knocks me back.

We're sitting outside at a little wine shop with three tables on the sidewalk in front of it. We each ordered the wine flight, and we're still on the chick wines. I also ordered a cheese plate and olives, but I'm the only one eating the food.

"You noticed my injuries?" Obviously, she's touched my scars. I wasn't aware she noticed the angry red raised marks. She'd asked for us to turn out the lights.

"You flinched when I touched." She reaches across the table, and the tip of her index finger points inches from my shoulder.

"Still recovering." Recovering from the bullets hasn't been as seamless as I'd like. But I've seen people survive much worse. The pain diminishes each day. I've still got all my limbs and digits.

"What happened?" There's a couple sitting all of two feet away. But they aren't paying us any attention.

"I was in the wrong place at the wrong time." It's half cop out, half truth.

"Is that why you left the military?" I gulp the rest of the pink liquid in a glass. It's fruity and burns a bit on the way down. "You don't have to tell me."

I'm not sure how this conversation turned into questions about me. Women from my past asked questions about where I toured, what guns I shot, how much I could lift. Questions I happily answered because they all indirectly conveyed the size of my dick. But saying I left the military equals saying I quit. And I don't quit.

"Do you like Santa Barbara?" Her high-pitched tone reeks of fake. That's not Stella. It's all she could come up with to change the conversation. I must have my mean motherfucker face on.

"I'm gonna head to the restroom." It's only once I'm two feet away from the table that I realize I've got three paper napkins balled into my fist. I toss them in the waste bin in the bathroom and splash some water on my face. If I'm going to have this day date carry on, I need to get into the game. Maybe I should've pushed my hiking idea. You don't really have to talk on a hike.

When I return, she's on her third tasting glass. There's a small amount in each taster, but I need to catch up.

"How long have you known Wolf?" she asks, continuing her string of questions.

"A long damn time. We went through BUD/S together."

"Buds?"

"It's a training thing." She seems interested. I like that she's unfamiliar with it. "It's something you have to make it through to become a SEAL."

"Are you in reserves now?"

"No."

"But you work out so much." She's right. I do.

"It goes with the job. Plus, I'm training for Iron Man." An hour later, she probably knows more about the Iron Man triathlon event and my training protocol than she ever could have possibly cared to know. Our whole conversation has circled me. And I'm not that fascinating. Not anymore.

"Stella, all right. How's one more winery sound? One more flight?" She's smiling, and there's color in her cheeks. Her eyes are hidden behind sunglasses, but her smile and laugh… they're growing on me. "This next flight, I want to learn about Stella."

"There's not much to learn. I'm pretty boring. Just your average middle-aged forty-year-old."

"Well, that's a sales pitch. I might need to help you spice that one up." She laughs, and it's loud and carefree. I'd like to record that sound, so I can replay it whenever I want.

When we locate a new place and order our second flight and a couple of appetizers, it's late afternoon and the shadows are increasing. Our new table is in the sun. But I wish we had never left our old table, because tension fills the space between us. It's uncomfortable as we face each other, searching for a conversation topic. In an hour, I can suggest an early dinner, or maybe some wine on my rooftop, but there's space to fill.

"All right, Stella Johnson." *Johnson.* She's divorced. "Is that your ex's last name?" My mom dropped my dad's last name.

"It is. Ethan still has his name, so I kept it. Easier if I have the same last name as my son."

"I can see that. So, what's your maiden name?"

"Sheldon." She wrinkles her nose. "I always hated that name."

"But you like Johnson?"

"It's a step up." She gives me a small smile.

It's ridiculous, but I don't really like that she's using another man's last name. It's nonsensical, and I shove the uncomfortable feeling aside when the waitress joins us and takes us through an explanation of the wine flight before us. Neither of us is out to get hammered. On a typical day, I'm not one to sit around drinking, but I do get the appeal of a lazy afternoon.

"And what are your plans when Ethan leaves?" Her chin jerks back. She doesn't like my question. But surely she has a plan. "He leaves in, what? Three years?"

"Yeah." She draws it out, sounding resigned. "I don't like thinking about it."

"I get that." She let my reason for leaving the military slide. I won't press her on something understandable. "Tell me about your favorite music."

An hour later, I've learned she's originally from Wisconsin and has no plans to return. She likes alternative rock, mostly nineties rock bands, and she's a self-professed television junkie. She works out to programs on a channel I've never heard of before.

"I force myself to do at least a one-hour show before I allow myself to veg on the sofa." If I were to guess, she does calisthenics while watching television. Based on her firm ass and well-shaped quads, I'd guess she does butt lifts.

Her teeth dig into her lip, and I'm fairly certain she is cutting herself short. Maybe she's self-conscious about rambling. But there's no need. We have time, and I like watching her. Light pink infuses her cheeks, probably from the wine. She has full, glossy lips that tease and taunt. She moves her fingers in the air, gesticulating as she talks. She's dressed conservatively, but her top is formfitting, and the outline of her bra shows beneath the thin cotton.

She picks Mexican, and once we're seated at a restaurant along the waterfront, she removes those sunglasses. Her blue eyes pull me in a way that's similar to the ocean outside. I've been drawn to the ocean for as long as I can remember. Her irises are a dark blue, and it's a mesmerizing color.

While she's clearly into hair experimentation, her nails are a subdued rose that doesn't match the bright pink on her toes. I don't recall any tattoos, but I sure hope to get a second look.

"So, your mom is in San Diego?" There's one thing about these long dates… you can learn a shitload about a person when you're forced to talk for hours.

"She is." I dip a chip in the fresh guacamole.

"You must see her a lot."

"I don't remember the last time I saw her."

"Oh, that doesn't sound good." She wrinkles her nose. "Do you guys not get along?"

"We just…" I pause, thinking about how to explain without the drama. "She married a guy I don't get along with. We usually speak on Christmas."

"Ew." Her nose wrinkles again. Her facial responses are more exaggerated than earlier in the day. She's not drunk, but I'd guess she's got a solid buzz. "That's one of my biggest fears. That… well, that first, Ethan will grow up and I'll only hear from him once or twice a year. And then, well, that I'd date someone, and Ethan wouldn't like him. Maybe that's why I don't date."

She dips her own chip, overloads it, and jams it in her mouth. She covers her lips with her fingers, all dainty-like. Instead of pointing out she's on a date, I choose a different tack.

"I don't see you ever choosing a man over your son." Those blues flash confusion my way. "And that's a good thing." I mean it, too.

My mother dated men who treated me like shit, and she simply looked the other way. To say she chose a man over me is probably a dramatic interpretation, but kids know when they aren't the priority. Leon is hands down the reason I entered the military the day I turned seventeen, so if you think about it that way, maybe I should thank them both.

"No, I would never choose a man over my son. Ethan is everything. But one day he'll go off to college. And if I'm dating someone, and he comes home… I'll be nervous. It'll be important to me he likes anyone in my life."

She's sincere in her statement. She's introspective, and there's honesty in her dropped gaze and her thoughtful tone. I believe her. And she rises about fifty notches in my book.

I've held off asking her about her ex. Just doesn't strike me as good date talk. But I am curious what kind of man could walk away from this woman. The mother of his child. And yeah, she's gorgeous. But it's more than looks. She's got substance. She's intelligent. Determined to provide for her son. To exceed expectations at work. She's got gumption. In training, we'd see it sometimes in the men you'd think wouldn't ever pass a challenging physical test. But they'd dig deep, and somehow they'd pull through.

The men who had never failed, who faced nothing hard in their lives, those were the ones who rang the bell. Dropped out during BUD/S. The pressure of continuing to be number one caused them to crumble. But this woman sitting in front of me, she'd had shit thrown at her. She hadn't been number one in school or athletics or in her marriage. But she survived. She pulled through. I could sense it, feel it. If you gave her a swim test, or an underwater test, or any kind of test, and she needed —no, she wanted to pass it, she'd be the surprise finisher.

"What are you thinking about?" The setting sun outside the window casts a golden hue over her dark reddish locks. I don't know how long I've been sitting here staring at her, but the urge to lean across the table and kiss her grows.

"You." I choose honesty. And it confuses her. Her brow wrinkles, and those eyebrows tilt down. I pop her nose with my index finger and grin. "You're pretty kick ass, you know that?"

The waiter arrives, saving her from responding. I pass him my card before he can leave.

"Can I convince you to stop by my place? We can catch the remnants of the sunset from the roof."

She tosses attitude with the crossing of her arms and the tilt of her chin. "Has this been your plan all along? Get me back into your 'hood and try to get me up for a drink?" She air quotes the word *drink*. If I recall, offering her a drink is also how I got her up to my hotel room.

"No pressure." But hell, yeah, I am hoping.

"I'll go. You only live once, right?" She bats those long eyelashes, and there's a hint of bashfulness.

When I open my front door, my dog Astra's nose juts out.

"You have a dog!"

"Well, technically, she's my buddy's dog." Then I remember she knows him. "Erik? When he came last week, he delivered her to me. She's my running partner. He says she missed me, but I'm not so sure she's digging this apartment life." I flick on the lights and open the door wide for her to enter.

Her mouth forms an "oh." The pad is nice, but it's not open-mouth worthy. Wolf hired a designer, and she did a decent job decorating. It's nicer than any place I've been in, well, ever. But Stella's house has more warmth.

Mine's pretty dark. There's a lot of black. In retrospect, I wish I'd been a little more involved in choosing the furniture. I would've gone more brown leather. All this black is a bit too edgy for my tastes. But I will say my surfboards look stunning against the one black wall. And the bike racks against another wall display my prized possessions to perfection.

Astra has her nose right up on Stella's thigh, and she bends down to scratch her.

"Why don't you think she likes apartment life?"

"When we lived up north, we worked from the house. She was never alone. I hired a dog walker to come and take her out twice during the day, and I give her long runs, but I watch her on cameras at work. She sleeps all day."

"Why don't you bring her to the office?"

"Really? You think that's okay?" Patel mentioned it, too, but no one else brings a pet in.

"Why not? I bet everyone would love her. I could help take her out sometimes if she needs to go to the restroom." I could see Astra trotting around the office. She'd probably still sleep a lot, but she'd be happier. "I can order dog supplies."

"You'd do that?"

"Well, yeah. It's my job."

"Not really. That's not your job. I can get my dog what she needs."

"It's office supplies." She shrugs. "I'd like to do it."

"Do you have any pets?" Now that I think about it, there were two small dishes on the floor in her kitchen, pushed up against the base of one cabinet.

"Smelly."

"Excuse me?" I take a deep whiff, but the scent I catch is fresh paint and new carpet.

"My cat. His name is Smelly. He's not one to come out and greet visitors."

Ah. She's a cat person. There had to be a flaw.

"What would you like to drink?"

"Oh, I don't know. Maybe water?"

"Come on, now. Let me pour you something for the sunset."

I step up behind her and shift her hair from her neck. A sweet floral fragrance fills my nostrils. I'm pretty sure the night I met her, she smelled like strawberries. But I expect with Stella, she's always changing. I press my lips against the arch of her neck. A little whimper escapes.

"If we do this, it doesn't mean anything, right?"

My palms clasp over her hips. I take a minute. Yeah, I want this woman. But there are some things we need to set straight.

"Stella." I say her name softly, so my breath flirts with her ear. "This means something." I press my lips to her temple as I caress her waist and up to her breast. "I haven't been able to stop thinking about our night together."

"Really?" Her tone has climbed multiple octaves, and I brush my lips over her neck and along her jaw. She drops her head back against my shoulder.

"Really. I loved our night together. But you know what I didn't like?"

She twists against me, and her brows angle over her nose.

"I didn't like how awkward it was between us afterward. This is what I want to happen this time. I want you to stay here. And in the morning, when you wake up in my arms, we're going to make love again, and then I'll drive you to breakfast. And there will not be any awkwardness."

"Because we're colleagues," she says, her words quiet and almost introspective.

I drop my hand over her pelvis, warming her through her jeans.

"I think we're more than colleagues." I could tease her by asking if she does this with any other colleagues, but she doesn't. And I don't like putting it out there.

"But, Trevor, you should date someone young."

There's no response to that other than to shut her up by claiming her. I angle her jaw and take those full lips that taunted me all afternoon. They're soft, supple, and fuck, the woman can kiss. And then the only thing I'm thinking about is bedroom, sofa, or kitchen counter?

# The One Where Stella Tells Ethan She Had a Date

Stella

The morning light pours through open windows. I stretch, alone in an enormous bed. The charcoal sheets and modern furniture bear a distinctly masculine quality. A black-and-white photo in a gleaming silver frame hangs on one wall. Smoke, or fog, rolls over crashing waves.

Ethan would like this room. He doesn't comment much on interior design. Hell, he doesn't comment much at all. But I can tell when he looks through the catalogs stacked on the coffee table. He pauses on the darker, masculine rooms with a surf aesthetic. Makes sense. He's a California boy, bred and raised.

And he'll be coming home today. I sigh and stretch. I am naked. And sore. Last night, Trevor proved his stamina. Holy fuck. I'm not sure I could have lasted, especially that third time, but

Trevor has this magical little bottle in his bedside table with an ointment that, holy fuck, did it do some magic on my aging lady parts.

"Do you like this?"

"What about this?"

"And if I lift you up like this?"

My answers had been yes, yes, and more. Just like this.

I've never had sex like I had with Trevor. I mean, our first night, I'd rather enjoyed it. Or I should say I enjoyed it in the moments I wasn't fixating on being in a stranger's hotel room.

Is this what a midlife crisis is? Hooking up with a twenty-something man? Doing something your younger self would have never had the courage to do? He asked me last night what I thought of anal. And what did I say? My skin heats several degrees, and my hand covers my eyes.

"Maybe." That's what I squeaked out. *Maybe*!

And he'd fit at least one, if not two fingers, with that magic ointment, in my ass. Holy shit. What if there had been shit up there? And how did it feel? At first, it pinched. Hurt. Then it felt… okay. Not great, but okay.

"One day, baby. We'll get that loosened up."

I'd thought he was talking about my butthole, but in the raw morning light, I can't help but wonder if he meant me. Jesus, he's already pulled me miles out of my comfort zone. I like things in the dark, and last night, he took me against a wall. Lights on. Fuck, his biceps rippled as he held me up, and god, his jaw muscles. Those hungry eyes as he pounded into me, over and over. It was like he couldn't get enough of me.

I squirm, remembering. One hand covers my breast, teasing the nipple, while my other warms my center. I close my eyes, replaying the feel of his taut muscles. Those ripped abs are straight out of a magazine. He's so hard and firm, even his insanely toned ass. And fuck, his cock.

"Well, well, well." My eyelids snap open. Trevor leans against the doorframe with a smug, cocky smile. He's holding two black ceramic coffee mugs. "I thought you'd want coffee when you woke up. But I like what you're thinking even better."

He's wearing pajama bottoms and no shirt. He's got tattoos on his arms and his chest. He's also riddled with scars. Some new, some old. But fuck if he isn't the sexiest man I've ever laid eyes on.

I am frozen in place. One hand on my tit, one far lower. His sandy blond strands stick out in different directions courtesy of my fingers tugging last night. Those strands aren't that long, but they're long enough to be disobedient. He hasn't shaved, and the dark shadow covering his face makes him unbelievably even sexier. My eyes travel from his well-formed pecs, down his eight-pack, to the smattering of hair above the plaid pants. The material is lightweight, and it juts out, showing the outline of a piece of his anatomy I am now intimately familiar with.

"Don't let me stop you," he taunts.

In for a pound, in for a bushel. That's the saying, right? My fingers get to work as he saunters across the room. Steam rises from the mugs. He sets them on the side table. His pants fall to the floor, and then the mattress sinks from his weight as he crawls across the king-size bed.

My eyes are glued to his. My embarrassment level barely cracks a three. All because his gaze is feral. He wants me. I lean forward, reaching for the ample evidence of that want, but he *tisks* me.

His lips fall above my bellybutton. The light touch tickles. I gasp and squirm. I dry my damp finger in his hair, and he trails kisses lower. I spread my legs, because I am not going to stop this. Holy fuck, does this man know how to use his tongue.

But he's also got that rough growth, and my swollen pussy is tender. We have abused it in the last twelve hours, and my pelvis tilts away. His velvety tongue over my most sensitive skin is divine, but I can't. And he reads me.

He jumps up and off the bed and steps into his adjacent bathroom. I watch in amazement as he slathers on white foam and slides a blade over that sexy five o'clock shadow. From my angle on the bed, I can see his chest and one of Phoebe's iconic phrases from *Friends* comes to mind. "Yes, please, take your shirt off and tell us all about it."

Could I say that to him in a meeting? Yeah, no. The HR director can't get away with that one. But damn if I won't be thinking it each and every day. This might be my midlife crisis, but as far as crises go, I'll take it.

The water in the sink splashes. He checks his jaw once in the mirror, and his fingers follow along the edge. On his return to the bed, he pauses and opens that drawer once more. The drawer that holds all his goodies. Condoms, magical ointments. I think I even saw a cock ring. This midlife crisis rocks.

He crawls across the bed, completely naked. His forearms strain from his weight, and his biceps flex. He holds himself over me, and I tentatively reach up to caress his smooth, freshly shaven skin. His lips press against the inside of my wrist. His gaze never leaves me, the heat both warming me and turning me on. His head dips, and he takes one nipple in his mouth and sucks. His tongue loops and teases. My fingers return to my center. A pop sounds as his lips release my areola.

Last night, he lavished my breasts with attention. I had a breast augmentation after Ethan was born. I'd always been flat, and after breastfeeding, I needed it. For me, for my self-esteem, I wanted them. But I'd always wondered how another man would react. By the time I got them, Jason had reached the point he looked for every opportunity to belittle me. But one thing is certain about Trevor. If he knows they're implants, he doesn't care.

My fingers trace the outline of his angular jaw, loving the feel of his silky smooth skin, and he rubs his chin down the valley between my breasts. His lips press a path back to his original goal. He never seems to forget his mission. His cock is hard, and weeping, and I curve my body, reaching for it, but once again, his eyes catch mine, and he *tsks*.

His tongue is tender. He eats me out like I am his breakfast. And then he finds my nub and sucks. I'm curling forward off the bed. And then he's over me and sliding inside, stretching me. It is heaven. He is heaven.

He freezes.

"Fuck, condom."

"It's okay. I'm on the pill." I bite back adding that at my age, pregnancy isn't as much of a risk. He remains frozen in place. "I'm clean."

He huffs. The blood vessels in his neck bulge. He's undecided. My hips urge him on, rocking into him, inching back and forward.

"You feel so fucking good."

"So do you." I reach up, careful to not meet his lips, because I have yet to brush my teeth, but I kiss his neck, and that whisper-soft skin below his jaw. Slowly, ever so slowly, his hips join the action, rocking against me.

He lifts up on his forearms, and we both watch as our bodies combine. The hypnotic dance lures us. A light layer of perspiration coats our skin.

"I've never… not without a condom." He grits his teeth. Closes his eyes. He rocks into me, over and over, lifting my ass, positioning me, hitting points so deep, I'm curling forward, vibrating, trembling.

His forehead falls to mine. He raises up, so we are almost nose to nose as we rock into each other. Those eyes are so close, and they are fixed on mine. His facial muscles contort.

"Fuck. Feels. So. Good."

My thighs squeeze around him and my legs loop, holding him in, and I squeeze. Deep inside me, he pulses his release.

He collapses over me, and we cling to each other. I love the feel of him, the safety and warmth. My fingers run up and down his back. *Holy shit. I'm officially a cougar.*

With a groan, he presses his lips hard into my neck, then my shoulder, and he slides out. He sits back on his ass and rubs his face.

"So, that was…"

"Amazing," he supplies.

"And unprotected," I say, staring at the ceiling, letting my breath come back. I offered it.

"Yep. Like I said. Amazing."

"Next time, we can be more careful. I don't know what I was thinking." I really don't. I lose my head around this guy. "You use a condom with others, and you should with me too."

I slap my palm over my forehead. I really wasn't thinking. Like, I know better.

"Ouch. You think I sleep around?"

"No, but I'm forty and too old to be dealing with STDs."

"There's a way to fix that." He pulls me onto his chest. "How about we just sleep with each other? Then I can go bareback all the time." He smiles and goes in for a kiss. I pull back and laugh at him in disbelief.

"Give it a week, and you'll change your mind."

"Ggggrrrrr." His teeth playfully gnaw along my jawline. "You are maddening, woman. While we're dating, it's just us, okay?"

His fingers comb my hair, which must be gnarly. What he's asking isn't unreasonable. I'm so out of the dating scene. But he's right. If we're going to have unprotected sex, we should be exclusive. It's not like I'd be out there finding other men, but he could easily find another woman. Tonight, in a bar down the street from his place, if he wanted.

"Are you sure you want to? You're in your twenties."

"What does that have to do with it?" He lifts my hand and places the tip of my finger in his mouth and sucks. Then playfully nabs the tip with his teeth in a play bite.

"I guess it doesn't. It's just… you could have anyone." I can't get over that. The man could model. He's got a body that would pass for a god. We live in Southern California where hot babes stroll the beaches in string bikinis. The world is his proverbial oyster.

"Hey. I don't want anyone. I want you." There's sincerity in his eyes. Albeit boyish and naïve sincerity, but it melts my heart into goo.

I place a soft peck on his cheek. It's almost motherly, but I swipe that thought and reach for my mug.

The coffee is cold. He takes it from my hand, sets it back on the bedside table, and promises a fresh mug after we shower. His shower is massive, with dual showerheads and enough space for a family of four. As the water pours over me, he soaps up a loofah and washes my dirty, filthy body. His gorgeousness occupies my attention. I'm not even the slightest bit mortified to be naked in front of him. Well, maybe mildly embarrassed and self-conscious.

When he's done, I take the loofah and return the favor, lathering his lean, fit form. Intricate artwork covers both biceps. On one, there's a massive tree with detailed limbs and foliage, and the root system trails down. A compass overlays the art.

"What does this mean?"

"Not much." I give him a look that says I'm not buying it. Expressive artwork of this caliber comes with a plan. His thumb brushes back and forth over my cheek, and he exhales.

"I've always been drawn to forests, to trees. The compass is to remind myself to stay true."

"And the constellations?" My finger traces the continuation around his arm through a field of stars and planets.

"The universe. A reminder of my place in infinity."

I press my lips to his chest and continue spreading the soap. His other tattoo isn't as expansive. While the other one looks like layers of tattoos added over years, this one has breathing room. My nail presses against the head of the skeletal frog with a spear.

"And this one?"

"It's for my team. Those we lost." A spread Eagle, or Hawk, flies over, at an angle, the sweeping wings arching over the frog, and slanting down to the underside. The effect is of a bird soaring overhead, swooping down, maybe watching over. I press my lips to the frog.

Trevor rinses off, playfully slaps my ass, winks, and exits the shower, leaving me under a powerful stream of water. I rinse my hair one more time, then turn the water off. When I step out, he's already dry, with a towel wrapped around his waist. He looks delicious. He's also on the move, ready to start the day.

While I towel off, he opens a plastic box. Inside are multiple packaged, new toothbrushes. I can't help but wonder if he keeps them around for his many lovers, but I will not ask. I will not ruin this morning. And besides, he's the one who brought up exclusivity. Not me.

For however long this lasts, I'm going to enjoy my secret midlife crisis.

His kitchen is gorgeous, but his refrigerator is noticeably sparse. Before I can dig in and whip him up breakfast from his random remnants, he slaps me on the ass and tells me he's taking me out to breakfast.

Sunday morning in Santa Barbara brings out the breakfast crowd by the dozens. But we easily find two seats at the bar of what he calls his neighborhood breakfast joint. While we wait for the bartender to fill our mugs, he leans into me and nibbles my ear.

"I've been thinking about the office."

"Yeah?" I straighten. Monday is looming. I've got a pretty full day of scheduled meetings.

"I've been thinking about you. Over my desk."

"Oh. No." I place my index finger over his lips. "Rules. Remember?"

He kisses my finger. The bartender pours our coffee and takes our order, which gives me time to get my mom voice on. These rules need to be crystal clear. After the bartender hustles away, I begin.

"My job is important to me."

"I know. I was just—"

"No. Let me be clear. I told you. I need this job. I probably shouldn't even be doing this."

"Hey." His husky tone stops my speech. "Your job is safe. I promise."

"What if things go sideways?" It's my worst fear.

"If it's ever awkward between us, I'll be the one to leave. I promise."

"This is your company." I shove his arm, and the bartender tosses a smile our way. "You can't say that."

"No, I can." He's all serious. So naïve. Young. "Look. What I love doing is training. One of our goals is to help vets find consistent, reliable income after the military. There's a lot of work out there, but it's project basis. Arrow has the funds to do it right. And I'd like to set up our men to be the best. Best training, best equipment."

"Men?" The hackles on the back of my neck, which he can't see, because he's all man, rise.

"Men. Women. It's a word. I don't give a shit what they're sporting in their pants." I raise an eyebrow. "Seriously. Patel is a teammate. Period."

"Good. Because women bring a lot to the team. We are capable. Diversity brings a lot to the team."

"I agree. You won't get any arguments from me."

And then he leans in and kisses me.

It's almost noon when he delivers me home and follows me up to my front door. He tugs on my fingers, and when I turn around, I discover we are eye to eye. I'm on the porch, and he's two steps lower on the ground. I fall into his kiss. His hands roam my ass and my back, and my fingers toy with the soft, short hair at the nape of his neck. A part of me, the part that is royally loving this midlife crisis, wants to lure him inside to christen my bed. And it would be christening the bed because the only action that bed has ever seen is of the vibrating variety.

But he backs up after one last press of his lips to mine. He pulls out his phone and reads it. He scowls and drops his phone back into his pocket.

"Thank you for an unforgettable date," I say. It's clear, he's got to go.

"You stole my line." He leans in for one last quick kiss and heads back to his car. My crazy insides flutter with his departure. He's wearing old jeans, running shoes, and a short-sleeved t-shirt with a faded PowerBar logo. He could so easily pass for a college student, maybe a grad student. And he's mine. For now.

My fingers wave goodbye as Trevor reverses out of the driveway. He's off to his training for the afternoon. He casually mentioned he plans to do a long bike ride, like seventy miles, this afternoon. I guess you don't get those muscles without sweat.

Just as Trevor's taillights sail out of view, a BMW pulls into my driveway. I'm wearing the outfit I wore yesterday. It's jeans and low sandals. It doesn't look like a date outfit, necessarily, but it's not my normal Sunday morning attire of a tee and LuluLimes either. My freshly showered hair is still damp and pulled into a top bun. Ethan gets out of the car and slams the door.

He passes me on the way inside and offers a, "Morning, Mom."

Jason steps out of his car. One arm rests on the top of his clean, shiny automobile. There's a woman sitting in the leather passenger seat. I don't remember if she's the same one I saw recently. I stopped keeping track years ago.

It's clear he plans to say something, but if he's not going to walk the ten feet across the yard, it must not be important. I wave and pause, giving him one last chance to speak. He doesn't, and I follow Ethan inside.

My cat greets me and circles my leg. I pick Smelly up and hold him in my arms, scratching along his neck. I fill his bowl with dry food and head up the stairs to Ethan's room. His overnight bag is in the middle of the floor, and he's already crashed, shoes on, on the bed.

"Did you have a good weekend?"

"Yeah."

"Good." I tap the doorframe and step away. I've got a ton of laundry to do, and grocery shopping before the week starts.

"Did you have a good weekend?" It's so unusual for him to ask me that I freeze for a few seconds. But then I turn around and give him my undivided attention.

"Yeah, I did." I could leave it at that, but I crave these moments of interaction. "I went on a date. It was good. We went to the Presidio."

"Cool."

"What did you do?"

"Nothing much." He glances up from his phone, then his gaze falls back to the device in his hand. "Do you mind closing the door?"

"Nope. Chicken tetrazzini okay for dinner?"

"Yep. Thanks, Mom." The door is almost closed when he adds, "I'll do the yard in a little while."

"Sounds good."

I lean against his door after I close it. My breathing regulates. Ethan really didn't seem to care. At all. Was he not listening to me? Did he not hear me? Or has Jason's constant dating made him immune? Or maybe teens are always immune? I'm not sure. But I hum as I proceed down the hallway. And I continue humming all afternoon. I simply can't stop.

# Cadence



Wolf leans over the railing on the roof deck. He likes it out in the open, so we come up here quite a bit. The wind is stronger today. Both wildfire and small craft warnings flashed across my weather app earlier. The small craft warnings incentivized me to adjust my workout plans and do a run and bike combo instead of an ocean swim.

"How's it going with Stella?"

"It's good." Since we're standing, I stretch. My shoulder and arm muscles are healing well, but I have to do extra stretching. Even with the stretching and physical therapy, my shoulder remains sore. It's a source of constant pain, but I refuse the pain meds. I've seen too many come undone with the seductive pull of a magical pill.

"You guys up for a double date?"

Both my hands are connected behind my back in a deep shoulder stretch. I shake my arms out and study Wolf. The guy doesn't date. When we'd be on leave, he gave me shit about my habits. Even coined the overused name for me—Casanova. Every team has one. But Wolf, with his oversized muscles and plethora of tatts, he was the true playboy. At least, if you consider always finding someone to take home the definition of a playboy. The king of the one-night stand and never a call back. In all the years I've known him, I can't recall him taking someone to dinner. Or at least, telling me about it. He does go down to San Diego frequently enough to make one wonder.

"Who are you seeing?" He's wearing sunglasses, but the way he inhales and smirks, I fully expect behind those shades he rolled his eyes at my high pitch. "Wait. Do you have a girlfriend?"

He proceeds to give me the dish on a woman who hunted him down at the gym. We both lift at Gold's. It's a muscle gym. It's no surprise, given Wolf's set of muscles, that a woman sought him out. His take on this woman is interesting. But before I can comment, he changes tact.

"That's why I'm taking her on a date." Wolf stands so ramrod straight you'd think he had a pole up his ass. "But what are your reasons? Stella is a find. If she quits because of you, I am going to be some kind of pissed. It's total luck we ever found her to begin with."

"That's the real reason you want us to go out on a double date, isn't it? So you can observe us in action?" He chuckles, checks the time, and gestures to the door. We've got a meeting in under five. "When are you thinking?"

"Check with Stella. I suspect Fiona will be available whenever I ask her."

"You are such a cocky motherfucker."

He's ahead of me on the stairs and, as luck would have it, he walks straight into Stella. She's wearing a tight black skirt and a white button-down blouse. I've been steering clear of her today, attempting to follow her rules.

"Hey, Stella, what night works for a double date?"

My throat constricts, which is a highly unexpected response. Yes, I wanted to ask her out myself, and I'm tempted to strangle Wolf for jumping in like this. What Stella and I have is new. Shouting about it in the office violates Stella's rules.

"It's just dinner," I add when those impossibly large eyes dart between Wolf and me. She's speechless. "Maybe Thursday night?"

Her son is fifteen. She can totally leave him at home for a dinner. But the question is, will she?

"I'll check my schedule." Her tone is highly professional. She rounds the corner, and I follow as if hooked on an invisible leash.

"If that's not a good day, we can pick a different time." Her steps slow, and she clutches her notepad to her chest. She looks over her shoulder at me, and it takes a significant amount of willpower to refrain from pulling her to me.

"So, I guess that means you told Wolf?" I'm not entirely sure what she means… Did she think I wouldn't tell Wolf? My business partner? My de facto brother? "It's okay. I mean, it's fine. Can we wait until we complete the paperwork for the company?"

"I didn't know there was paperwork for the company."

She lets out a little huff. It's cute, but it also puts me on higher alert. "I haven't formalized the process yet. Or created the forms." She's muttering to herself. I think. "I'll tell Ethan I have a business dinner. I won't be able to stay out late."

"That's fine."

"Fine."

Haven't I heard that the word *fine* has multiple meanings?

I spend the next few days attempting to discern what Stella's *fine* means. She's polite. Professional. And if she didn't have her son with her after hours, I am somewhat certain I would have confirmed I'm in the doghouse.

But I focus on work and hope she'll calm down all on her own. I've located an old gym a few blocks away in a less desirable area that I'm aiming to convert into our private training facility, so that's taking up more of my time. Plus, I've had a few meetings with the woman chairing the upcoming Santa Barbara Vineyard Expo. They have selected some mega-millionaire's estate for the event but said mega-millionaire doesn't want us visiting for an on-site inspection. From a security perspective, this isn't okay. And the woman in charge is a volunteer, which means she takes my calls between luncheons and tennis matches.

Kairi and Erik and their team are listening for Spectre activity. They are mining all the learnings from the brief access to Kane, the head of Spectre's phone. But it's a slow-moving program. We've laid traps...but it's a waiting game. Waiting games try my patience.

Thank god I'm training for an event. It allows me six or so hours a day to clear my head and focus on physical training. I've always excelled at physical challenges. My body is something I can control. There are no project variables or decisions up the chain. It's all on me.

Wolf tells me he'll handle all the plans for our double date. I don't ask him much more about his gym stalker. I assume he's banging her regularly if he planned a date several days in advance.

This isn't prom. I don't need to compare corsage notes, but I think the last time I went on an official double date might have been in high school. I don't count hanging with David and Kairi, because in those situations, I'm a third wheel. That's a very different situation.

On Thursday, a few minutes before eighteen hundred, I lightly rap on the doorframe to Stella's office. There's a notable neon blue chunk of hair that flows from near her ear down to her chest. Her full lips reflect the light. They look wet, like she recently licked them, but I imagine it's a thick gloss. Her cell phone vibrates, and she holds a finger up in the air.

"Hey, Ethan." She's silent for a quick beat. "There's a frozen pizza in the freezer, or there's leftover lasagna. Or there's plenty of sandwich stuff." She's silent again. "Who do you want to have come over? Sierra? Yes, of course, that's fine."

"Does Ethan have a date?" I ask the second she ends the call. I lean over the chair in front of her office desk. A waft of a heavy, sweet fragrance fills my nostrils. So far, Stella hasn't smelled the same twice, but I like all of her fragrances. So far.

"Oh, not a date." She clicks over and powers down her computer. It's one of the safety procedures we require all employees to follow. "She's like his sister."

I don't argue with her, but I don't recall anyone being like my sister when I was fifteen. But, hell, for all I know, her son is gay or bi. I've read that a lot of this younger generation is bi. Kairi, who's genuinely like a sister to me, is bisexual. It's all cool with me.

"Thanks for coming out tonight." Those deep blue eyes flash with surprise. "I know you'd rather keep things on the down-low with us. But Wolf's like family. And, I have to say, I'm curious about tonight."

"Oh, why?"

"Because in all the years I've known Wolf, he's never taken a woman out on a date. I only mention this because if it's weird, or he's weird, I want you to be prepared."

The restaurant Wolf chose is around the corner from the office. We leave at the same time Patel is closing down the reception area. I am careful to maintain a physical distance between Stella to not arouse Patel's suspicion. Patel heads in the opposite direction we do, and it's not until she rounds the corner onto the back alley, and Stella and I approach the front door to The Goat, that I place a possessive hand on Stella's lower back.

We have little time tonight, but I'd love nothing more than for our dinner to pass quickly and for Stella to join me back at my place. It's been almost a week since she spent the night, and all the professional cold air hasn't been doing anything but increasing the lewdness of my nighttime fantasies. All Stella-centric. It's proof my hormones have fully recovered from the trauma of three bullets.

Wolf and his date are already at the hostess stand. Wolf didn't exaggerate. She's all over him. She has one arm around his back, and she's pressed to his side. Her free hand roams his chest, then his abs, and dips lower to pat his crotch. From the expression on the hostess's face, I'd guess she saw that, too. *Classy.*

To Stella's credit, she's cordial. She offers her hand to Wolf's date.

His date introduces herself as Fiona, but the song from The Knack pulses in my head and I want to call her Sharona.

The women carry the bulk of the conversation. That is when Fiona isn't sucking on Wolf's neck like a vampire. If I were in his shoes, I'd be uncomfortable. But he's relaxed. He openly peruses his date's breasts. Which is remarkably easy to do given they're spilling out of her dress.

All during dinner, I compare Fiona and Stella. Stella wins by a mile. Both women dye their hair, but Fiona's is a saturated blond so dry it resembles straw. Stella's warm auburn offers peeks of color and personality. Stella's breasts, while the perfect size for my palm, aren't displayed for the entire restaurant to see.

The two women go off to the restroom, and I wish I could accompany them.

"You've got it bad," Wolf says.

"What do you mean?"

"Watching her walk across the restaurant. Watching her eat. What is it? She keep you on a short leash?"

"What's wrong with you? I'm just worried about her reaction to your date. She's a viper." There are worse words I could use.

"She's something." Wolf raises his eyebrows, and the disgust I see on his face calms me down. He's not into her. That's a relief. I couldn't fake being nice to that woman for the long haul.

"Before they come back, did you see the latest from Logan?"

"Spectre leaked data about a Taiwanese firm? Are we working on that?"

"No. The point is they aren't laying low anymore. Signs of life. Activity."

"Good. And in the meantime, we're working a wine festival."

"A celebrity-filled event. Don't forget the celebrities." He clinks his water glass against mine. Stella exits the restroom, and Wolf signals for us to go quiet. As if I would ever talk about business in front of the woman he brought to dinner.

I stand and hold the back of the chair for Stella. Her cheeks flush pink, too pink. As if she's been running. Fiona settles into her seat. Wolf does not get up from his chair. She casts an annoyed glance his way but then settles right into his side.

Beneath the table, Stella fidgets with her napkin. She doesn't lift a fork or take another bite. She also can't look in Fiona and Wolf's direction. Her gaze scans the restaurant in the direction of the exit door and down at her lap, anywhere but across the table.

After we finish our meal, Fiona tugs on Wolf, and when he leans down to her, she openly tongues him, once again, one hand below the table. It doesn't require a heightened sense of imagination to figure out what she's doing. But she's Wolf's project.

Those deep blue eyes look up at me, still trying to look anywhere but across the table, and that flush of color remains in her cheeks. I wave down the waiter for our check. It's time to remove ourselves from this situation.

After we pay, Stella can't get away from me fast enough. I'd like to stop by her house and talk it out, but with her son home, I won't do that. Instead, I get home and pull out my laptop and review Arrow's multi-pronged plan. It's thorough. One of these tactics should work. But I don't yet have a handle on this damn festival, so I skim the event notes and properties and run through security plans one more time.

# THE ONE ABOUT SWINGERS

STELLA

The car door shuts, I flutter my fingers, and Ethan tosses his head in his signature see-ya-later move, and I dial Jenn. She's ahead of me in the car drop-off line.

She answers with a direct, "So, last night not so fab?"

"Oh my god," I groan loudly so the car speakerphone will convey my agony. "I don't even know where to start. First, she had to have been, like, twenty-two. Her dress was so short that when she sat down, I could see her crotch. Like, see her panties. And I swear I think she gave Wolf a hand job while we sat at the table. I am not exaggerating."

"And Wolf is…?"

"Trevor's friend. My boss."

"That's a weird name."

"It's short for his last name." I rest the back of my head on the headrest then flip the blinker.

"What was Trevor doing?"

"He was like me. Being polite. Being normal. That girl… I swear, if that's what kids do these days, I don't want Ethan ever dating."

"I don't think high school girls are that forward."

"Yeah, right. Have you noticed how short those shorts are on the girls heading to school in the morning?"

"You sound like such a pearl clutcher." Jenn's laughter brings out my smile, even though inside I'm still pretty damn flummoxed.

"Seriously, Jenn. I always knew going out with my boss had 'bad idea' written all over it. I guess, on the bright side, that'll be over now."

"How do you figure?"

"There is no way he sat there and thought… I'm cool with this old-as-fuck chick sitting beside me."

"Shut the fuck up."

"No, seriously. Any man in his right mind would think… I want some of that twenty-two stuff."

"It sounds to me like any man in his right mind would want to go wash his hands. What a skank."

"Yeah, you go ask Terrell how he'd feel about it. He'll tell you to your face he's appalled, and don't get me wrong… if it was Sierra, his daughter, acting like that—"

"Oh, shit. He'd go ballistic."

"Yeah. But, deep down, so deep down he'd never admit it to you, he'd be totally jealous of a date like that."

"Nah. You're wrong. He wouldn't. He'd be mortified. She sounds like the women Jason dates, and he's appalled by them. I've seen it. I've been there. Terrell squirms."

The highway traffic has picked up, and a silence fills the line as I focus on weaving between the lanes. There's an uncharacteristic fog hanging over the freeway this morning that's creating an LA vibe.

"Hey, I shouldn't have mentioned Jason."

"Oh, please. Like I care. Just be grateful you've got Terrell. Dating sucks. But I didn't even tell you the craziest part. She followed me to the bathroom. Suggested we swap partners."

"Nuh-uh."

"Yeah-huh. Color me flabbergasted."

"What did you say?" She's laughing inside… I hear it in her tone. She thinks it's funny. I mean, I do, too, but not when it was happening. No, when it was happening, I'd been mortified.

"Nothing, really. I stood there, probably looking like a shocked high school parent, and maybe she realized I am technically old enough to be her mother… I don't know. But it was awkward. And weird. And she seemed to get way too much enjoyment out of it. Someone else entered, and I rushed out. And it was over. She went back to mauling Wolf when we got back to the table. I am telling you, I was right from the beginning. I am too old for that shit."

"Bull— Good morning!" Jenn's overly exuberant greeting means kids and parents are arriving, and the call disconnects.

Jenn doesn't get it, but I am absolutely serious. I can't compete with twenty-two and overly horny. I'd need three or four drinks to be anywhere near that aggressive. And, more than that, it's just not me. It'll never happen. And if swapping partners is what Trevor and Wolf do, that's fine, but I am so not the one he needs to be seeing.

Last night, after the dinner spectacle, Trevor walked me to my car like a gentleman. He tried to get me to come up to his place, no doubt horny as all get out after that little table display. But, even with his sweet goodnight kiss, it's not like I was born yesterday. He probably texted Trevor for little Ms. Volpe's friends' contact numbers before my headlights were out of view. And he should! He's twenty-eight. I can't forget that. He should be with women in their twenties.

"Morning." Patel sits behind the glass reception area. She smiles, but based on her hand movements, I can tell someone's speaking to her on the headset. She waves me through, and I head up to my office.

There are several client meetings scheduled today. I have yet to hire an assistant, as I want to have a good idea of what resources they need before I hire anyone. But that means I'm the one ordering food for the meeting and ensuring the conference room is cleaned and food refreshed between meetings. They have invited me to attend two of the meetings on today's schedule.

One meeting is with the Santa Barbara Police Department to coordinate safety plans for the upcoming Vintner's Weekend. They have officially selected Arrow to handle all security matters for the event. I love that we're doing it because it gives legitimacy to what we're doing and something I can describe to Ethan so he'll understand what Arrow does.

There's a soft rap at my door. My computer is powering up, and I'm standing over my desk, seconds away from pursuing coffee from the office kitchen. Trevor fills the doorway. He's wearing a white oxford button-down and dark slacks. And he's holding two coffees with to-go lids.

"You look nice." He often parades around the office in shorts and a t-shirt. The man looks insanely hot no matter what he wears. After all, he is superhero worthy. But this business attire look might be my favorite. Especially the way he has his sleeves rolled up and how the thick black band and silver watch face highlight his muscular forearm and wrist.

"I brought you a coffee." I blink. *Right. Coffee.* "Cream. Half a pack of sugar?"

"Thank you." Surprise he remembered I asked about cream for my coffee at his house filters through. The warmth from the paper coffee cup heats my hand, and, well, the entire room.

"Did you get everything done last night?"

"Huh?" I sip the coffee as I attempt to follow his train of thought.

"You said you needed to get home—"

"Oh, right? I did. Yes. Tuna casserole ready to go." Yes, I forgot about the lame excuse I created as my reason I couldn't go up to his apartment. It had nothing to do with the bathroom episode or the skank at the table.

A dog trots into my office and sits obediently near Trevor.

"You brought Astra to the office."

"Yeah. She's been checking the place out. I think you're right. She's happier here."

"Well, I'm sure she is."

"What are your weekend plans?"

"Nothing much. I've got Ethan."

"Yeah. I have nothing planned, either." He scratches the top of his dog's head. Her mouth opens, and her tongue lolls to the side. She's a cute dog. She's also a German shepherd, and I make a mental note to buy dog treats to keep her on my good side.

"Well," I push out my chair and sit in it, since I now possess my required coffee, "I'm sure whatever you find to do will be better than tuna casserole."

"I doubt that."

The timed code for our intranet appears in my cell, and I enter it before the code refreshes.

"Yeah, right. Friday night at the Johnson house. Wild times." Yes, I let the sarcasm drip.

"I'd love to. What time?"

"Huh?" An error flashes on the screen. *Fucking typos.*

"How about I bring dessert and wine?"

"Ethan will be home." I didn't mean to invite him over. Twenty-somethings await him. Did I even invite him over?

"What kind of dessert does he like?"

"Trevor—"

"You can introduce me as a friend from work. You have friends over for dinner, right? I promise, I'll be on my best behavior. I'll bring Astra. Ethan will like her."

"Ethan is fifteen." Astra wags her tail. "The only things he likes involve sitting on his bed in his bedroom."

"I won't bring Astra, then? Seven p.m. good?"

My phone rings, and in an out-of-body moment, I see myself nodding. Am I really having him over for tuna casserole on a Friday night? After the worst double date in the history of double dates?

The day flies by as it always does with back-to-back meetings. However, this afternoon feels a tad more manic as we host about twenty different Santa Barbara town officials who arrive to discuss the security logistics of the upcoming festival. The town hosts events all the time, so I'm surprised by the number of interested parties. And that's just the town officials. Our next two meetings involve representatives from area wineries and trade groups.

I'm not the secretary, but I dutifully take notes in all the meetings and collect business cards from anyone who has them. The men gather contact information on phones, but I'm a little old school. If someone has a business card, I'll happily collect it. Besides, I've heard horror stories of people losing their digital contact list.

Trevor maintained complete professionalism throughout the day, as he always does. He didn't mention another word about dinner. And he'd been in a closed-door meeting in the conference room when I left the office for the day. They have a lot of closed-door meetings, but I imagine they needed to regroup after the abundance of information they received.

Trevor said seven, but I don't really expect him. The pads of my feet throb, and I kick off my shoes. Whether or not Trevor shows, I have a son to feed. But who am I kidding? Trevor backing out is wishful thinking. It would be easier if he didn't show. I wouldn't have to talk about the bathroom incident. And everything at work would be good. He'd be nice to me, thinking he dissed me. We have a good work relationship. If he decided to take Fiona for a whirl, it would actually be a much better situation for all involved. Easier. For me, much easier.

The side door slams shut as I slide the casserole into the oven. A familiar thud indicates the enormous backpack Ethan hauls has landed on the floor.

"Hey, hun. How was school?"

"Fine."

"How was the volleyball game?" He stayed after to watch the girls' volleyball match at school, and he caught a ride home with a friend.

"We won."

"Did Sierra get to play?" Jenn shared she'd been bummed recently as she spent more time benched than playing.

He grunts, and I interpret it as she played some. He sidesteps me, opens the fridge, and pulls out a soda.

"I'll be upstairs."

Of course he will. I debate mentioning a friend might stop by. But it's silly. Trevor will not spend his Friday night eating tuna casserole at the Johnson house.

Upstairs, I change into my comfortable jeans with rips near the knees, a thermal, thick socks, and downstairs I flip on the television. There's a *Friends* marathon tonight. This is the kind of Friday night I like.

*Knock. Knock.*

The sound is solid and loud. It's so loud my whole body jumps to answer. Up the stairs, I get one glance of Ethan's closed bedroom door as I bypass the stairs and open the front door.

Trevor has changed into jeans, but he's still wearing his button-down shirt with the rolled-up sleeves, and he's holding flowers, wine, and a brown paper grocery store bag.

"Hi. I wasn't sure you'd come."

"Why?" He looks genuinely surprised.

"Because." I twist a strand of hair and open the door wide. I don't have a good reason. I guess I should have known Trevor is a man of his word. It was just, I suppose, my wishful thinking.

"Mom?" Ethan calls from the landing at the top of the steps.

"Hi. Honey, I forgot to mention. We have a guest for dinner. Mr. Thompson from my office."

"Hi." He gives a quick nod but lifts his phone, indicating he's got someone on the line. "Can I go out to a beach party tomorrow night?"

"Yeah. Sure." My hand curls around the doorknob, and the muscles cramp.

"Can you talk to Aunt Jenn about letting Sierra go?" *Oh, no.* My spidey sense comes to life.

"Does Aunt Jenn not want Sierra to go? Where is this party?" It's a question I should have asked first.

"Mom, it's just a group of us getting together on the beach. A bonfire kind of thing."

"With no adults?" Trevor leans his shoulder against the door. Shit. "Here, come on in," I tell him.

"Tommy Lawlor's parents are going to be there. It's sort of in front of their house." I look him up and down. I trust Ethan. And the fact is, if I said no, he could go to his dad's and do it.

"Okay."

He smiles. It's a little shocking to see that full smile.

"And you'll talk to Aunt Jenn?"

"Yeah, I'll talk to her. But no promises." His bedroom door closes as I add, "Uncle Terrell might want to attend."

Trevor grins.

"I don't envy you with teenagers."

"Right? But the beach party is fine." Doubt nags at me as I say the words out loud. I'm a little embarrassed my son and I were shouting at each other, but it's normally only the two of us in the house. We have a routine that works for us.

"We used to do them all the time."

"Beach parties? Down in San Diego?"

"Yep."

"And they were okay?"

"Well, define okay." He grins, and I do not. "How're his grades?"

"They're good. Really good."

"And does he seem to have good friends?"

"Yeah. Pretty much the same crew he's hung out with since elementary school."

"You're probably good." He lifts a cake box out of the brown paper bag. "Dinner smells delicious."

"Tuna?"

"Do you have any idea how long it's been since I had a home-cooked meal?"

The man has zero soft cushion. He's all sinewy, hard muscle. I doubt that's possible on take out, and I express my skepticism with one raised eyebrow and a hand on my hip.

"Seriously. I don't count grilled meat, steamed broccoli, boiled eggs, or protein shakes as home cooked."

"I'll grant you that. But if you saw the steps I take to compile this casserole—"

"It's going to be delicious." My insides roil as his hungry gaze takes me in. Heat radiates all around me, and it is most definitely not excess heat from my contractor-grade oven.

He presses me against the counter, and his lips cover mine. It's soft and tender. His rough palms cup my cheeks, and his forehead brushes against mine.

"I've wanted to do that all day." Me too, if I'm honest. Sort of. I can't get the bathroom scene out of my head. My palm flattens on his chest. He's inches away, and he wants to know what's wrong.

"Do you and Wolf swap partners?" His lips scrunch all together as if he thinks I've lost my marbles. "Are you swingers?"

"Why are you asking?" He backs up, arms crossed. His brow furrows, and I think I screwed up.

"Fiona asked. It just threw me. But I guess… based on your reaction. Maybe it's just Wolf? Or just her?"

He rubs his hair vigorously back and forth, but he's smiling. He's amused. It's good I can amuse people.

"That's what she asked you in the bathroom, isn't it?" Both my hands find the counter behind me, and I grip it for stability. "I knew something went on in there. When you came back, you were quiet for the rest of dinner."

He steps closer, removing the space between us. His fingers caress my throat, and he gently eases my chin up.

"Let me reassure you. I. Do. Not. Share."

His lips fall to mine for a soft, gentle, reassuring kiss. He is warm and comforting and strong. My fingers explore his chest, his biceps, and along his shoulders. Our kiss deepens. My ankles rise off the ground, and my fingers comb through his fine hair. Our tongues slow dance. He cups my ass and pulls me against him. A thud on the stairs breaks us apart in an instant.

"Mom, what time's dinner?" Ethan rounds the stairwell, his phone pressed to his chest. "I'm gonna go over to Ramon's to work on a project after dinner."

Ramon lives two blocks over. But still…

"On a Friday night?"

"He has extra poster board."

"You didn't tell me you needed any."

He shrugs. "He has it. We're gonna watch a movie after. Will we be done in, what? Thirty minutes?"

I check the timer on the oven. It's true, Ethan and I can consume dinner in under ten minutes.

"Yes, that's fine."

He lifts the phone to his ear and charges back up the stairs.

"Welcome to my life."

"Seems nice."

"Yeah." I bite back any kind of twenty slam. There's no way to come across as funny. Sure, I'd expect more vibrant plans from the stereotypical twenty-something. But Trevor isn't stereotypical. He's a former SEAL. He's served in war. He's a partner in a security firm. I don't know exactly what he did in the military, but my impression is he kicked ass. And he continues to do so. And what was I doing at his age? Doing the pre-school jig. Oh, and my marriage was falling apart.

The drawer with my placemats sticks, and I jiggle it. Once it opens, I lift three matching brown wicker placemats.

"Can I pour us some wine?"

"Sure. That would be nice."

When I set out the casserole, along with a tossed salad that Trevor bought from the market, and freshly baked garlic bread, the dinner table looks adult. Especially when combined with two wine glasses.

"Ethan!" I call up the stairs. Stampede noises as he gallops down announce his impending arrival. When he rounds the corner, he pauses.

"It's a real dinner tonight," I supply.

"Cool."

Out of habit, I dish casserole onto Ethan's plate, then Trevor's. I'm on the second spoonful when two sets of eyes slow me down. My cheeks burn.

"Sorry. I'm such a mom."

"Looks good." Trevor probably doesn't mean for his statement to sound sexual, but he has me squeezing my thighs. I lock eyes with him for a quick second, then dish out the salad on my plate. I let the men handle serving the salad on their own.

"You work with Mom? Mr…"

"Thompson," I supply.

"You can call me Trevor." He pauses and seeks my gaze. "If that's okay with your mom."

"It's fine."

"We're driving your Tesla, right?" Ethan asks.

"Well, it's the company car," Trevor answers.

"I like it. I'm hoping we still have it when I get my learner's permit."

"Ethan," I admonish. Jeez. I have no plans of continuing to drive Trevor's car for another three months. Actually, that's one thing I should do this weekend—car shopping.

"It's a good car. Have you been doing driver's safety?" Trevor asks Ethan.

"Well, I should already be driving. But I was late signing up for the book part of the class. I'm ready."

"Where do they teach you driving skills?"

"It's part of the class I signed him up for," I say.

"I can take you out if you like," Trevor offers. "There's an old development that I think lost funding. It would be great to learn on. The roads are paved, but no one's up there, at least right now."

Ethan inhales his food and avoids looking at Trevor. The silence that follows is awkward. For me.

"I'll take him out." I've been meaning to. There's so much I mean to do. Story of my life. Jason doesn't want Ethan driving his precious BMW.

"Have you ever taught anyone driving skills?" Ethan directs his question to Trevor, and I hold my breath, watching the dynamic between the two. It feels like Ethan is administering a test.

"In the military. Yes. We had some advanced training components. Courses we had to master. Once we did, I helped some of my teammates."

"What branch?"

"Navy."

"That's cool." Ethan serves himself a second helping of casserole. "But you're not in now?"

"No." Trevor stuffs a large forkful of casserole into his mouth.

"Did you ever serve?" Trevor's chewing slows, and Ethan expands. "I mean, like abroad? Afghanistan or whatever?"

"I did." The corner of Trevor's lips turn up slightly. "Afghanistan."

"Trevor is training for an Iron Man."

"No way. That's cool. My track coach did that. One out in Hawaii."

"That's a good one."

"What kind of bike do you have?"

And then I'm lost. The two of them speak a different language. But I am also mesmerized, because Ethan is alive and animated. He's engaged in the conversation. Ethan's phone rings. It's one of his rings for his friends. It's a song, and to me it sounds like screeching guitars.

He doesn't answer. Simply declines and types out a quick OTW.

"I gotta go." He picks up his plate from the table. His phone rings again when he's standing in front of the dishwater. This time, he answers.

Trevor meets my gaze over the rim of his wine glass. My stomach flips and flops. *Yes, we're about to be alone.*

"Hey, Mom. Ramon is gonna come over here. Is that okay?"

My stomach flutters get smashed, but I whack a smile on my face. "Sure. That's fine." I love it when Ethan has his friends over. They're welcome anytime. "I thought you needed poster board."

"Nah. We'll get it later. And Mom? Will it be a problem if we watch a movie down here? Sierra and Lateesha are going to come, too."

"Absolutely." I smile at my son, to reassure him it's fine. "I'll make you guys popcorn."

"I think we need more soda," he says.

"Make a list, and I'll run to the store." Trevor lays his fork down. "I told you Friday night in the Johnson house is a blast."

"Mom, I'm gonna run upstairs and get a quick shower. If Ramon gets here, you can send him up. Mr… ahm, Trevor, it was nice to meet you."

"You're getting a shower?" That is so not like my son.

"Real quick."

"Hey, Ethan." My son pauses, one hand on the stair rail. "Tomorrow I'm planning on hitting some trails. Mountain bike riding up through the hills. I've got an extra bike. Any interest in joining?"

Someone who doesn't know Ethan well might miss how he brightens.

"Yeah. That'd be cool. But I'm like… I don't have a lot of experience."

"We'll go at your pace. I'm doing my training in the morning. This is just for fun. To get out. I can swing by after lunch, and we can ride up?"

"Cool." It's the three jerky nods that in Ethan-language is essentially the equivalent of jumping and down that relays my son's excitement.

Trevor and I haven't yet loaded the dishwasher when my phone dings with a shopping list.

"I'm sorry," I say as I peruse the shopping list. "I should probably run. I'd like to be back here before the girls come over." Ethan isn't one to invite girls over. Sierra is like family, but this will be two girls and two boys. I need to be home.

"No worries. I'm aiming to be up by around four."

"In the morning?"

"Saturday's my long day."

"Wow. That's unbelievable."

"Thanks for dinner."

I follow him out to the carport, and he leans down to give me a chaste kiss.

"See you tomorrow?"

"You know you don't have to take him mountain bike riding, right?"

"I wouldn't have offered if I didn't want to. He loves bikes. It'll be fun. You don't mind, do you? He just seemed really into bikes, and it's kind of my thing."

"No, it's fine. Thanks."

Trevor climbs in his Jeep and drives away, and I complete a quick run to the U-Save market. When I return, Ethan joins me in the kitchen and helps to unload the bags. He's freshly showered, and his damp hair shines in the light.

"You know, Mom, if you're dating someone, it's cool." I simply stare. My son has been taller than me for a couple of years, but his shoulders seem broader. "Dad dates women all the time. I've had years to get cool with it. You don't need to shelter me."

"I'm not."

"He was here for work?" There's a knowing smile there that both teases and reprimands. Damn. I think it's a lot like the one I give him from time to time.

There's a knock on the door, and Ethan greets his friend. All I can bring myself to do is refresh my glass of wine. Have I been sheltering Ethan? Is that what I've been doing?

# Sweat



Iron clinks on iron. I survey the room. Ten new hires are doing my version of a welcome wagon routine, proving they are indeed as fit as they claim before we send them out on assignments. Flash and Ghost are on the kettlebells. Sweat drips down Vader's forehead as he kills it on the row machine. I check my watch. The others are doing sprints. When the buzzer goes, they'll switch it up. I need to ensure these guys haven't grown complacent. They've got to have fire in the belly—passion for the job.

Scorpion runs inside and hits the jump rope. His shorts and shirt are drenched with sweat.

"Where's Mustang?"

"Ate my dust."

I bury the urge to wipe his smug-ass smirk off his face. This isn't a mission. It's not even a drill. There's no danger out there. But I don't particularly care for the way he left his teammate behind. I make a note on my phone app that Scorpion flies solo.

Five hours later, I'm sitting inside Arrow's offices and recapping with Wolf.

"Had to send Mustang to PT. Came back limping after a three-miler. Pulled muscle."

"Happens," Wolf says. "In other news, press release is out. It's official." Wolf sets down two highball glasses and pours Macallan. He hands me a glass.

"Dog-and-pony show worked," I say.

"Eh, last piece needed to seal the deal."

"Always gotta blow the egos on the powers that be." He moves in front of the project board. It's a whiteboard. Erik hates it. He'd prefer it all on the network, and shit's there, too. But Wolf and I are old school in some ways. We like to see it all laid out.

"We'll need a hiring list. And I'll need to think about training."

"Dude." Wolf crosses his beefcake arms and frowns. "We're getting complaints. The men say you're killing them."

"Bullshit. They can't take it, we cut 'em."

"Man, this isn't BUD/S."

"The more you sweat during peace, the less—"

"Are you fucking shitting me right now? Is that your attitude when you're with our new hires down at the gym? The less you bleed during war? Get over yourself. We'll never keep anyone on staff."

His attitude really pisses me off, given I'm still doing PT on my shoulder. The only reason I'm alive today is my training. Four against one. And I'm the sole survivor. But I keep my calm. There will be no fisting, no slamming my chest into the overgrown ogre. I drain my glass in one burning swallow.

"That shit's meant to be sipped."

"You're going soft." Outside, the sun falls closer to the horizon, and the remnant voices of passing pedestrians carry through the glass. It's the end of the workday.

"Erik wants to coordinate in ten."

One glance at my wrist tells me the office will shut down by the time we end our call with our team in the vines.

"I'll come back." I'm two steps from the door when Wolf speaks.

"Stella already went home."

"What?" I spin around. I couldn't care less if she leaves the office early, but I wanted to say goodbye.

"That's where you were going, right?" His shit-eating grin does nothing but irritate me.

"Yeah." If he's going to give me shit about it, I'm going to toss it right back at him.

"Family emergency," he says. The word *emergency* grabs my attention.

"Ethan? Is he okay?"

"Yeah. You know her son?"

"Went mountain bike riding with him on Saturday. Good kid."

"Just the two of you?" Wolf perches his ass on the edge of the desk, the picture of relaxation as he swirls the golden liquid.

"Tried to get Stella to come, but she didn't bite."

"She doesn't seem the mountain-biking type."

"No. But I think I can get her to do some road trips." Mountain biking isn't for everyone. I get that. Ethan shared she enjoys hiking, so that's an option.

"Be careful with her."

"Let me stop you at the pass. I get it. Besides, she has this idea in her head that I'm too young. She's got a wall up."

"Age is relative."

"You think I don't know that?" The thing is, I expect Stella knows that, too. Only thing I can figure is she's still smarting from a failed marriage. But I'm not in a rush. Taking it day by day and seeing what happens works for me.

My hand twists the door handle when another thought crosses my mind.

"What about Fiona? You're..." I let my words trail.

"Still seeing her."

I nod and exit.

"You're gonna be back for the meeting, right? It's in five minutes."

I don't bother answering him. Besides, I'm not sure of the answer. Family emergency? Ethan? I push through the stairwell door and come up on Patel from the back entrance. Big mistake. The barrel of her gun greets me.

"Have you got a bloody death wish? Why are you coming in behind me? No one enters that way."

"Sorry. Just wanted to ask if you know what's up with Stella. Is her son okay?" Patel opens a drawer and places her pistol in it.

"School called. He was in a fight."

"What?" The kid I spent Saturday with had been level-headed. Solid focus on the downhill. Determination on the up. He didn't strike me as a hothead.

"She had to go meet the principal. I'm glad mine are toddlers. Don't get me wrong. Preventing injuries is a full-time effort, but the teen years. I'm dreading them."

My phone buzzes.


Wolf: *Charlie Mike*


Continue Mission. Military code. *Yeah, yeah. Yippee Kai Yay Motherfucker.* I don't bother with a response and slide the phone back into my pocket.

"You going to go check on Stella?" Patel leans back in her chair. She's smug. Entertained.

"Later. I have a meeting I've got to get to." I huff out a sigh that sounds like a spoiled teenage kid doing a chore he doesn't want to do.

"BOHICA?" she asks with one carefully arched brow. I shoot her with my thumb and index finger.

It's the military acronym for *Bend over, here it comes again.* Patel is funny.

"Yeah, something like that."

# The One with the Boy Toy

Stella

My front door swings open and bounces against the back wall. The sheetrock vibrates.

"Where is he?" Jason's throat bulges above his white pressed collar, red and inflamed.

"What the fuck, Jason?" Thanks to the asswipe, there's a hole in the wall.

"I got a call in the middle of the sales pitch. And that dumb bitch from the school told my secretary what happened." Ah, now I get the anger. Jason's day was interrupted, and the call embarrassed him. Double whammy.

"I got the same call, had the same workday interruption, but I didn't show up at your house and sling the door into the wall."

"You need a fucking doorstop." *Yes, it's my fault.*

"Need I remind you? You don't live here. Knock." I grit my teeth and jut my chin out.

One of the protruding veins in his bulbous neck curves outward, and I visualize the blood pumping at a monstrous volume. It's the angry demon look that once wobbled my knees and cobbled me. But I've traveled that road so many times that my body reacts differently. No longer do I shake. Inner fortification holds me ramrod straight. Repulsion smothers any nerves.

"Is he upstairs?" He steps past me, not waiting for an answer. I grab at his elbow and tug on the sleeve of his suit jacket.

"My. House." I'll call the cops. I do not care if I make a scene.

"Did you even speak to him? He's suspended for three days. What's mother-of-the-year doing about it? Or let me guess. You took him out for ice cream, didn't you? That's why I need to show up. He needs a parent that will lay down the law. Not pussyfoot and coddle him."

I grit my teeth and force my shoulders back. Breathing through my nose, I gather all my control. I need it. Jason is an asshole to the nth degree, but we have to parent together.

"Do you want a drink?" He's not one to say no, and I need one. I also need the time to gather my thoughts.

Ethan isn't the kind of kid to throw punches. Ever. And all I got from him were grunts and one-word answers after I picked him up. He's still angry. Still boiling. Over what? I don't know. All I got was a barrage of mumbled epithets and the sense

Ethan believes he is in the right. And he's not ready to talk about it.

I'd love to say his issues stem from his dad. But no, the holding things in? That need to process internally before sharing… that's all me. Which is why I let him go upstairs without telling me much of anything. I trust that he'll open up in a few hours, or tomorrow. He's grounded until we work this out.

The bottle bears a slight shake as I pour the red wine into two glasses.

"He's going to have a bruise below his eye. Right above his cheekbone." The facts are a good place to start. "The other boy has a black eye, and a swollen lip."

"What kid?"

"Thomas Ellison."

"Are you fucking kidding me?" I slide one glass across the counter and lift mine, nonplussed at Jason's reaction. I don't really know Thomas Ellison, but I am quite certain his identity will be revealed with no prodding on my part.

"His father is one of my clients. Not my biggest, but he's got a solid practice. Two days a week he's down in LA." I can't imagine Ethan knows this. The wine has a sweet tang, and I swirl it, wondering if maybe it's gone stale since I opened it two days ago.

"Well, what did you say to him?"

"About?" A calm force field falls over me.

"The tooth fairy. What do you think? The fight. Did you punish him?"

"He's grounded."

"Why did they get into a fight?"

The last thing I want to admit to Jason is that I don't yet know. But I don't know. Jason sips his wine, then steps to the sink and spits it out.

"Jesus. What is that? Two-buck chuck?" He dumps the wine into the sink and sets the glass on the counter. Red residue stains the white porcelain. "I'm going to talk to him."

Ethan's father pounds up the stairs. I rinse the sink, then collapse into the chair in the living room. There's no knocking sound, but at least there's no sound of a door slamming into a wall. I'm not sure what I should be doing. There's no manual on how to handle these incidents. I want Ethan to open up and talk to me. In three years, he'll be off at college and on his own. I want to give him the room to learn to navigate life's issues on his own, beneath my roof, so when he's really out there on his own, he'll succeed.

Maybe I should go up and join Jason? But no, I've already had my time with Ethan. I should be thankful Jason is involved and showing an interest. In past years, he's been uninvolved, to the point it hurt Ethan. Jenn used to tell me I was projecting. She said Ethan seemed fine to her. That he didn't notice when Jason missed his games, or when he canceled on weekends. She said I felt hurt by it, and I projected that hurt onto Ethan. But he was fine. She said even with married couples, sometimes a parent missed games or had to go away on business trips.

Jason wanted fifty-fifty custody, but he only wanted to see Ethan every other weekend. For years, that worked out to about one weekend every other month. Jason has a full life. But in the last year or so, he's been much more involved. I'm not sure why, but I suspect it's because college looms overhead. Of course, if Jason wants to raise another child, he can. The women he dates are so young he'd probably need to wait a few years to start a family.

Jason's deep tenor vibrates through the ceiling. He's not yelling, but his loud booming voice travels through the floorboards above. He's talking to Ethan, not listening. That's a trait Jason has possessed his entire life. He speaks to people and expects to be heard. He is the sun in his own universe, and everyone orbits around him.

There's a soft knock on the front door. I hope it's not one of Ethan's friends. I'll either have to turn him away or keep him downstairs until Jason comes down. Jason won't think twice about embarrassing Ethan in front of his friends. He might even leap at the chance to mortify him. Cutting people down in front of others is a weapon Jason wields with precision.

Concerned aqua eyes greet me when I open the door. Trevor? He's holding a leash, and Astra stands dutifully beside him, her tail flitting back and forth.

"Hey." *Why are you here?*

"They said you had a family emergency. And you left your pocketbook. I thought you might need it."

He holds my pocketbook out, and a wave of shock filtrates.

"I didn't know. I haven't needed it." In my discombobulated rush, I carried my phone out in my hand. That's all I needed.

The ceiling creaks from steps above.

"Is everything okay?" Trevor asks.

"There was an incident at school." He nods, and it's clear Patel told him that much. "I don't know." I swing the door wide to allow him to enter.

"Is it okay? With Astra?"

"Sure. Just keep her on the leash in case she smells Smelly."

Astra sits on her haunches beside her owner, ears perked forward. Her dark eyes are watchful. Normally, I'd be on the ground loving on her. But instead, I collapse back into the club chair.

"Ethan didn't say much. Other than the other guy deserved it." I study Trevor's eyes for any slant or sign of judgment because my son hasn't opened up to me, but he's nonplussed.

"He probably did." Trevor's nonchalant approach lifts my confusion fog. "Sometimes punches are deserved."

"It's never okay to fight. Especially at school."

Trevor's lower lip protrudes. The ceiling creaks.

"Jason is here. He's speaking to Ethan."

Rapid thumping down the stairs slows as Jason realizes another person is in the den.

"Jason, this is my friend Trevor."

"Friend?" A maniacal smirk I know all too well flits across Jason's face. In three broad steps, with a hand outstretched, he reaches the sofa. Trevor stands and takes his hand. Ethan stops halfway down, one hand on the banister.

"You were here the other morning, right?" Jason asks.

Trevor and I glance at each other. I didn't realize Jason saw Trevor drive away. That was weeks ago. "So, you've got yourself a boy toy." He's smiling, but it's an angry smile, one that some might describe as sinister. "No wonder our son is acting out."

Astra's lips lift, exposing her incisors, and a low, intimidating growl fills the room.

Trevor utters a succinct, "Heel." The growl halts. But the dog's ears and focus remain trained on Jason. Smart dog.

"Is he living with you now? Is that why his dog is here?"

"Jason, I believe you're done with Ethan, right? You can leave."

"You know, if you're living with someone, I don't have to pay you alimony."

"Jason, you haven't paid me alimony in years."

The dumb twat has to consider this. I don't know why or how. He views the child support he pays me as a fine he has to pay instead of what it is and always has been—paying for his son's expenses. Money that admittedly I needed in the past, but my dependence on his funds is drying up thanks to a once-in-a-lifetime job opportunity.

"Do you have anything else you need to say?" My words are so much calmer than the internal combustion raging within. The tips of my fingers are ice cold. I push up off the armrests.

Jason and I face off. There's a surly German shepherd with sharp incisors and a former SEAL behind my back. Never have I ever felt so strong.

"If he doesn't get his shit straight, he's coming to live with me."

I'd love to say it's an empty threat, but I know Jason plans to hold his college tuition and probably an automobile over his head. At fifteen years of age, where he lives will ultimately be up to Ethan. But I don't like at all the underlying implication my parenting skills are the reason he's threatening it.

He's such an asshole. How on Earth was I ever married to him?

# CHARLIE FOXTROT

TREVOR

Stella's skin color blanches. Red blotches mar those smooth cheeks and slender throat. Her shoulders are back, and there's a whole lotta hate in that glare.

Her ex is wearing a suit that's cut a little too tight for my taste. His pants are a little too tapered, and judging by his flaming red neck, I'd say his tie verges on a chokehold. He glances between Stella and me. I know his type. All bravado, giant ego, no substance.

"Is there anything else you needed?" Stella asks. "If not, you need to leave."

"This doesn't happen again. Do you understand me?" Jason doesn't wait for a response. He storms out, and the door slams behind him so hard the wall vibrates.

There's a lot that can be learned observing how a divorced couple interacts with each other. Sometimes there is mutual respect, and then you know that no matter what happened that ended their commitment to each other, they've moved past it and there's an underlying healthy relationship. I think I can count on one hand the number of friends I've had who reached that level of maturity. All military, all families for the most part torn apart by the distance or the job. The couples grew separately rather than together.

Sometimes there's a level of hatred so intense bystanders risk collateral damage. Some might question if the hate line will cross back over to love. Those are the couples that the wise say little, in case they end up back together.

And then there are couples where you realize one member of the couple is highly toxic, and you feel grateful the other survived. My mom had a few of those relationships. She's in one of those right now, which is one reason I don't see her often. I can't stand her husband. He's one in a string of assholes. The difference is I didn't grow up under this one's heavy hand.

It's clear Stella has an asshole in her past. But she stands up to him. I hope she's the one who ended the relationship. There's strength in kicking toxic human waste to the curb. My mom did it once or twice, and the rebound afterward is heartening. In her case, it wasn't enough.

Stella's back is to me. Her shoulders are so erect it's as if her commanding officer is facing her, but her dainty white fingers are curled into a fist. No doubt her nails are pressing into her skin. She faces her asshole ex with solid strength. She didn't resort to screaming. Her tone remained level, even-keeled. Ethan never had to cringe upstairs, listening to the yelling between two parents who lost their cool and forgot voices carry.

I fucking admire that. Every fiber quivers with admiration. I don't doubt she wanted to lose her cool and scream like a mad banshee, but she prioritized. Her son came first. I love that. In my life, I haven't seen that often enough.

Unfortunately, Ethan stood on the stairs and observed his old man be a complete and total dick. That's not a comfortable place to stand.

Minutes tick by, and she's frozen, lost in whatever emotions are ricocheting through her. I've had missions where I needed stillness afterward. I get it. So I give her the time she needs. It's no sweat. I'll be there for her however I can.

A creak on the stairs breaks the silence.

In slow motion, Stella turns to her son, blinking as she returns from wherever she'd been collecting herself. With hooded eyes and guilt I recognize, Ethan faces his mother. Silent acknowledgement passes between mother and son. Then his gaze falls to me. His expression is void of emotion. Shell-shocked. Then his gaze falls to Astra, and he transitions from a young man to a boy. He's still at that age where one can, in the right circumstances, cross the line back and forth. Because he's only fifteen.

Ethan sprawls on the floor in front of Astra, ruffling her fur and scratching behind her ears.

"Hey, girl." Astra came with us on our trail ride. Ethan had been in awe of how dutifully she tracked beside us. And of course, boy and dog bonded. She licks his face with one long, wet swipe of tongue. The action dispels the emotionally laden cloud in the room.

"Are you all right?" Stella's question is soft and full of concern.

"Fine." Astra lifts her paw against Ethan, and he takes it in his hand.

"Did he come down on you?"

"Dad being Dad." Ethan huffs it out like that's enough said. I'm curious about what the definition of coming down is in this household, but I am the interloper, so I remain quiet.

"Hey," Ethan directs his question to me, "I was thinking I might go for a run. Can I take Astra?"

"Fine with me." She's been on a run already today, but I went light with only three miles and a swim. I doubt Ethan will exhaust her.

"You're grounded." Stella places her hand on her hip, but the right side of her lip is curled up, and I sense this is the way she and her son communicate.

"Mom, I'm not going over to any friends'. I need fresh air."

"Okay." She checks her watch. "Can you be back before dark? Where are you going to run?"

"Through the neighborhood. I'll stick to sidewalks."

I could drive him to trails, or pull out an app to create a route, but as the interloper, I remain mute.

"Do you mind?" Stella asks me.

"No. Astra will love it."

He jumps up and throws on running shoes. His shorts hang below his knees. That would drive me bananas on a run, but he's not running for the workout. He's running for escape. Out of all the methods available for escaping one's emotions, physical exertion is the healthiest. I clap him on the back after giving him a tutorial on Astra's commands.

A neighbor empties her mailbox, and I nod while watching Ethan and Astra jog out of sight. Stella stands on her front doorstep, one hand over her eyes, shielding them from the sun.

"You okay?" I ask.

"I am." She sighs. There's an unmistakable sadness about her. "Want to come in while we wait for them to come back? I've got chili in the Crockpot, but it won't be ready for a while."

Wordlessly, I follow her inside. My phone vibrates, and I read the message. It's Wolf, telling me he has updates. He'd like to get together this evening. He's my next-door neighbor. Catching up with him is easy. This situation in Stella's home is feeling like a clusterfuck. I don't bother responding to Wolf.

She lifts the glass lid on the circular pot on her counter, and a potent, mouth-watering aroma fills the kitchen. With a long spoon, she stirs it, then places the lid back down. I take her hand and lead her over to the sofa. Sitting as far back as I can, I place her between my legs. I shift her hair to the side and press into her shoulders. She whimpers and ducks out of my grip.

"Sorry." I hold on to her shoulders. "You're tight. I'll take it easy, but let me work through those knots."

My thumbs knead the muscles on the sides of her neck. I position her head downward, as if she's looking at the ground, stretching those tight muscles. Gently, I massage and knead. Then, using the thumb-crawling technique, I press into her shoulders and work my way toward her spine.

"This is heaven."

"Normally, I would have you strip and do a full body massage. But I think we both know where that would lead. And you've got Ethan coming home."

"Hmmm." She leans into my hands, and her head lolls to the side. "I can't remember the last time someone gave me a shoulder rub."

"Seriously?" I frown. "I'll have to add that to my daily to-do list."

The noises she emits sound like muffled laughter. She's a skeptic.

"I'm serious. When I deliver your coffee, I can do a quick shoulder rub. Or maybe I can catch you at the end of the day before you run out the door in a mad rush."

She has one tight knot on her right shoulder, and the pad of my thumb presses into it, eliciting another moan. All her sexy noises are sending my blood southward, but I'm determined to ignore it.

"Why are you always rushing out? Do you pick Ethan up after school or something?"

Patel has that situation. Her kids are in a daycare, and she watches the clock with the focus of a sharpshooter.

"Nah. He usually gets a ride home with a friend. He can walk too. But I'm usually rushing home to get dinner ready. Ethan's a growing boy. He gets hungry. Sometimes he has sports to get to. Or he needs to be driven somewhere. His schedule… he's at the age where he plans it and more or less assumes I'll make it all happen."

Stella always makes it happen, so he's only expecting what she's always delivered. He's fifteen. He's not going to apply deep thoughts unless she prompts him. I remember that age. Girls and sports filled my head. Not much else. Even the jerks my mom dated didn't occupy mental real estate at that age, because I'd just close the door. By then, I'd become a master at avoidance. It wasn't until my mom had a meltdown one day because of a stain on a new piece of furniture she really loved and tears streamed down her cheeks that I saw her as more of a peer, and not just a parent.

I lean forward and press my lips to the slope of Stella's neck. Goosebumps rise along her arm. She leans back, into my chest, and I wrap my arms around her, holding her close, and she relaxes into me. I've never done this with a woman. I've never held a woman, or offered a massage, without an ulterior motive. In the past, once I achieved the end goal, I always moved along.

When I joined the military at seventeen, my primary aim had been to claim my independence and put distance between me and my mother's boyfriend. It didn't take me long to let the competitive bug drive me to an ongoing climb of increasingly challenging trainings and courses until I received the ultimate designation. I earned my place as a SEAL.

Throughout those years, relationships made little sense to me. A few of my teammates tried them, but fuck if they didn't struggle. Not to mention, when deployed or on a mission, it seemed to me, we were fuck-all better off being out there without the worry of leaving a wife or kid behind if things went haywire. No one to worry about meant greater focus on the mission. It meant I served as a stronger team member—or so I thought. Didn't seem to help my team in our final ambush. Wolf and I had been the only two to walk away.

Leaving the military didn't lead to a quiet life. Wolf and I went into a bar and got drunk with a harmless-looking guy who offered us consistent pay. Erik needed security and offered Blackstone-level salary. That choice led us down a squirrelly path, but I wouldn't change a thing. Erik, Wolf, Kairi, and I are all partners in Arrow now. And I believe in what we're doing.

A calm washes through me. Maybe over the years I maintained my single status because I'd never had this. I'd never felt this warmth toward someone. This desire to hold and protect. This sense of peace.

Stella's fingers comb through my hair. My spine tingles. I could sit like this for hours, holding her, rubbing her arms and legs, letting her fingers toy with me. She tilts her head back against my shoulder, and I kiss her. It's a soft kiss. A slow kiss. One more thing that feels new. Different. Holding a woman, treasuring a woman, it's different. And I do treasure Stella.

She's like a lot of women from my past. Attractive. Sexy. But there's more too. At work, she has a no-nonsense approach to managing the entire office. She's corralling our wild west ways into a semblance of the corporate world. She's turning our start-up into a legitimate business. She prioritizes everyone else in her life—at home and at work. She's a force. And she's always changing. Her hair color, her fragrance. But those dark blue eyes are steadfast. Constant. And each day I see them, she pulls me deeper in, to the point unusual sensations flutter through my chest when she's near. And this, right now, holding her, it's bliss. This, right here, on her sofa, might be the most intimate I have ever been with someone.

The side door swings open, and Astra trots in, her leash trailing behind her. Ethan freezes, his eyes on his mother and me. Stella sits up, her back stick straight.

"Did you have a good run?"

Ethan unfreezes and toes off his shoes.

"Yeah. It was good. Thanks for letting me go."

"Sure thing. You want to shower real quick? Dinner should be ready soon."

"Yeah." He's two steps up when he pauses. "Trevor, are you staying for dinner?" Stella is already halfway across the kitchen, presumably to stir that chili.

"Nah, I need to head." I wasn't invited, and I'm not about to force my way in. Yes, I forced my way in on tuna casserole night. But there's a lot going on in the house tonight.

"Are you sure? We have plenty of chili." Stella's invitation sounds genuine.

"If you two don't mind, I'd love to stay for dinner."

"Cool," Ethan says. It seems to be his favorite one-word response. "I'd like to get your take on what happened today." He shoots his mom a tentative glance. She softly smiles. "Since, you know… you, well, you might… I mean, you used to… I don't know. Never mind." His hand falls on the stair handrail.

"Hey, Ethan, any time," I say.

He nods and clicks his tongue, which isn't one of Astra's commands. But he adds, "Come on, girl." That's not one of her commands either, but she dutifully trots up the stairs after him.

I get up and find placemats and plates to help Stella. The normalcy of it all is… comfortable.

My phone vibrates. It's Wolf again. This time, I tap out a quick response.


Me: *At Stella's. I'll check in later.*

.   .   .

Over dinner, Ethan clears his plate in record time. In the military, we'd come down on him for that. You've got to chew your food, or it can lead to bad things. Cramps, for one. But there's enough going on, so I don't harp. He gulps half a glass of water.

"You know, I remember my first fight," I say, and Stella's eyes dart to me. But more importantly, Ethan has looked up from his plate. I give Stella a look that says "trust me," and I can see a tiny flash of panic across her eyes.

"I was really scared to talk about it. It triggers a lot of feelings, you know. I think, as a man, it unleashes this scary side. And what was worse was my mom wasn't an easy woman to talk to. I could never tell her about my fights, and then things got worse for me for a while. Guilt and shame just make life harder. But looks to me like your mom is a lot more understanding."

Ethan glances over to his mom's face and she just smiles weakly at him. There's a plea in her expression, but she doesn't want to push. I give Ethan a wink, and he looks down to his plate. A few more seconds of silence go by, and I reach for Stella's hand beneath the table.

"Um. Mom?"

"Yes, sweetheart?"

"Well, today, I... there was this guy. He said some things to Sierra. I told him to leave her alone. He got all up in my face. Told me it was none of my business. Anyway, that's what happened." He shrugs, and his gaze is on me in a nervous way, like he's worried I'm going to come down on him or judge him. "She'd been upset about it. But I told her the only reason he was being a jerk is because she turned him down when he asked her out. He'd been nice, and then he just flipped. He's been a jerk for days."

"Who threw the first punch?" Stella asks.

"I did." He meets his mother's gaze head on, but he bows his head and hunches his shoulders under the weight of his shame.

"Why?"

"He chest bumped me. Then he asked me if I have a thing for slutty mulattos. I don't think I've ever been so pissed, and I know you're gonna say it's just words. And it is. I shouldn't have thrown a punch. I stooped to his level. And I shouldn't have. I should have… just walked away. It's just words."

"Why didn't you tell Principal Esteban what happened?"

"It didn't matter what he said. I punched him. I was still going to get suspended."

"Well, thank you for telling me what happened. And, while I would have preferred that you keep your cool, I'm also proud of you." He squints in disbelief, as if uncertain he is hearing her correctly. "You stood up for someone you love. You are a good person."

The moment between the two of them catches me off guard. There's a thick current of emotion crossing that table, and I back away from it. I rinse my plate in the sink while the two of them hug.

"I've got homework. Gonna head up. Good to see you, Trevor." Ethan offers me his fist to bump. Our knuckles tap, and he steps away. Ethan runs upstairs, and as soon as we hear the bedroom door close, Stella's smile disappears.

She sighs. "I should have said more, or…" She huffs and walks back to the kitchen. I pull her against me and breathe her in.

"You did great. You're…" She looks up at me, waiting for how the sentence ends. And I let my eyes say the rest.

My phone buzzes again, serving a reminder I need to get back. We stop by the front door.

"Bet you wish you didn't stop by tonight." she says, staring at the floor. There's no tease in her tone. She's for real.

"I loved tonight."

"Yeah, right." She rubs her forehead. "What a cluster."

"Still loved it." I can tell she doesn't believe me. There are foreign sensations swirling, and my phone vibrates once more. I get out of there, but a part of me stays behind.

# The One with Affirmations



Saturday morning, there are noises down the hall. Outside my window, a daze of daylight infiltrates the cracks in the white plantation shutter bifolds. The dim golden light accentuates the thin layer of dust. I really need to dust all the blinds. I check the time. It's barely six.

Ethan said he and Trevor were going out to the beach this morning. My expectation had been that I'd hear knocking, and I'd have to wake up my son and maybe fix Trevor coffee while Ethan rushed to get ready. But, based on the cabinet door slamming shut, the water running, and other assorted sounds of a fifteen-year-old brushing his teeth and getting dressed, he's doing it all on his own.

Relief he's fulfilling his end of an agreement with no nudging from me fills me. That's what you want as a parent—independence. Or at least, that's one of my daily refrains. I also have a few other favorite ones.

I am strong.

I can do this.

I am one person.

My back muscles are sore. And this morning, there's another pleasant soreness. My face heats, just remembering. It must have been something about seeing a man interacting like a friend with my son. Watching that blessed dog trail behind Ethan. Because Friday after lunch, in the office, a demon came to roost. My hand falls over my eyes, as if by covering my eyes I can block the memory of this girl gone wild.

*"You all have been in lots of closed-door meetings." Trevor's silky V-neck short-sleeved tee fit him like a glove, and it became hard to swallow as I visually traced the outline of his muscles. "Is everything okay?"*

*A waft of deodorant soap hit me, and I leaned closer to get a better whiff of Trevor's freshly showered aroma. I pushed his office door closed. I, Stella, pushed his door closed.*

*He may have raised an eyebrow, but I can honestly say I have no idea if he did or not, because I solely focused on his pecs and his biceps. He crossed his arms but rolled his chair back from the desk. He wore shorts. Black shorts with a thin material. I might have backed up. I might have sat in the desk chair and conducted appropriate business. But those shorts hid nothing.*

*All morning, I'd been squeezing my thighs, thinking about him. I'd struggled to focus on another meeting with the lawyer reviewing yet another version of our employment contract. Like a horny college girl, I'd drawn curly designs in the margins of my notepad during a staff meeting. I fantasized about him pressing me up against a wall in my den or taking me on my sofa. Both actions that could never ever happen when Ethan might come home. But in the office...*

*His shorts, while sitting, rose high above his knee. Golden hair mixed with darker hair curled along his skin. I came around the corner of his desk. My heart palpitated faster, not with nervousness, because I don't think my cognitive processes registered a plan. A noticeable bulge filled out the right side of his crotch, pointing to his elbow. The loose material allowed movement, and for a brief second, I considered he must be more comfortable with that extra movement than in jeans. His chest raised and lowered. He uncrossed his arms and rested his forearms on the armrests. His fingers curled around the edges. He swallowed, and the lines of his clean-shaven throat reflected the movement so clearly I felt the pull to him, and a desire to press my lips against that soft, smooth skin strengthened. His lips remained in a flat line, even as the expansion and contraction of his chest quickened.*

*Those aqua eyes unveiled my inner bad girl. The one I locked away so long ago I considered her six feet under. But in that closed door room, whatever demon-like wild child infiltrated my body gagged the stuffy, rule-following soccer mom.*

*My ass rested on the edge of his desk, and he rolled his chair closer, so his spread legs were on each side of mine. My finger traced his clavicle. My touch seemed to lift the corners of his lips.*

*"How can I help you, Stella?"*

*My brain short-circuited, and the only thing I could focus on was him and that bulge and the unmet need my vibrator had done nothing to quell the night before.*

*"Is office sex on the table?"*

*His eyes widened, and a full smile crossed his lips. "I believe I can accommodate."*

*He kept his line of vision on me. I've read about a heated gaze, but damn if I didn't feel his gaze on my skin. Hot and salacious. Clicking sounds filled the silence. Out of the corner of my eye, his screen went dark. Powered down. A faint click near the door made me wonder if he locked the door through a command on his computer. But that thought fled when he stood and his chair rolled against the wall.*

*His muscles flexed as he repositioned me on his desk. His large hands clasped my waist and made my hips look half their size.*

*"Do you have any idea how good your ass looks in these tight skirts you wear around the office? How well this fabric hugs your curves?" I whimpered for the briefest second before his lips claimed mine. Sexual need coursed between us. I'd love to say there were emotions flip flopping too, but I'd be fooling myself. No. Sexual need unleashed would be the best description.*

*He cupped my head as he ground his kiss into me. Our tongues danced and teeth clashed. I curled my hips against his thigh, seeking pressure as my blouse opened and the rough pads of his fingers teased my bare breast.*

*He lifted me, and my skirt rose over my hips, exposing me, then he fell to the floor, on his knees, and spread my thighs. A tight tug burned for* seconds as he tore at the thin black lace of my thong. The fabric rubbed my ass as he dragged it under me and tossed it behind him.

"I like this trimmed pussy." Light blue flashed upward, and I sucked in air. "Do you know I dreamed of this?"

I licked my lips. Words escaped me. It had to be a fantasy. He had to be a fantasy.

"Well, I did. I jacked off in the shower, thinking about this dream."

He inhaled, and I spread my legs wider. So unlike me.

His tongue ran along my seam, then he went deeper. I rocked my hips forward, straining to give him better access. My palms flattened on the desk behind me, propping my chest up. Cold air blanketed my exposed breast, with my blouse partially unbuttoned, the cups of my bra pulled down and pushing my breasts out. If someone walked in, we would've been quite the sight, with his head between my legs, my heels on his shoulders, my bare chest thrust out with wild abandon.

He added two long fingers and sucked and blew over my bundle of nerves. I pressed my lips closed, holding in the squeals and cries and moans aching to come out. And then his teeth grazed over my clit and I curled forward. The entire room darkened, and I lost my sense of place and time, and not that my sense of propriety had ever been in the room, but at that moment it vacated the city.

My arms vibrated, the pressure of holding me up finally doing them in, combined with the interstellar glory rocking my world. He stood and captured my face, one palm against each cheek, and he kissed me. Deeply, possessively.

My fingers curved around his erection, and he let out a low groan. I pushed his shorts down and wrapped my fingers around his smooth, *silky flesh. The pad of my thumb smeared the wet cum around his tip.*

*"Fuck. I want you, Stella. I'm going to take you bare."*

*"Yes," I panted.*

*He kissed me again, holding me in place while I stroked him and he rocked into my tight grip. His kiss held a promise. I wanted him inside me, and I squirmed to get closer.*

*With an indiscernible growl, he lifted me, flipped me around, and said, "Grip the desk."*

*My palms pressed against the cool desk, and my fingers gripped the underside. He stroked my thigh and my ass. He smacked it once, not enough to hurt, but enough to send moisture pooling. Holy shit.*

*"Little seductress."*

*He rubbed my spine, the pressure firm, silently commanding I lean forward. He positioned me just right.*

*He placed his cock between my butt cheeks. The smooth skin of his very hard erection moved back and forth. One hand gripped my hip, and with one hard thrust, he forced entry. We moaned in unison, and fuck if that wasn't hot.*

*"Hold on," he reminded me. And then he proved his strength as he pressed into me, over and over. Crap crashed to floor as he pressed my spine and I flattened across his desk. With each push into me, the hard edge of his desk manipulated my mound, sending spiraling sensations. The tantalizing tingles curled through me, lifting me up, raising me to an unprecedented, exhilarated state. The cool of his desk, the slap of skin against skin, the smell of my sex blending with his soap, the paper desk calendar scraping my nipples, the gleam of the silver*

*handle on an office door with me splayed across a desk, legs wide as he pounded into me, it all served as a cyclone of sensations.*

*With a firm grip on each hip, he heaved me back, creating space between my body and the edge of the desk. The butt of his palm massaged me in a complimentary rhythm to his hips, and then he somehow pinched. Holy mother. The orgasm ripped through me with so much force, my arms quivered and my hips jolted.*

*"That's it, baby." He huffed, his breathing loud and winded. His hips slowed, once, twice, then I felt him pulse deep within me. Seconds passed. When he collapsed over me, his shirt still on, my blouse half on, my skirt over my hips, and...*

The downstair door slams shut, and I jolt out of my recollection. My eyes dart around to check I'm still alone. *Fucking hell.* My grin is so wide it makes my face ache. The skin along my hipbones is still tender, as are other parts. Evidence my fantasy happened.

When I tell Jenn, she's going to be shocked. She'll open her mouth wide, and her first response will be something like, "Nuh uh!" because that is so unlike me. I still can't believe I did it.

I don't know what I'm doing. I guess this is what a mid-life crisis looks like. Having a fling with your boss. Your twenty-something boss who will one day get married and have children with someone who recently reached the legal drinking age. Not that Trevor is jonesing to have children. He's too young, and he's a man. Men don't think like that. It won't be until several of his friends have kids that children will enter his radar.

He's close to his friend and partner Kairi. The way she and her fiancé, David, are together, I wouldn't doubt they'll have children soon. David's a pediatrician, so he clearly loves kids. And she's, like, thirty-three. Women, we have to think about children even if we aren't necessarily ready for them mentally. Yes, I'd bet those two will make an announcement in the next couple of years.

Apparently, Erik, one of the Arrow partners, is newly married. I've met him, but never his wife. They got married in a small wedding on her family vineyard with only immediate family and business partners present. But I've been told her grandfather is pushing for a larger celebration. Vivi is younger, so I'm not sure how long it will be before they spawn.

Wolf, Trevor's closest friend by far, the man he considers a brother, has a girlfriend who clings to him the way you wish Saran Wrap would cling to a plastic bowl. But I don't think she's it for him. He treats her like she's a for-now flavor. I recognize the look because Jason gives it to whatever young woman finds herself in the front passenger seat of his high-priced luxury sedan.

This entire thought process is silly. Mentally running through his friends, trying to determine at what point he's going to realize he wants children and I can't be his baby maker. I mean, technically, sure, it's possible. But I don't want to. My son is fifteen. I loved being a mom and doing all those mom things, but I didn't love it enough to repeat the eighteen-year cycle.

No, there's an end date on Trevor and me. We both know it. Like so many things in life, it's all timing. And I think I might be able to sell myself on having fun for now, but how stupid is having a fling with your boss? It's stupid. It's bananas stupid. It's like throw-me-a-sarcastic-quote-from-Chandler stupid. "Okay. You've got to stop the Q-tip when there's resistance" level stupid. That's what it is. I have my dream job. I mean, I really enjoy what I am doing. I'm about to hire people who report to me. And while, yes, Trevor could be mistaken for a Norse god, there's no universe where he and I work out. He'll want children. Look how good he is with Ethan. Of course he's going to want children. And he should have children.

And yet yesterday we had condomless sex because we are in an exclusive relationship.

Fuck me, he's just so… amazing.

My palm slaps against my forehead.

This is so stupid. It has to end; it's going to anyway. My heart starts to beat in protest. My mind is giving me flashes of that smile and those eyes I—

No. I'm practically arguing with myself in my own mom voice. *No. Come on, now. Don't be so silly.* I know what I have to do. I need to end this. My mind obeys, but my heartbeat compensates by thumping in my head. The sadness starts to creep in as reality sinks. There's just no good way this works out, is there?

The whole morning, my brain waffles back and forth between Trevor's firm, fit torso and my paycheck. I need my paycheck. I have credit card debt to pay off, and Ethan's college tuition is less than three years away.

When Trevor's Jeep crowds my short driveway, I'm sitting on the front step with my third cup of coffee. I'm wearing an old sweatshirt and enormous flowing pajama pants. I have a speech planned.

"Mom." The passenger door opens, and an enthused Ethan hops out. "Guess what? Trevor knows all about lifting weights." This information is not a surprise. "And he's going to help me get a routine going. Isn't that cool?"

"How was the beach?" I don't respond to the gym thing because I doubt Trevor will want to go to the gym with my son after I execute the planned speech.

"Cool. He's a machine. You should see him slice through waves." Trevor comes around the front of the vehicle. He's hanging back.

"I smell," he offers as explanation.

"Oh, me too, Mom. We did a bike, swim, run routine. I'm gonna run up and get a shower."

"Okay."

"Thanks for today. Appreciate it. I had fun," he calls out to Trevor.

"Sure thing." Trevor smiles at my son as they bump fists.

They nod at each other. It's interesting watching my son and Trevor interact. I rarely see the interaction between Jason and Ethan. Usually, Ethan's head is down, and he plows into the house and I'm left interacting with the asswipe.

"See ya tomorrow," is Ethan's salute. The door creaks, and he's gone. Trevor remains by the hood.

"I'm gonna head on. Any chance I can take you out to dinner tonight? Ethan said he's going to the movies with some friends."

Trevor is across the lawn. This is not a good time to unload my speech. Maybe dinner will be? In a flash, his long strides cover the distance between us. Sweaty man smell fills my nostrils, and instinctively my nose scrunches. He ignores my reaction to his stench and picks me up, pressing me up against his damp shirt, and twirls me.

"Yes, I smell."

Laughter spills uncontrollably. He's not tickling me, but he's twirling me about for the entire neighborhood to see. He kisses the tender area on my neck, just above my shoulder, and I squeal and squirm from the tickle. He slows to a standstill and catches my eye. The seriousness in his expression has me blinking. I force myself to maintain eye contact. I force myself to hear him. I focus on breathing.

"I'll see you later?"

Half a nod is all I give. His lips cover mine, and suddenly my olfactory sense shuts down and I truly lose myself in his soft, slow, warm kiss. Then he sets me down, swats my ass playfully, says he'll call me after he showers, and climbs into his Jeep.

He blows me a kiss before driving away, and it physically warms my heart. Yes, it sounds insane. But I feel the kiss he blew. It finds its way inside my ribcage, and the temperature elevates in that center spot, serving evidence that when he leaves, my heart is going to explode into fragments. No one said a mid-life crisis would be casualty-free.

# Lima Charlie

Trevor

"You spent the rest of the weekend at her house?" Wolf's Monday morning greeting doesn't faze me in the least. He passes me my coffee and the breakfast sandwich he ordered for me.

"After your little update, what did you expect?" He cornered me upon my return Saturday after I dropped Ethan home. "Anything new?"

"Not on Kane." Photo recognition software picked him up at LAX. Which means he's stateside. No more staying on the down low. He's here. Somewhere.

Astra and I spent the remainder of the weekend with Stella and Ethan. Thankfully, she's coming around to accepting us. It helps that Ethan loves working out. I also suspect there's a girl who has caught his eye. That's about the time I started putting time in on weights. I think his crush is the same girl who had him throwing a punch last week at school, but Stella swears she's like a sibling.

"How's her son handling you sleeping over?" Wolf's background isn't much different from mine. He had a stepdad with a heavy hand.

"Ethan and I get along. He's a good kid. I was about to beg to sleep on her sofa… trying to figure out how to explain why I wanted to stay overnight, when he pulled his mom aside. He told her to not be ridiculous. That his dad has women stay over all the time, and it doesn't bother him. I heard the whole conversation. Her place is pretty small." I unwrap my bacon, egg, and cheese croissant. There's avocado on it too. I didn't ask for avocado, but it's healthy. Since my breakfast sandwich has avocado on it, I douse it in Tabasco.

"And then she let you stay? Last night too? On a school night?"

"Well, last night I took Ethan onto the beach to do some navigation by the stars. Purposefully did it a little late." I got up wicked early for my workout, so in a way it was like I didn't stay the night. I pretty much work on the same premise my neighbor, an old vet, used to crow about. In the early morning hours, you cross over between all the drunks into those getting up early to go fishing. My adaptation follows along the lines of in the early morning hours, the assassins stop working and the soldiers are up sweating.

"FBI and NSA? They have nothing more?" It's frustrating. We have these massive forces working with us, yet shit slips through the cracks.

"No. And it was a couple of hours after he'd been through the airport that surveillance picked him up. They're still working to figure out what passport he used."

Sometimes I believe our government works at a snail's pace, but then I remind myself that the databases are more complex than Hollywood portrays them.

"They should have an answer on that soon, right? He had to go through customs." Visual recognition should pull that footage quickly—in theory. The pick-up we got was an image of him stepping out from baggage claim.

"Kairi's on it."

That's good. Over the weekend, while Stella watched old *Friends* episodes, I gave the matter a lot of thought. Unlike Kairi and Erik, I'm not afraid of Kane. For one, I could end him with my bare hands. But if he's back in the States, he's about to bite some bait. It's a good thing, but I still needed to be near Stella and Ethan. Simply an instinctual need to protect. But do I think he's been watching me closely enough to know I have a girlfriend? To know he now has a way of hurting me? That, I don't know. I doubt it.

The men who shot me posed as utility workers. We believe all they wanted was to plant surveillance. If they had lived, we could have confirmed that. All things the same, the need to be at Stella's should any unsolicited worker stop by bound me to her house. Thankfully, Ethan fully welcomed it. And for once,

I was thankful Erik purchased a well-trained attack dog. When Ethan and I went to the gym, I found it comforting knowing Astra remained with Stella and she would kill an intruder.

"Donovan is complaining about you. Loudly." Wolf wipes the grease from his country biscuit off his fingers. He's nonplussed, but I am confused.

"What?" He's one of our agents. "He and I have had zero disagreements."

"He's corralling some of the guys. Says the workouts you're requiring of them are too rigorous." Now Wolf is full-on smiling. This amuses him. "He says it's like you haven't accepted you're no longer a SEAL. He implied he's going to go to HR to discuss the matter. Wanted to give you a heads-up." I grimace. He grins. "If you want, we can give him the code name Liza."

Liza is the code name for drama, after Liza Minelli. Yeah, I'll call him Liza. Wolf might think it's funny, but I don't. He dives into a few other status updates as we head into the office. My frustration level remains high. A strong burn to punch something surfaces. Maybe for my lunch routine I'll do a round of kickboxing.

Sure enough, after our morning status meetings and a review of some hires we want to extend offers to, Stella enters my office. Unlike last week, she's not looking at me like I'm chocolate cake. Those deep blue eyes are too serious. Her full lips rest in a flat line, and she clutches a notepad to her chest. Her reddish hair is pulled back into a low mess, and the way it weighs her hair down, dark chocolate roots show. It's the first time I've noticed what must be her natural color. When grown out, I imagine it really sets off those spectacular irises.

She closes the door. Instead of walking around my desk with fuck-me eyes, she pulls out a chair and sits, demurely crossing one leg over the other. I brace myself. This might be where she tells me we had a great weekend, but she can't do that again. She started something along those lines during dinner, but I navigated the discussion well and let her in on enough to understand that I need to be around them, at least for the short-term. But maybe she's thought more about that.

I understand she wants to protect her son. I love that about her. I spent the weekend extremely cognizant of Ethan's where-abouts. I remember the discomfort of a creaking bed, knowing your mom is in it and what's happening at that moment. I wasn't about to do that to Ethan. Stella and I did discreetly shower together. Her tight shower tub wasn't conducive to much, but it allowed us to release some sexual tension. The layout of her house is not ideal, with the two bedrooms right beside each other separated by thin walls.

Stella clears her throat. She pulls me back into the moment. She sits in the chair across from me as formal as one can possibly be. *Here it comes.*

"I am coming in here in my role as Human Resources Director." All the tension that had been building in my chest disperses. This isn't about us. It's about that fool, Liza. "It's not something to smile about. I need you to take me seriously and to hear me as the HR voice for this company."

"No problem." She's about to tell me about that dipshit's complaints. That's worlds better than what I feared.

"I'm serious."

"I understand. I am, too." I force my superior officer expression, the one I used to give to, well, superior officers. This seems to satisfy her, although her right eye squints. She might be trying to figure out what I'm up to.

"Donovan Drudge came to see me. He didn't file a formal complaint, but he has expressed concerns about the physical training requirements of the position." I don't say anything but keep my superior-officer-expression pasted on. She fidgets with her pen. "He believes you are extreme, and this could end up costing us exemplary employees."

She waits.

"Is this where I speak?"

"Yes." She looks flabbergasted. "I want to know what you think. I'm not sure I fully understand what all he's talking about, but the training requirements he shared did sound… extensive."

By some miracle, I resist the urge to call her Ms. Johnson. "If he doesn't like the training requirements, he can quit."

"He said you would say that. But, you know, he claims there are at least ten others who feel the same but didn't want to come to HR."

"Then ten others should quit, too."

She sighs. "You recognize we have a growing list of clients, many international. We're having trouble locating prospects who meet your list of qualifications as it is. Once someone passes our background checks and interview process, we've invested in them. We don't want them to quit. Arrow's employees are its greatest resource." Her shoulders are back. The notepad now lies flat on her lap.

"Let me be clear. I value our employees. Apparently, more than some of those employees value themselves. This isn't mall security. The only reason I am alive today is because of my training. And that is not an exaggeration. Not by a long shot." Now those eyes lock on mine. I've got her attention. "We used to have a saying in the military that more sweat in peace times means less blood in war. If we need to type that up and put it as a company motto on the wall, do it. When the NSA hires our group, it's for a job they can't be associated with. That the US government can't be associated with. We are black ops. If a mission goes sideways, they issue denials. You think I give a rat's ass if he thinks my expectations that he can run seven miles is extreme? Or that I expect him to continue target practice every single week? Or that he needs to fine tune his hand-to-hand skills because, to be quite frank, they suck? No. If he can't take it, then we'll send him on an assignment, and he'll die. He may die anyway, but at least I'll know I did everything I could to keep his ass alive. So, you get anyone coming in to complain, you can figure out what the best HR terminology is, but the answer is, they're fired."

She scribbles on her notepad. There's a soft rose over not just her cheeks, but her entire face, almost up to the hairline.

"Who names their kid Donovan Drudge?" My question earns a smile.

"You know, we could use him for a desk job. We have surveillance needs—" A loud, hard knock on the door interrupts her, and the door opens.

"He's here." Wolf is on alert. The hair on the back of my neck rises, and my chair hits the wall behind me as I stand.

"Santa Barbara?"

"No. Here. In the conference room."

My hand falls to my desk drawer to retrieve my pistol.

"You don't need it. He's got two tangos with him, but Patel took their weapons. He says he has a business proposition to discuss."

I pick up the gun.

"Seriously. No weapons. Let's see what he has to say."

I don't want Stella anywhere near Kane. Even if Wolf and I don't carry, that doesn't mean every agent on the floor doesn't have weapons. There's potential for a storm of bullet fire to rip this floor apart. Fear flashes. I wish she wasn't working here. I want her far away.

"Go down to Patel," I say to Stella. "Ask her for access to the safe room. Tell her I told you." She glances between Wolf and me.

"Go. Now," Wolf barks.

We watch her hustle down the hall to the stairwell.

"Come on," Wolf says.

The conference room glass divider is clear. Erik and Kairi are standing at one end of the conference room table. They both arrived yesterday for a planning session. Two goons are about ten feet behind Kane while he takes in the view of Santa Barbara and the Pacific Ocean. Kane wears a suit. Gleaming gold and diamond earrings hang all along his earlobes. Those are new.

Wolf enters first, and Kane spreads his arms out wide with an over-the-top smile. Rings line his fingers. I am halfway surprised he doesn't have two scantily clad women on each side. If we lived in a northern climate, no doubt he'd be in a full-length fur coat. I never liked this guy.

"Look-ah here. The Wolf man and his trusty sidekick." He's still got his arms out, as if he's being filmed and there's an audience. Technically, he is being filmed. We have security cameras all over this room. "The family is back together again."

"What do you want, Kane?" Erik looks like he wants to kill Kane with his bare hands. And he could. He has the skill set. Kairi is pale.

"Here's the deal, motherfuckers. You all betrayed me. As you know, I don't take kindly to that. But I'm willing to let bygones be bygones. All I want is for you to do one last thing for me."

"Why would we do anything for you? What's stopping us from making a citizen's arrest right now?" Erik leads the charge. I'm trained on the two men in the back of the room. I am not down with this weapons-free approach. Wolf should have let me bring my damn gun.

Kane's fingers dramatically fly to his chin, and the fucker laughs. Then he gets serious.

"Let's see. Would I really come in here without having thought of that scenario? Anything happens to me, and one Vivianne Rossi goes missing." One of his goons holds up an iPad, and there's video footage of Vivi in her bookshop behind the counter on the screen.

"One Dr. James meets with a bloody end." My insides coil at his emphasis on the *bloody* and the cold way he stares down Kairi. The video on the iPad shows David in a white lab coat walking down a hall in a setting I presume is his clinic. Kairi's hand covers her mouth.

"And let's see, Wolf. I know you don't care too much for your stepfather, but there's a special someone you visit on every single trip to San Diego. Amiright?" His roll through of the slang is all Kane. Obnoxious to the end. The frustrating thing is, his lard ass wouldn't physically do any of it. He's all hired guns.

"And Mr. Sidekick. California golden boy. God, I wish you were even just a little gay. Any chance at all?" He pokes his bottom lip out and holds his thumb and index finger out to indicate an inch. Stoic, I wait to hear what exactly he plans to hold over my head. "Yeah, I didn't think so. So sad. I'd love to know what you're packing."

Mostly, I see Kane with women. He's attempting to taunt me. If he's pegged me as the kind of guy who will get upset with this kind of talk, he's got me all wrong. But he gets a lot wrong.

"Well, let's see. I have video footage of you murdering a man in Shanghai. Something happens to me, that goes straight to

China. They don't like unsolved murders at all. When they ask to extradite you, how long before you think the US government trades you?"

I cross my arms. The answer is obvious. Not long. I can only guess he's referring to the time I killed his gun for hire. But it's possible he's referring to an earlier job. Do I care? I take quick stock. No.

"You're a tough one to threaten, love. I thought about your mother, but you speak to her so rarely I'm not sure she's proper incentive. But there's a soccer mom who caught your eye, right?" The goon's iPad screen flashes to Ethan and a friend in a crowd in front of his high school.

Every muscle in my body tenses. I would like nothing more than to tear the little man apart limb by limb. But he's got us. No doubt he's got a small army in the area.

"Don't get so fretful. Remember? I came here with an offer. You do one little teensy tiny thing for me, and I'm gone. Out of your lives forever. Unless you all decide to take me up for a fun little Spectre reunion on my yacht in the South Sea. For old times' sake."

The goon in the back closes the iPad. The show is over.

"What do you want?" It's Wolf who speaks. Erik appears choked with rage. Tears fall down Kairi's cheeks. I wish I hadn't seen her tears, and I focus on his henchmen.

"Arrow Securities is handling the security for an upcoming wine event."

"We do security for several events. You'll need to be more specific," Wolf says.

"The Santa Barbara Wine Exposition. It's a month away."

"Since when do you care about wine?" I ask, but we all know the answer. Thanks to Phantom, we've known he bids on expensive wines around the world.

"Well, I do love an excellent wine. And look at you, Erik, marrying into the Rossi family. Well done." Kane feigns clapping over the famed Rossi wine name. Unamused, the rest of us wait for him to finish his performance and get to the job. "All I need you grumps to do is to install a teensy tiny bit of code into the auction system. That's all. And then you're done with me. The score will be even."

"Who is bidding that you want to rob?" Wolf asks.

"What do you care? It's a bunch of wealthy people. No nation states. Shouldn't be an issue for your most powerful client." He's talking about the US government. To him, NSA, CIA, FBI… you name it, it's all one entity.

"Have you forgotten your roots?" Kane directs his question to Erik, standing a foot in front of him, close enough he has to tilt his head upward.

"We add your patch of code, and we're even? No more threats?" This is important to Erik. He glares down the psychopath.

"We're even until you do something stupid like release decryption software for crypto."

Erik and Kane face off. I half expect Erik to say no deal. It's no secret he's been working on decryption software for over a year. And he's had success with the government reclaiming ransom payments.

"Fine. We're even. For all past events, we're even," Wolf says, breaking the stare off.

"How do we confirm for you we've implemented your patch?" I ask the question that Erik is supposed to ask, but I suspect he's overwhelmed with rage.

"Oh, cutie pie," he singsongs. "I'll know."

Kane flutters his fingers in the air. A half-ass wave goodbye. His two employees flank him on the way out. Our agents scatter across the open cubicle area. Guns out, angled up. Prepared.

The scene transitions into slow motion.

One. Two. Three.

And he's gone.

# The One with a Girl's Night

Stella

Outside my doorway, an eerie silence prevails. My desk phone rings, and I welcome the distraction. It's one of the recruiters we work with. She has updates, as do I. When we finish going through the list and I've shared who we want to extend offers to and who we don't, I glance back out the door.

My phone rings again. This time it's Patel confirming a delivery from an office supply store. She is clipped. There is zero familiarity. Her work tone amplifies my jitters.

Earlier, when Wolf barked for me to join Patel, she wore both a gun shoulder strap and one around her waist. She said little.

"What's going on?" I asked.

"Stay in here. I'll be back." As the door cracked closed, she added, "Don't worry." *What the what?*

A safe room. It's crazy. Insane. What are we doing with a safe room?

When I finish my call, I round my desk and peer outside. The conference room glass is frosted over, but the door is open. The heavy door to the conference room shuts with a bang, and the sound echoes.

Kairi Morrigan crosses the bullpen to the break room. I need a coffee refill and take off to join her. She's been in the executive meeting all morning. She can tell me what's going on. And if she won't, at least I can gauge her mood.

"Hey. Welcome back," I say. She's in front of the coffee machine, reading the buttons.

"Hey." She smiles, but it's brief. Her attention returns to the confusing machine in front of her.

"Is everything going okay?" I want to add "in there," but I don't. It's not my place.

"Yep." It's an absentminded answer. I cross my arms and step back, waiting for my turn at the machine.

The silence in the room revs up my self-conscious monster. Most adults are fine with silence. But the silence in the room has me checking my nails, crossing my arms, and looking up at the ceiling.

I get that I don't have clearance for information on all of their projects. I am helping to draft employment agreements that clarify the legal aspects, given some of our clients are government entities with strict rules and regulations. And yes, I am not blind. I have seen the gun racks near Patel and in a room upstairs. I've heard Trevor go on about training and risks. But today shit got real.

Kairi's skin is pasty white. She's chewing on a thumbnail that barely exists. I won't push her for information. But I can distract her. She looks more distraught than I was when the safe door closed on me.

"When did you get in?"

"Yesterday." She jabs a button on the machine.

"Good trip?" It's the worst cooler conversation ever, but better than silence.

"Hhmmm."

I am uncertain how to translate her answer, but I think it's a softly murmured yes.

"Are you and David still considering moving down here?"

"Maybe. One day."

"If you decide to, I can help with relocation. Just let me know." It's my job. She probably is fully aware I'll help her.

The machine hisses, and a hot stream of dark liquid and a cloud of steam shoots down into her mug.

"Did David come down, too, or is he still in Napa?" I ask. She seems lost in thought, and I should just shut up, but that's not how I'm wired. I should have never followed her here.

She lifts her full mug, and whatever cloud that had been over her lifts, and it's like she's seeing me for the first time. "You doing okay?"

"Of course." My response is eager and weird. But I can't help it. I've been jumpy since being asked to hide in a safe room. "Do you have dinner plans? I'm supposed to meet my friend Jenn for dinner, but I can cancel, or you could join us. You know, if you want company for dinner. I mean, if you don't have plans. I know those guys don't always think about dinner plans, and you're out of town. But don't feel obligated. I just thought I'd offer."

She squints and chews on that butchered thumbnail. I get the uneasy feeling she's returned to her deep thoughts.

"Sure."

Her mystic, one-word answer unsettles me. Something heavy is still going on. After letting me out of the safe room, I was informed everything is fine. The man they were worried about is no longer on the premises. But there's an undeniable weight in the air.

When I exit the break room, the conference room door is closed. The frosted glass blocks any view inside. Three agents hover around one computer. No one else is on the floor. Trevor's office door is open, so I assume he's sequestered in the conference room.

It's a strange morning, and that's the understatement of my year. But as my scheduled list of phone meetings begins, the spine-chilling vibes rescind. Outside my door, the men in the bullpen move around, some sit, some stand, now and then a phone ringtone sounds.

I'm in the middle of a scheduled call with our health benefits rep when a harsh rap against my door snags my attention. Trevor stands in the doorway. His jaw muscles are flexed, and there's an intense energy ricocheting off his form.

"Lila? Can I call you back? Something just came up."

"Oh, sure. Should we schedule something now?" Lila lives her life with back-to-back client meetings scheduled.

"Why don't you email me some times that work for you?" I end the call as Trevor places two pieces of paper on my desk. He's all business.

"These are agents we are relocating here for the wine festival." His finger taps the sheet. "Where are you on new hires?"

"We extended five more offers. I have a list of new candidates to review." I've put in place a process, but it takes time.

"Once offers are accepted, send them to me. We'll need every single one of them to cover for the agents we're pulling down here. Where are you on hiring a staff manager?"

"Ahm, I'm reviewing resumes—"

"Make it a priority. We need someone who can manage resources. Someone who knows skill sets by the back of their hand and who can be moved and who can't. I don't know if everyone on this list can be moved or not. You'll need to call them all and find out. If you'd staffed your department, you wouldn't need to clear your day. Now you do." I stifle a "yes, sir" response. "Wolf said you are using his recruiter?"

"Yes." My stomach rolls. He's not scolding me exactly, but…

"Tell her we need twenty new hires within a week. If she needs to sub out, we'll do it. Also, this list." He taps the second sheet and waits until I look up into his commanding eyes.

"Yes?"

"These are European assets I've already reached out to. They're coming here. You'll need to work to cover their positions."

"Got it."

"Handle this. Then get your department staffed."

"Yes, sir." I cringe. I don't like saying sir to any boss, but especially one I'm sleeping with. My answer doesn't faze him.

"And Stella, one other thing."

"Yes?"

"The weekend of the festival?"

"Yes?" I lift a pen, ready to take notes.

"I want you and Ethan gone."

"What?" It's going to be a huge event. As an Arrow employee, I have a ticket to attend. They are saying members of the British Royalty might attend.

"Is there a college Ethan needs to visit?"

"He's not going to… that's his dad's weekend."

"Stella." He drops my name with a seriousness that brooks no room for discussion. "Tell Jason you need Ethan that weekend. Either the two of you will be far away from here, or you'll be holed up in a safe room. Your choice which one is easier to explain." My mouth drops. Trevor is already backing out of my office, but he pauses, and his fingers scrub his scalp. "Actually, I'll think about that. I might need you in a safe room."

A nerve-wracking buzz accompanies me for the rest of the day as I clear my schedule and hop on to the project dumped on my desk. I don't yet have direct employees, but I have vendors, and I have them all hopping. The only thing I can guess is that we have some enormous VIPs attending this wine festival, and he's nervous that someone might target the event. Maybe he's worried about a bomb, like the Boston Marathon bomb. They have contacts with several government agencies, including the FBI and NSA. Did they tip them off? Are they afraid of terrorist activity?

I don't get into the details of our security work. I know a lot of the projects strike me as boring. But, as Erik has informed me, Internet security is boring until the weaknesses manifest. We consider the physical security portion of our business high level. I know that some of the men and women we hire are extensively trained in combat. I know Trevor treats training like a matter of life and death. But I do not know the details for any of our covert operations. I don't have the clearance, and until today, I didn't have the interest.

By the time I exit the office, Patel is long gone, and the night-time shift is on duty. My stomach lurches. It's been unsettled all day. A couple of crackers was all I could manage at lunch. I've been jumpy, reactive to every noise. Every sound that infiltrated my office had me scanning the cubicle area for movement or, I suppose, information. Since joining Arrow, they have included me as an executive team member. Whatever is going on, whatever happened in that conference room this morning, has everyone on edge. I spent the whole day on the phone, reaching out to people, discussing travel and back-up needs, putting as little in writing as possible.

My throat is dry and scratchy. My muscles are tense. It's been a long time since I left the office and craved wine, but I am more than ready to step across the street, meet Jenn, and unload. As much as I can, that is.

"Stella. Hold up." Kairi hustles along the sidewalk. "We're going to dinner, right?"

"Oh my god." My palm slaps my forehead. "I totally forgot."

She smiles. The setting sun reflects on freckles I hadn't noticed before. She's wearing flip-flops and is a few inches shorter than I am in my work heels.

"It's okay. I would've forgotten, too, but Trevor saw you leave, and he reminded me."

They've been holed up in the conference room. I forget that while I can't see in the glass when it frosts over, they can see out.

"I'm surprised you guys aren't working late." I look both ways and charge across the street. Kairi follows along.

"It's gonna be busy until this wine festival is behind us." One glance confirms she will not give away any information I don't already possess. It's fine. These guys are under contract with multiple government agencies, and they have to follow clear protocol outlined by those agreements. I won't push. If I need to know, they'll tell me. I trust them. Who would have ever thought I'd work at a company with covert operations? But I do, so I need to go with the flow.

Jenn waves from the sidewalk hostess stand in front of the Goat. She suggested this place since it's close to my work and she wanted to get out of Goleta. All I care about at this point is that the place serves wine.

"Jenn, this is one of my bosses, Kairi Morrigan."

Jenn's eyes widen, and she holds out a hand. She's wondering why I brought a boss with me to our dinner. I told her I needed to talk.

"I'm not really her boss." Then Kairi looks at me. "I'm not your boss."

"You are, kind of. I mean, I don't directly report to you, but you're one of the partners."

She waves her hand, pushing that fact aside. "Meh. We're not that kind of organization."

We're seated on the outdoor patio near a stainless steel heater. The bright orange filaments glow. The waitress hands us our menus and moves to leave us, but I stop her.

"I'll take a glass of your chardonnay."

Kairi glances at the menu, then at Jenn. "Are you drinking chardonnay, too?"

"I think so."

"Bring us this bottle." Kairi points on the menu. I don't know what she ordered, but it doesn't matter to me. I buy my wine from Trader Joe's. Whatever she ordered is going to be fine. Jenn remains silent, tentatively glancing between the woman I introduced as my boss and me.

"Kairi lives in Napa. She's down here for work, so I invited her to join us. She's considering moving to the Santa Barbara area. Jenn is a kindergarten teacher at an elementary school in Goleta."

"You guys don't live in Santa Barbara?" Kairi asks.

"Well, it's Santa Barbara County. It's not far," Jenn explains.

"You know, David and I looked around in this immediate area. Near State Street."

"That's a beautiful area," Jenn says. It's near the touristy area. It's also wicked expensive. Technically, Jenn and Terrell could move into that area now if they wanted, but she didn't want to change schools, and there are some ritzy areas in Goleta, too. They moved into one of those areas years ago. As did Jason.

Jenn answers several questions Kairi asks about schools. Her fiancé is a pediatrician. Since Kairi is in her thirties and she's fascinated by area schools, it doesn't take a rocket scientist to draw the conclusion kids are on the radar. My theory the other day was spot on.

The waitress arrives at our table with our wine. The Goat is a relatively expensive, swanky place, and she does the whole small amount in a glass thing to taste. Kairi approves it. The moment my glass is filled, I lift it to my lips. When I set it down, it's almost empty.

"It's been one of those days," I say.

"That's an understatement. Maybe we should've started with cocktails," Kairi says.

We should have, but I've got to drive home.

"Is everything okay with Trevor?" Jenn's question puts the spotlight on me. But I can't blame her for automatically jumping to the conclusion any issues at work are boy-related. I told her I spent the weekend with him and needed to talk to her.

"It's fine," I say. Kairi crosses her legs and holds her wine glass out. I don't know what she knows about Trevor and me, or what she thinks. But I know it's a temporary thing. And it's better if she's aware. "Like I told you, we spent the weekend together. Ethan was totally cool." Kairi doesn't know me well, so I add, "Ethan's my son."

"I'm sure he was fine. Jason goes through a girlfriend a month, and they always stay over."

"Jason is my ex," I say, for Kairi's benefit.

"He's an asshole," Jenn adds.

"Oh." Kairi's pale cheeks flush. I assume it's from the wine. "Well, it's a good thing you've found Trevor. He's a really good guy. I can vouch for him."

"You trust him?" Jenn asks.

"With my life," Kairi answers, as solemn as can be. I remember she was there the day he got shot three times. Her serious expression raises questions about what else happened that day… questions I probably should have thought to ask earlier. But Kairi brightens, and she squeezes my knee. "I'm serious. You've got a great guy in Trevor. It's obvious he loves you."

"Oh. We aren't like that," I rush. We haven't used words like love. We're much more casual than that. I can't read her expression, but her reaction isn't positive. Jenn has crossed her arms, and she seems ready to fight me. "Ladies, seriously. He's twenty-eight. I am forty."

"So?" Kairi blurts.

She can't be serious. She's scoping schools.

"She's never watched *Cougar Nation*," Jenn says.

"What is that?" I ask, appalled at the name and fearing it's a reality TV show.

"It's a show. I watch it. The age differences are twenty or thirty years. Twelve years is nothing."

Kairi laughs. I do not.

"Thirty years? That has to be a younger person going after money. I mean, one person is fifty and one is eighty?"

"I'll admit that, so far, on all the episodes, the older woman is wealthy as fuck. On one hand, you do kind of want to bitch slap those young men for playing her until she dies, but then when you take a step back and think about it… that shit's been going on in reverse for centuries. Why can't a wealthy woman buy a younger sexual partner?" Kairi nods and clinks her glass against Jenn's. "But, to be clear, that's not the case with you and Trevor."

"It sure as hell isn't. He's seen my home and my defunct car. If money is his motive, my credit card bills will send him running."

They both laugh. Again, I do not.

"Trevor likes you." Kairi bellows it, as if raising one's voice makes it real. "I can tell you, he doesn't care about your age. All he sees is a sexy-as-fuck woman who is intelligent, driven, and a fantastic mom. He told me about Ethan. You should hear how he talks about you."

"He's going to want kids." It's self-explanatory. I can't believe I'm having to explain this to these two women.

"You don't want any more kids?" This is Jenn asking. She seems genuinely surprised, but given she worked so hard to have number two, maybe she's always assumed I wanted a second kid one day.

"No." She tilts her head like she doesn't believe me. "Seriously. I've got one almost out the door. I'm done. Like, mentally, I'm done. I've scraped by long enough. I'm ready for my next phase. And it doesn't involve diapers and the PTA. I'm done." I refill my wineglass and almost empty the bottle. The waitress passes, and Kairi orders a second bottle.

"I get that. Honestly, there was a time when I wasn't sure I wanted kids at all. Not too long ago, actually. Kids are a huge responsibility and an enormous commitment." Kairi clinks her glass against mine. "You do you. But don't let the kid thing bar something more with Trev. I'm not sure you are correct when you assume he wants kids. You should ask him."

Like that's going to happen. Like I'm going to be the one to bring that up.

"He'll be a great dad one day." I will leave it at that. Jenn's phone vibrates, and she excuses herself to take the call and to go to the restroom. I down about half of my second glass. From here on out, I will drink water.

"A few things about Trevor. He enlisted at seventeen. He's served on missions overseas he can't talk about. He's seen things you haven't even dreamed of. He's not one to boast, but his career in the military spanned almost ten years and is impressive. And in the last two, he's been working to build a company. He's not your average twenty-something." Kairi cares for him. And I feel like I'm being put on notice. "I can promise you Trevor is serious about you. He's told me. He's like a brother to me. If you're planning on ending things with him—"

"I'm not planning—"

"If you are holding him at arm's length because of this kid thing, you've got to talk to him." I open my mouth to interrupt, and she holds out her index finger. "And another thing, before Jenn gets back." Her voice drops, and she glances around the patio. "No matter what. Over the next two weeks, you do what he says. Do you understand me? Your safety and your son's safety depend on it. Don't get girlfriend head." Her grip on my arm tightens. Despite the patio heater, my skin chills.

"What's girlfriend head?" I'm going for light with my question. I want to go for the light.

"It's thinking he can't tell you what to do. It's being stubborn. Which is all fine. I heartedly endorse girlfriend head. Women rule the world. But not until after the festival. If he asks you to jump." With the abrupt end of her sentence, she lifts her glass and swirls the golden liquid.

"You want me to ask how high?"

"Yes. I do." She glances back in the restroom's direction. "Trevor may think I'm being overly cautious, but if he asks you and Ethan to stay at his place, at least until the festival is over, I'd encourage you to seriously consider it."

"Kairi. What is this? What's going on?" I've been trying so hard to follow guidelines and not push for information. But she's taking all the nerves I had earlier in the day and amping them up to a level that has my knees jittery below the table. "Is Ethan in danger?"

# FPCON Alpha

Trevor

"Good work today." Wolf holds his fist out, and I bump it with mine.

Today didn't go how I expected. We planned for three dozen different scenarios while we laid out traps for Kane, and not one of them included him waltzing into our offices with a proposal.

I'm drained. Astra sits, alert. She's tracked me all day, never letting me out of her sight. Her allegiance is to me, but I need it to be for Stella and Ethan.

"Tomorrow, we need to sit down and review contingency plans." I push the stairwell door open and hold it for Wolf to pass through.

"Should our plans go sideways," he needlessly adds.

"Yep."

"What did you think of Kairi's idea?"

I let out a sigh. Kairi suggested I move Stella and Ethan into my home. She's not wrong. It's secure. There are other benefits. The guest bedroom I would give Ethan is one flight up and opens onto the roof deck. The master bedroom is on the main floor and not directly below the guest room above. It would allow for so much more privacy than Stella's home offers. But I can't imagine what Ethan would think, or how to go about explaining it to him. If my mom had told me she and I were going to live with one of her boyfriends, I would have fought it tooth and nail. It was bad enough when they moved in with us.

"I don't think it's a bad idea," Wolf says, giving me his opinion without my asking. "Going FPCON Alpha makes sense. We've lost him again. FBI and CIA… they don't know where he is. It's like he walked out of our office and disappeared into thin air."

"Kairi's always going to be the most cautious of us." With good reason. A couple of years ago, one of Kane's hired assassins killed her girlfriend. But still. FPCON Alpha? Everyone on base?

"Cautious is good. Erik has Stella's home and your home on the security detail list right now."

"I don't see any reason he won't stick to his word. If he does something before the festival, his plans fall to shit."

"True." Wolf and his one-word response annoy me to no end. "Should we add security to your person in San Diego?"

I've been curious for a while who he is visiting down there. But he's been secretive for so long, I respect his need for privacy.

"I added security the day we were alerted he landed in LA."

Right. Wolf is cautious. I don't know who Wolf has down in San Diego, but he assumed Kane would. We already went over this extensively, but one of the biggest issues I've got is how much Kane knew. We'd always known he could be ahead of us. But how did he get so much information on us? How did he know I hadn't been in touch with my mother? The inverse of that conclusion is that he knows everyone I've been in touch with. It's an unnerving conclusion. How long has he been monitoring me? All of us? Does he have access to Phantom? Has he been using it on us?

Or worse, does he have another source inside the FBI or CIA? For that reason, we've decided to move forward without looping our partners in on this recent development. During the West Coast Blackout, we discovered he recruited someone within the NSA. She's in custody awaiting trial, but there could easily be others. Double agents have existed for decades.

Wolf and I return side by side to our condos, both of us deep in thought. We've got a skeleton plan. We must flesh it out. We must account for all potential scenarios. I've worked on countless missions, but I've never felt like so much rode on tactical analysis before.

A dark, empty apartment greets Astra and me. My bikes hang neatly near the entrance. Surfboards decorate another wall. With an enormous television set on one wall, leather sofa and complimentary lounge chairs, the layout says "bachelor apartment." Ethan wouldn't mind living here for a bit. It's just coming up with a reason. What are reasons people vacate homes temporarily? Fleas. I've seen homes in the area tented for fleas or pests. But Stella wouldn't want her home fumigated. A gas leak. But those are dangerous.

I open my closet door and grab an overnight bag from the top shelf. I throw workout and work clothes in the bag.

Water leak. Those are messy. I can't do anything that would require the neighbors to move. And is it necessary? I can't blame Kairi for being frightened and bottoming out on the worst-case scenarios. I haven't slept well since Saturday when Wolf gave the update. After this morning? The only chance I have of getting any sleep is if we're in a secure location.

I can go days without sleep. But not two weeks. I'll need to get Stella and Ethan to stay with me temporarily. We can be secure in my condo up off the street. It'll lighten the overnight security detail, too, given Wolf and I have adjoining condos. But how do I get Stella to agree without sending her running for the hills?

It's after ten when I pull into Stella's short driveway and park. The Tesla is charging in the open air since the carport is open on three sides. There is a back wall, and that's what we placed the charging station on. I have underground parking at my condominium, and there are charging stations. But it's not like bad weather is on the horizon and I can use that as an excuse for her to move. This is Southern California. Bad weather means Santa Ana winds, fire, earthquakes, or maybe an hour of torrential rain once a year.

The side door is closer, so I tap it lightly. The outside light flicks on. She swings the door open. Her gaze drops to the bag hanging off my shoulder.

"Kairi wouldn't tell me much. But I assume you're here because you don't feel we're safe on our own?" She steps to the side to let me in. "I assume that's why you stayed around so much this past weekend?"

She's speaking in a hushed tone. She doesn't want Ethan to hear, so I follow her lead and respond in a similarly quiet voice.

"I wanted to be here." Those deep blue eyes slant, and she frowns. Her right hand falls to her hip. She's one of those women who can't believe a guy is into her. Ironic, given the only reason she's in any danger is because I do care, and somehow surveillance conducted by strangers picked that up.

"Stella, can we talk? Outside?"

"Let's go to the front stoop. If Ethan's bedroom window is open, he won't be able to hear us."

I drop my bag on the kitchen table and follow her through to the front of the house, taking the sixty seconds to plan. The success of our plan depends on it being close to the vest. I trust Stella, but I don't trust that anything I say isn't being overheard. We're on a need-to-know basis, and all project discussions occur in our secure conference room. But the cat's out of the bag on how I feel about Stella. And she shouldn't be the last one to know.

We sit side by side, our thighs inches apart, our feet flat on the path that leads to the porch. We both face the road, not each other. I take her hand and weave her fingers through mine.

"Stella, there are a few things you need to understand."

"Hit me." There's a resignation in her slight smile that makes me wonder what the heck Kairi told her. *Stay on mission.*

"I'm not a bullshitter. Never have been. When I met you at the hotel bar, I wasn't looking for a relationship. What happened between us?"

"You wanted a one-night stand?" She tries to pull her hand away, but I tighten my hold.

"That night? Yes. That's typical for me. At least, before the shooting. I didn't count on seeing you at the office. Had I known? We probably—"

"Wouldn't have gotten together. I get it. I understand."

"No, I don't think you do. I didn't understand it myself at first. But I like you. When I have spare time, I want to be with you. I like waking up next to you."

"You leave in the morning before I wake up." Here she goes, calling bullshit again.

"Doesn't mean I don't like waking up next to you. Doesn't mean it doesn't make it hard as hell to drag myself out of that warm bed. Hell, I'm not saying this right." I drop her hand and scratch my head. "Stella, I think you're amazing." She edges away with a look of disbelief. "Dammit. Listen to me. I don't have experience with this. I want a relationship with you. You're smart, and driven, and independent. You don't give a shit I was military. You ask me zilch about life as a SEAL. You've raised a son with a good head on his shoulders. That's not easy, especially when his dad is a total dick. Look, at the end of the day, I might not be what you want. But you seem to find it hard to believe I want to be in this. And I need you to believe me. I want you. As my girlfriend. In a committed relationship. I think you're gorgeous, but that's not the reason I want to be with you." Her elbows are on her knees, and she places her head in her hands. Her hair cascades down over her shoulders. The moonlight highlights two chunks of color near the base of her neck. Bright pink, and two different hues of blue.

"Are you testing colors?"

"You know I'm a lot older than you, right?" She's still holding her head, and she's speaking down to the ground.

"Why do you give a damn? Why does it matter?"

She lifts her head, and those blue eyes are sad.

"It's not so much the age. It's where we are in life. I like you, too. I really do." Her emphasis on the word *like* feels good. "But we're at different stages. I'm preparing to send my son off to college, and you have yet to have children." Children? That's not really what I was proposing.

A lightbulb flickers within the deep recesses of my brain. "You think I want kids?"

"Maybe not yet. But you will. One day." Her tone rises with each statement.

"You can't have more children?" I'm a little slow piecing this together.

"I'm forty!" Her hands, palm open, wave in the air.

I suppose forty sounds old to be having kids. Not that it matters to me.

"Stella. Is that why you've been keeping me at arm's length? I thought you were protecting Ethan."

"I am. Trying. But now you two are friends."

"We are friends. I'm not trying to be his dad. He's got one of those. But we are friends. And whatever happens between us, I'd like to stay friends with him. He's a good kid. You should be proud."

"I am." There's a touch of defiance in her tone.

"Why do you think I want kids?"

"Why wouldn't you? Look how great you are with Ethan."

"Stella." Frustration rises. Do people normally have these conversations when they've been dating for a month or two? I huff out a deep breath. "Children aren't on my radar." It's an honest response. I told her no bullshit. "They haven't been."

"Well, you're young. You can change your mind."

"So, what? I'm out of the running? Because I might, at a later date, decide I want children?" This is not the direction I expected this conversation to go. "What about adoption?" Not everyone can have kids the natural way. Couples don't split because of it.

"You're missing the point. I don't want children. I'm done. If you envision children as a climb up a mountain, well, I'm almost at the peak. I'm almost at the top. And it hasn't been easy. And… I'm sorry. I like you, too. A lot. But I don't want to make that climb again. I am one and done."

I take a minute and stare at the house across the street to assess. The house needs a good paint job. The grass needs cutting. It's uneven, and there are bare, sandy spots in the middle of the yard. Children? I need to recap what I am hearing.

"Let me get this straight. I like you. And you like me." I pause, waiting until she nods in agreement. Her upper teeth sink into her lower lip. "I've never wanted kids. I had a shit childhood and have no parental role model to speak of. My next-door neighbor was a retired vet. He's the closest to a true parent I ever had, and he gave me my first beer and taught me how to chew tobacco. Kids aren't remotely on my radar. But because you believe one day I might want them, you don't want a relationship with me. Because, presumably, one day I'll change my mind and I won't want to be with you?"

Her neck cracks when she twists it from side to side. "That sounds crazy, doesn't it?" Her voice is weak.

"To me, it does." I told her, no bullshit. She hasn't said one mean word, but I feel like someone took a two-by-four and bashed my sides with it. "Can I ask you a question?"

"Sure. Anything."

"Why did you and your husband get divorced?" I've only been around him twice, but I have a growing suspicion he left her for someone else. He changed his mind about her.

"We had a lot of issues. We were too young when we got married." Now she's staring across the street. I edge toward her, eliminating the couple of inches between us. She leans into my side, and I wrap my arm around her. "And there was a colleague," she mumbles.

Uh-huh. Exactly what I thought.

"Stella, I can't guarantee the future. No one can. I could go out on a…" I stop myself. I was about to say mission. But that's in my past. Still, I could take on dangerous work for a client. "You know, not too long ago, I was in the ICU. They didn't know if I would live or die."

"I didn't know it was that serious." Her lips press to my neck. She means what she's saying, but it's only because she didn't really think about it before. One bullet can kill.

"My point is there are no guarantees in this life. I still take on high-risk jobs." I lift her chin with my thumb. "No one gets married believing they'll get divorced, yet half of all marriages end in divorce. There are no guarantees. But we like each other. There are no guarantee it's gonna work. But there's no guarantee it won't. It is possible we are each sitting on this step right now with the love of our lives. It is possible we'll still be sitting together when I'm ninety and you're one hundred and two." She huffs out an amused sound, a squelched laugh. "Life's about taking chances. The future is the great unknown. Will you take a chance on me? On us?"

"We are dating, right?" Her lips scrunch. "We were together all weekend. You're spending time with Ethan. I'd say I'm taking a chance." She's right. Why did I even go on this tangent? Because she was putting up a wall. Because I had to lay my cards out on the table. "What more do you want?"

Her question cuts straight to the heart of the matter.

"There's a shit storm brewing. It could be nothing. But it could be something. We're dealing with a criminal we can't predict. And he has a lot of resources at his disposal. A lot of the work we do is overseas. This isn't a normal situation. That guy this morning?"

She nods. Her arm presses softly against my thigh, grounding me.

"He threatened you and Ethan. He's been watching us, and he knows you are both important to me."

"Threatened us?"

"He's blackmailing us into doing something."

"What does he want?"

"I can't tell you."

"You're not going to do it, are you?"

I shake my head but put a finger over my lips. It's paranoia at its finest. But I'm not saying it out loud.

"We're going to do what he wants." I wink at her. It's the only slight signal I can think of to reassure her we won't be doing what he wants, but if someone is out there watching us, they won't pick up on the subtle signal in the shadows. "But I don't trust him. At all. I need you safe. You and Ethan. I can keep you and Ethan safer, more easily, if you move in with me. For a couple of weeks."

"Until after the wine festival?"

"Please?" I can't force her. We'll have to come up with a reason to share with Ethan.

"Is this guy a terrorist or something?"

Terrorists. In Santa Barbara. Her theory would be more amusing if one couldn't argue that it's correct to some degree. There are different kinds of terrorists.

"In the military, we assign codes to threat levels. It helps to create a set of expectations for how operations run on military bases, and what we do to keep our loved ones safe. Right now, we're at FPCON Alpha." Her brow furrows. "Forced Protection Condition Alpha. It's one level above standard operations. There is a small and general threat that is not predictable."

# The One with a Move



Trevor drops his bag on my bed. His gaze meets mine briefly before he enters the bathroom and closes the door.

Ethan's bedroom door is closed. Without opening it, I use mom x-ray vision and see him sitting on his bed, back against the headboard, legs straight out, laptop on his lap. There's about a fifty percent chance he's kicked off his shoes and the pads of his socks are dingy. My nerves zing. Going before my son with this debacle isn't easy.

I've gone ten years without bringing men around. It's been Ethan and me as one team. For a lot of those years, Jason's escapades didn't even play into it, because he so rarely saw Ethan. As that changed, I gritted my teeth. I didn't say anything because what would be the point? The law doesn't provide any recourse. Even if it did, he'd out-lawyer me.

If I'm honest, bringing men around has felt hypocritical. I've hated Jason for parading women around our son. And here I am, bringing a man ten years younger into our lives. And I'm about to suggest we live with him temporarily.

Behind me, I hear the click of the bathroom knob. Once again, Trevor meets my eyes across the hall. I haven't moved. He stands, watching me, his expression solemn. He hasn't said it, but I believe he hates that he's put me in this situation. Whatever this situation is. FPCON Alpha. Would I be in this same place, talking to my son about moving out of our home for a couple of weeks if I hadn't been dating Trevor? Would being an Arrow employee alone be enough to put me at risk? If the answer is yes, I don't want to hang that guilt on Trevor. He's got enough weighing him down.

With a deep breath and a secular Hail Mary, I rap my son's door. I wait for him to tell me to come in. He's fifteen. And male. I'm aware enough to know that smart mothers wait for the all-clear.

"Yeah," he calls. I push the door open and find that he's in exactly the position I imagined. His shoes lie in the middle of the floor, and the bottom of his socks are surprisingly bright white. He glances up from his laptop and waits. I sense his desire to return his attention to the computer on his lap.

"Can we talk?"

His eyes briefly glance at the screen. He speaks to it in a mumbled voice that sounds like, "Gotta run." He snaps the lid closed and tosses it to the side. He crosses his legs, creating a spot for me on the end of his bed. I take it.

"What's up?" he prompts.

Trevor and I planned what I would say. If you don't count things like Santa, I've never lied to my son. A dull throbbing in my head and the state of my stomach are the ways my conscience is telling me I'm about to do something I will regret.

"Mom?" Now he's concerned. I have to speak.

"Our plumbing is a mess. I need to get a plumber in here…" He is squinting at me. He doesn't believe a word I'm saying. We're about to enter the high school years when we have to trust each other. My hand grips his jumbled comforter. His bed is never well-made. It suffices in a state of tossed.

"Scratch that." There are things Trevor told me I can't say, but I'll work around them. My son comes first. "You know I work for a security company, right?" He only nods. He's still squinting. "There's a high-profile wine festival coming up. It's getting a lot of attention. Mostly because of the attendees. And Arrow is doing the security for it. Now, what I'm about to tell you, you can't repeat to anyone. Okay? I'm not supposed to tell you this."

"Okay." His lower lip protrudes. It's his "okay, that's fair" face.

"There have been some threats made to Arrow employees."

"What kind of threats?"

"It's probably nothing at all to be concerned about. But, in an abundance of caution, Trevor thinks it would be safer if we moved in with him." His head tilts and his eyebrow cocks upward. "Just until after the festival."

He stares. I wait. Patient. Letting him process. My hands grow cold. I fidget.

"I know what you're probably thinking. This is crazy, and you're supposed to be with your dad next weekend. But it's just until after the festival. You don't have to pack yet. I still need to sort a lot of things out, and I know this must seem like."

"Mom, Mom, Mom. Chill." He huffs, and I watch his face carefully. He has little patience, but I watch him take a breath. "I'm okay with it. What? Are you worried I'd rather stay at Dad's?"

The question splatters my innards up against the wall. That never crossed my mind. I never once considered he might prefer Jason's home. Or that that might be the safest place.

"Mom. It's cool. I don't wanna stay at Dad's. I don't even want to go over there next weekend." I need to tread carefully. I do not want to be the parent who turns her son against his father. I make a point of keeping my opinions about Jason to myself.

"Technically, next weekend is his weekend. But I'd feel better if you were with me until this situation is over. Trevor's condo is more secure than our house. But I don't want to tell your dad about what's going on." I probably should not say that. "It's just, the more people who know, rumors might spread. We need to keep this on the down low."

"You don't want people to freak and for it to hurt attendance?" His conclusion is a good one. That makes a lot of sense.

"Exactly."

"Cool. When do you want to go? You want to pack now?"

God, I love my son. This went so much more smoothly than expected. He's such a great kid.

"Let me ask Trevor. I think he was thinking tomorrow." He brought an overnight bag. Probably expecting I wouldn't even consider uprooting tonight.

"'Kay." He pulls the laptop back over his lap. "Was there anything else?"

"No." But while we're talking… "How're things at school? Any more tension?"

"Nah. That guy has a girlfriend now. It all blew over." His hair falls over his brow, and he swipes it away. "Guy's still a jerk, though."

There's a scratching at the door. I get up off the bed and open it. Astra trots inside and straight up to Ethan.

Smelly's back arches. He hisses. Astra freezes. Smelly leaps off the bed and scrambles under it. Ethan disinterestedly watches our cat disappear.

"Hey, girl. I didn't know you were here." He pats his bed, and Astra jumps right up, tail wagging.

"I'll let you know if we need to pack now."

"Cool." He's scratching behind Astra's ears, and she licks his face. I love seeing him interact with her. Sometimes he seems so old to me. But when he's interacting with the dog, it feels like a few years get erased. With one last glance at my boy, I head down the hall.

Trevor is in the same position on my bed that Ethan had been on his. Only he's wearing flannel pajama pants, a muscle hugging white t-shirt, and he's barefoot. His shoes sit lined up together on the floor at the end of bed.

"Well, that went better than I thought." Trevor's lips turn up at the ends. His blue eyes are lighter than Ethan's and mine. They stand out in a way that they pack a punch and grab you. "I ended up telling him the truth. I couldn't pull off the plumbing line. But I told him not to tell anyone."

"Okay." He's unaffected. I suspect little gets Trevor riled up.

"He asked if we wanted to pack and go tonight." It's late. I'd rather not deal with packing tonight, but I am relaying Ethan's response.

"Tomorrow is good." He glances at his wrist. "I'll be up in less than five hours as it is."

"Busy training day?"

"Always."

"We have several new agents starting tomorrow." It'll be a busy day for me, too, double-checking paperwork and getting all the signatures I need. But those new agents are meeting Trevor in the morning at the gym. I have yet to visit, but it's a temporary facility Arrow is using for training. Trevor and Wolf have been scouting for a location to retrofit for Arrow's sole purposes. There's little available, and land is expensive.

I head into the bathroom to brush my teeth and wash my face. The head of Trevor's toothbrush hangs over the sink. I pause, taking in the normalcy. The muscles along my ribcage spasm.

"Tomorrow, I won't make it into the office until after noon. Do you think you could take Astra in with you?"

I pop my head out the bathroom door to look at Trevor when I answer.

"Sure. Do you want us to pack up tomorrow, be at your place later?"

"That would be great. I'll take care of dinner."

I give a quick nod. It's unnerving how normal this feels. But it shouldn't. We're not moving in together for real. This is a military guy's protective streak coming out. The circumstances are extraordinary. After removing my makeup, I step down the hall and knock on Ethan's door.

"We're going to pack up tomorrow, okay?" He nods. Astra is curled up on the foot of his bed.

"Hold Astra. I'm going to get Smelly out of here. Okay?"

"I don't think Astra will do anything to Smelz."

"Well, let's not push it," I say from the floor as I latch on to one of Smelly's paws.

"Smelly has his claws. From what I've read, cats usually win against dogs."

With Smelly secure in my arms, I rise. Astra's pointed ears leave no doubt the dog is fully aware of another animal.

"Maybe so. But, again, no need to push it."

"Will Smelly move with us?"

I hadn't thought about it, but yes, he'd have to come, too. I nod, and Smelly squirms, so I speed to the door. When I set Smelly down in the hallway, he scurries off.

"Don't stay up late, okay?"

Every night I say that to Ethan. It's been a couple of years since I actually knew what time he turned lights out. Every year, he grows more independent.

When I return to my bedroom, I close the door behind me. Trevor gets up off the bed.

"Which side do you want?"

"You're fine where you are." He's on the side he ended up with over the weekend when he stayed over. "I mean, if that's okay for you." Some people are picky about sides. Maybe he'd rather have the other side?

He pulls the comforter back and climbs in the bed between the sheets. Fully aware he is watching me, I open my pajama drawer and sift through my options. There's a long t-shirt pajama top that falls to my knees. I wear it pretty much every week, and if Ethan sees me in it, he won't think twice. With my front to the dresser mirror and my back to Trevor, I unbutton my blouse. I don't have the nerve to check if he's watching. But I imagine he is.

My cheeks are hot. But the last thing I want is for him to see my flushed face, so I keep my focus on the dresser countertop, astutely avoiding the mirror. I unclip my bra. Cool air circulates around my breasts. I hurry to slip the pajama top over my head and shoulders. The hem falls below my waist, and I have to lift it to unzip my skirt zipper. The skirt falls to the floor. Temptation to leave it on the floor, and my blouse on the dresser, is strong. But Trevor's pair of shoes lined up so neatly at the foot of my bed taunt me. I pick up my clothes and drop them in the hamper in the corner of my closet.

I go to my side of the bed. It's not really my side. When I'm alone, I sleep on the side Trevor currently fills. But I don't care which side I sleep on. You would think after sleeping in a bed by myself for so many years, I'd now sleep in the middle. But I don't.

My legs are cool, and I am drawn to the warmth of Trevor's body. I shift closer until our thighs align. He palms my thigh. His rough skin caresses up to my ass. He shifts my panties to the side, so it's skin on skin.

He kisses me. A soft press of his lips. Then his tongue dips, and our kiss deepens. I fit my leg between his and roll my hips against his unmistakable erection. I reach for it, fondling the bulge through the flannel pajama bottoms. He groans into our kiss. His hand falls on mine, and he lifts it and presses a kiss to my knuckle.

"Not tonight." Embarrassment filters through, and I roll back, reclaiming my leg, moving it away from him. "My place. He won't hear us." He brushes his lips across the tip of my nose. "Tomorrow night," he promises. "Just rest."

I roll over, facing the wall. I should have thought of my son. Trevor is correct. I just spoke to my son. He's up, lights on, walking around.

Trevor's warm body curls around me, and his touch soothes. I stare at the white wall for a long time, my back to Trevor's chest, until sleep finally comes.

* * *

"Hey, Mom. You overslept. Get moving."

The bright stream of gold light hurts my eyes, and I squint into the harsh rays. I roll back, and my hand brushes across cool linen sheets. Trevor is long gone. The clock on the bedside table has me lurching out of the bed and charging for the shower.

"I forgot my alarm," I shout.

Ethan says, "I'll put the coffee on."

Fifteen minutes later, my heels clatter across our linoleum floor. My makeup is on, my hair is wet and pulled back into a low bun, and my blouse is untucked. Ethan hands me a steaming coffee mug with a grin.

"When did you learn to make coffee?" He doesn't drink the stuff.

"Dad's." He shrugs. "Astra's still here. Is she going into the office with you?"

"Yeah. She is. Trevor had a full day this morning. He couldn't have her tagging around."

"I'd take her to school with me if I could." As I'm tucking in my blouse, I consider that. It would be nice. Astra wouldn't let anything happen to Ethan. But we both know that's not possible.

"You know, you've got to be aware at school. I know it's such a slim chance anyone would come after an employee's son. But just… be smart, okay?"

"Stranger danger?" He's smiling, like it's a joke.

"I'm serious." At the sink, I pour the coffee mug into my thermos. We say nothing else about it until he's jumping out of the car and waving at a friend.

"Be careful," I remind him.

"Love you, Mom."

# Home Base



Wolf shows his ID to the security guard. The guard peers up and studies the ID and Wolf's face. Then he asks for my identification. He carries both of our licenses into the tiny guardhouse. The gate comprises bars three inches apart, and it connects to a solid wall covered in stucco. The wall itself is tall and prevents anyone from seeing inside easily, but it's also two feet wide and presents a great perch for a photographer or anyone seeking to roam the perimeter before jumping inside.

We've been told they have sensors on the wall, but we need to check out the system ourselves. The billionaire who owns this estate already has a security team in place. But when the owner agreed to offer her property for the ball on Saturday night, she understood her security team would need to work with additional festival and town security. Much of the three-day festival will occur throughout the Santa Barbara area, with various vineyards hosting events. All the walking wine tour areas within town have ongoing events for ticketholders. The Saturday night ball costs an additional five thousand per ticket and will only be attended by those wealthy and influential enough to score the invitation.

"How'd this morning go?" Wolf asks.

I spent my morning assessing the physical fitness of a crew of eight men we reassigned for the upcoming festival. For a situation like this, there are jobs we can provide someone who hasn't maintained an acceptable fitness level, but I want to ensure we don't put someone in a role that might kill them.

"All good. One guy, Jamison… Code name Squawk… he's a subpar swimmer."

"He was Air Force."

"I checked his file. He's good. If we were doing anything near the ocean, I'd think twice. But he's a good hire. I'd like him stationed near our chopper."

"We aren't going to need to fly anywhere."

"You never know."

Wolf and I can both pilot a helicopter. Arrow owns four helicopters, but we can only keep one here at the event. I scratch my jaw, brainstorming potential scenarios that might require air support.

The security guard approaches the window with our driver's licenses pinched between his thumb and index finger.

"You're going to go through that gate, turn right, follow the path around the fountain. Our head of security is going to come out and meet you. His name is Simon Garcia."

Pavers line the long driveway. The landscaping is immaculate. As we round the fountain, parked automobiles come into view. The estate sits up on a cliff, like so many estates in Santa Barbara. An uninterrupted view over the Pacific extends as far as the eye can see. A dusty gray fills the horizon where deep blue blends into the sky. Farther up, there's an enormous modern house. The ball will be held outside and in tents.

Simon Garcia approaches as we exit Wolf's vehicle. He's wearing a dark suit and tie, sunglasses, and an earpiece he hasn't bothered to hide. If I saw him on the street, I'd assume he was a security detail or FBI. We exchange introductions.

"Santa Barbara police arrived earlier and took a tour of the grounds. I've been told you're taking lead for the event?"

"They have hired Arrow Security—"

"I got that." Garcia cuts Wolf off and waves his hand. His jacket rises when he does, and I get a glimpse of his Glock. "Before we go in with the others, all I want to know is what's really going on here?"

Wolf and I exchange glances, but we're also wearing shades, and I can't read him as well. I bow my head ever so slightly, letting Wolf know I'll let him take the lead on the response.

"Look, we do a lot of events here. I've never had the NSA and the FBI do drive-bys. If there are specific guests you're concerned about, I'd like to be aware. You can see my men's files if you like. But we can do our jobs better if we know what's really going on."

"You had visits from both the NSA and FBI?" I ask. Unbelievable. Arrow is supposed to take the lead. Garcia just nods.

"What's your background?" Wolf asks Garcia the question, and even though I can't see his eyes, I know without a doubt he's scanning him, sizing him up.

"Green Beret. I've been doing private security for the last ten years. I read about you both. SEALs?" It's on our website. Mutual respect passes among us.

"There will be an auction Saturday night," Wolf begins. "Part of it will be live."

"Part virtual. Yeah." Garcia looks to the house. He's telling us we don't have long until we're joined by others.

"That's the big event," Wolf concludes. "The threat might be in the crowd. Might be only online. It's probable it will be both. I don't think the auction is going to go down exactly as people expect."

"And you don't want all hell breaking loose at the ball during the auction?"

"Right."

"All the proceeds are going to charity, right?" Garcia seems genuinely stumped. Something tells me he's spent the last ten years worried about obsessive fans. The NSA and FBI flashing badges has him flustered. He's trying to add it all up.

"There are some prized vintages going up for auction. Registration closes on Monday. We'll be going through the attendee list. You're welcome to comb through it with us. We're still piecing together why the auction specifically is targeted."

"But it is targeted?"

Wolf only nods. A group of suits exit the house on the hill and head our way. We spend the next hour getting a tour of the estate. It's expansive. What I'm most impressed with is the security system Garcia has implemented. This estate is secure, even if the wall is climbable.

On the way home, we hit traffic, and I flick my wrist repeatedly, checking the time.

"You got plans tonight?" Wolf asks.

"Stella and Ethan are moving in. Until this blows over. I told her I'd fix dinner."

"You should grill a filet. That's your best dish." He should know. He's eaten pretty much every dish that's in my repertoire.

"Have you heard from Erik?"

"He's holed up. Working on that code."

"He's not going to botch it, is he?" Kane instructed us to insert the code into the auction tool. It's the auction tool they hired us to ensure is secure. Kane's desire to install code into an online auction isn't unexpected. But his need to send a personal warning to ensure we follow orders worries me. I don't trust him.

"We've got to trust him," Wolf says, as if reading my mind. But he's talking about Erik. And he's right. We're a team. And we have to trust our mates to do their part. Neither Wolf nor I know enough to check over Erik's work.

"Kairi said she and David are staying with you?"

"David arrived last night. He'll be here until this is over. Erik and Vivi too. Vivi arrives today."

"Good."

"I'm surprised you didn't pull a Kairi and push Stella and her kid away."

Wolf's referring to Kairi's desire to push David away when they first got back together. We all understood her reasoning, but she came around. Traffic has crawled to a slow churn. I could outrun the car easily.

"I thought about it. But what's the point? Right after threats were made, he wouldn't buy a breakup. They're safer with us. You know, it's funny. You've been with Fiona about as long as I've been with Stella, but he didn't threaten her."

"I'm dating other women too. I don't let her stay over."

"She's tried?"

"That girl leaves shit every time she comes over. I have to do a sweep before she exits the place."

"I don't think Stella is her biggest fan."

We both kind of chuckle. Fiona is a piece of work.

"What's bugging me is how he knows so much. We've searched for cameras. How would he know how I feel about Stella? What's his source?"

"Yeah. That's the threat that bothers me the most. I don't know. Kairi and I discussed it, too. I don't think he has anyone on the inside. Which leaves someone following us and being good enough at it we didn't pick up on it."

I've thought about that. But we're good at what we do. Situational awareness is a strength. We've been trained by some of the best in the world. It's unlikely we would be duped for months.

"Tomorrow, I'm going to come out and train with you." Wolf does that several days a week. There's nothing new there.

"Okay." We get past a fender bender taking up the right lane and finally pick up speed.

Patel greets us when we arrive back at the office. "Stella said she needed to get home early and to tell you she'd be at your place by six." I check my watch. I have ten minutes. "She left Astra with me."

She buzzes the door, and Astra exits her receptionist cave. Patel hands me her leash.

"You can leave her with me anytime."

"She's a good dog." I look down at the furry canine and her pointy ears. "You're a good dog, aren't you?" She wags her tail like she knows what I'm saying.

When I return home, I'm greeted by the distinct aroma of Pine Sol. I requested the cleaning service come today and go through all the bedrooms and bathrooms, change out sheets, and give the entire place a thorough scrub. I've had them on a bi-monthly schedule, but I've moved them to a weekly rotation now that there will be three of us, a dog, and a cat. I'm not entirely sure how the cat is going to adapt. Where to put the litter box is another nuance I'm uncertain about, but Stella told me she'll find a place.

I'm thinking the upstairs area with the roof access is best, as long as the cat isn't suicidal and wouldn't try to leap off the roof. Or maybe the guest room downstairs.

My phone vibrates with Stella's text telling me she and Ethan have arrived. With one last glance around the orderly, clean condo, I charge down the stairs to help them with their stuff.

Ethan and Stella have the trunk open when I arrive in the garage below my building. There are hissing sounds coming from the carrier. I've never actually laid eyes on Smelly cat. I'm not a cat person and have spent little time around them, but judging from the high-pitched whining noises coming out of the carrier, Smelly is not a happy cat.

Ethan and I fist pump while Stella drags a heavy suitcase out of the trunk. I rush to help her before she scratches the enamel on my car. Ethan and Stella each have one suitcase, plus Stella has a shoulder bag. The cat has about as much stuff as Ethan does.

"Ethan, thanks for agreeing to stay until this passes."

"It's cool." He shrugs and grabs as much stuff as he can. I lead them to the elevator. I like stairs, so I never use the elevator, but with the luggage, it is a nice feature.

We unload everything right inside the front door. Astra smells the cat, but she's such a well-trained dog, with one hand movement she moves to her dog bed and sits. Erik has no idea what an amazing dog he gave up.

"Hey, so, I have two guest bedrooms. I'll show you them both, but I was kind of thinking you'd like the one upstairs. It has its own bathroom and an attached area that's sort of like a small den. I thought we could set the cat up there, too."

"He likes to stay under my bed, so that works," Ethan says. He ducks his head into the basic small guest room that is right next to the master. For obvious reasons, I don't want him picking that one. It's a room I use for gear storage. I lead the way up the stairs. Ethan immediately opens the sliding door onto the roof deck.

"Whoa," he says.

It's a nice view. I've got a few pieces of furniture up here, but it could stand a bit more. He leans over the bar rail. There's a wall that wraps around the roof, and there's a painted metal bar on top of the wall. Never once did I consider it dangerous. But as Ethan grabs the rail and halfway hoists himself up for a view down, I second guess the roof. Four floors up.

"Ethan. Get down." It used to annoy me to no end when my mom's boyfriends reprimanded me, but when he drops back down flat on his feet, he's grinning.

"This place is great."

"Come look at the bedroom. And let's set some ground rules. One, no hanging over the edge like a fool."

He chuckles and charges inside. I'm serious. There's no need to laugh. Stella is smiling. It's like it doesn't faze her that her son was just looking down from a rooftop. I squeeze her hip when I pass her to catch up to Ethan.

"Second rule, that sliding glass door gets locked at night. Once we're asleep, I don't want you coming out here. You got that?"

I'm not entirely sure what I think will happen, but the rule makes sense. Ethan doesn't question it.

"You can set up your desk for school right here." I point to a desk I cleared. I had thought I'd use this space as my home office, but I haven't really needed a home office.

"Does Wolf's apartment have this same layout?" Stella asks.

"It's almost identical." There's a wall built on the roof to separate the two condominium's roof decks. We've talked about removing it since we're buds. But I don't think we will because there's no need to risk lowering the resale value.

"He's got a full house right now, too," Stella says while she watches Ethan kick off his shoes. One sneaker thuds against the wall.

"Ethan. Be careful," Stella reprimands. The wall is painted a stark white. She bends at the wall, running her finger over the spot where his shoe hit.

"Why don't we let you get settled? I'll go down and work on dinner."

"I'll get Smelly set up here, and I'll be down to join you," Stella says.

"Where does Astra stay?"

"She has a dog bed in my bedroom."

"Can she stay up here?"

"That's fine with me. But what about the cat?"

"He's pretty old. He stays out of the way. If there's an issue, I'll keep Astra out."

"You gonna be okay up here?" I ask Ethan. He beams. He's a pretty happy kid, but I've never seen him smile quite like this.

"Yeah. This space is great." The way he emphasizes the word *great*, you'd think he was Tony the Tiger. There's a surfboard hanging on one wall for decoration, and he points at it. "Can that be used?"

"It's real." It's not one I've used. The designer Wolf hired asked about decorations, and I told her I'd like to have racks for holding things where possible. Surfboards, bikes, and guitars are the only items that met her designer criteria for acceptable wall decorations. The only other thing I would've hung up is guns, but now that I have guests, I'm glad I don't have walls of easily accessible assault rifles. He runs his fingers across it. "Sure. You can use it. Also, any of the bikes downstairs. The boardwalk's not far."

He's still grinning when I leave. It's good to see.

Dinner goes well. Of course, who doesn't like baked sweet potato and filet mignon? Ethan eats the steamed broccoli too.

That night, as I enter my bathroom, I pause at all the bottles lined up along one counter. There are two sinks. And plenty of cabinet space.

"Why don't you put your stuff in a cabinet?"

"I can if you want. But, I mean, we're not permanently moving in."

"Get comfortable. Set things up however you want."

Until this evening, the condo felt like a hotel suite. A place to shelter at night. With bodies inside, at the dinner table, in the den hanging out, it feels more like Kairi's place back in Napa when we all lived together. When I check the locks, turn on the alarm, and turn off the lights, creaks and thumps drift through the apartment as everyone prepares to turn in. There is a peace to the noise.

Attached to the master bathroom is a walk-in closet with a center island. It's a good size. My clothes don't fill it up by any means. Stella didn't pack much, but her work clothes fill out a section of vacant space.

I leave her to finish getting ready on her own and slide into bed, resting my head against the canvas headboard. My normal routine would be to turn off the light and get some shuteye. Instead of turning off the lamp, I pick up my phone and flick through news articles. There's nothing of great interest.

The bathroom light goes dark, and Stella steps through the doorway. She's wearing a t-shirt that falls mid-thigh. The material is thin, and while it's not see-through, the cotton drapes over her nipples, leaving little unseen. She looks at the floor as she crosses the room and comes around the bed on the other side.

"This must really be different for you." She climbs into bed and copies my position, legs forward, back against the pillows and the bedframe.

"How do you mean?"

"I mean, you're probably used to…"

"What?" A blush lights across her cheeks. She tucks a loose strand of hair behind her ear.

"You know. Like crazy monkey sex."

I can't hold back a full-on smile. "Have we had crazy monkey sex I missed?"

"No." She places a hand over her face, and she laughs. It's carefree and girlish. I take her wrist and pull. "It's just that you probably aren't used to having someone over with their teenage son upstairs." Those dark blue irises finally look up. "I'm ruining your game."

"My game?"

Her teeth sink into her lower lip as she smiles right back at me. I let out a groan as I caress her hip and her waist, and then massage her breast. My thumb flicks back and forth over her nipple, through the t-shirt.

"You have a good game." She sinks back against the pillow, resting on her side. She is both tempting and welcoming.

"I don't know if you've picked up on this, but you're the only one I want to use my game on. And lucky me, you are right where I want you." I press my lips to hers briefly, then pepper her with kisses along her jaw. She strains to give me a better angle of her throat, and I oblige. "But this?" I tug on her shirt. "I think we need to remove this."

She grins and sits up. She pulls the shirt over her head and throws it to the end of the bed. Her breasts are full and luscious. Her dark hair spills over her shoulders. The comforter falls over her hips, but from my angle, I can see her black silk panties.

"Did you hear me mentioning rules to Ethan?"

"Uh-huh." I lean forward and place my mouth over her nipple. I circle my tongue, then suck. She squirms.

"We need a rule in here."

"We do?" Her nails scratch over my jaw and through my hair.

"No clothes," I tell her before I administer attention to her other nipple. She lightly touches my shoulder, then my bicep, and she's on the verge of tickling me as she explores my chest until she finds the band of my briefs.

"I thought you said no clothes."

It doesn't take us long to remove the offending items. Our kiss heats as I roll on top of her. She spreads her legs, wrapping them around me, welcoming me. This right here, what we have, what I feel, it's not a game. There's absolutely nothing gamey about it.

I want her here. I want her below me. I want inside her. I want her squirming, and moaning, and reacting to my touch, and my tongue, and my fingers. I want her quivering and whimpering. I want all her noises, all her reactions. I want her hesitancy, her teasing, and her desire.

I grab her wrists and hold them over her head as I pound into her, claiming her in the most primitive way, in my bed, in my home, in my life.

She tugs her wrists free, and her nails scratch my back. She tugs on my ass, as if trying to pull me deeper into her. I want to hold her forever, to feel her soft curves, to be a part of her.

The familiar pull at the base of my spine, the tightening sensations, warn me I need to slow it down or it will be over too soon. I slow my thrusts and pull back. My thumb caresses her flushed cheek, and when I look her in the eye, it's tangible. A warmth, a fire within. My lips fall to hers. Our tongues clash and meld, much like our bodies. She tenses around me, and I reach between us and coax her, massaging her, finding the secret to her release. Her nails dig into me. Her head dips back. She quivers, and her muscles spasm, gripping my cock. With a loud growl and one more thrust, my release rushes through me in a blast so powerful I almost black out.

I collapse on top of her, gasping for air. Her fingers comb my hair and trace along my back. Her legs remain wrapped around me. I don't want to move. I want to stay like this forever.

My weight is too much, and I roll to my side. We lie like that, side by side, fingers tracing each other. I want to fall asleep like this, but Stella eventually forces herself up and walks naked to the bathroom. I need to follow her, but I flick off the lamp. I double-check my alarm, since after this late-night activity, it's conceivable I might oversleep without one.

Once we're both back in the bed, she cuddles up next to me. I close my eyes, ready for sleep to take me.

She presses a kiss to my chest and says, "Thank you."

"For?" If she says sex, I'm going to explain that I will be more than happy to do that every day for the rest of her life.

"For having us here. For being concerned about us."

I open my eyes. I caress her face, and my fingers tangle with her hair. I angle her chin up so she can see me.

"I want you here."

She rests her head back down my chest, and I stroke her hair.

"Ethan may not want to leave. He's got a full-on suite upstairs."

"It's a good condo." I hadn't planned on having this conversation for a while, but she might as well know what I'm thinking. "I think we'd be better off finding a place in Goleta. Maybe in Jenn's neighborhood? He'd still be near friends in his school district. We'd have a yard. Would be good for Astra."

Her teeth graze my skin, and she bites down.

"Ow." I pull back, just an inch. She didn't really hurt me.

"You are too young. Delicious. But you don't know what you're saying."

I thread my fingers through hers and place kisses on each of her knuckles. With a heavy sigh, I aim to both let her know my position and wrap this up for sleep.

"Here's the deal. If I was still a SEAL, I probably would have carted your ass to the justice of the peace already, so I'd know you would be taken care of if anything happened to me. This is what I want. And if you can't accept it, I'll wait until you do. I've already had my lawyer adjust things so if something were to happen to me, you and Ethan will be taken care of. I'm not in the military now. I don't need anything to be legal to ensure you're taken care of." She lifts her head and I gently press her to return to my chest. "There's no rush. I'm not going anywhere. I'll keep showing up until you see what I see, until you feel what I feel. Until you focus on the positive possibilities."

I press my lips across her hair, breathe in a faint strawberry scent, close my eyes, and fall into a deep sleep. It's a peaceful, restful sleep. The kind of sleep that comes from a feeling of safety and being right where you're supposed to be.

# The One Where Stella Stands Up



My phone on my desk vibrates. I flip it over and cringe. If I didn't have it set on silent, the Death Star tune would play. Even with the phone set to silent, I hear the death toll beat.

I could let it go to voicemail. But given Ethan told his dad he's not going over there next weekend, I should answer. If he's angry, I might as well hear him out. I probably should have called to discuss the change in plans, but he's canceled so many times himself and informed Ethan, not me, it felt like we effectively transitioned to communication via Ethan. And there's also the small fact that I can't stand my ex. I'd rather not speak to him.

With one quick glance at my day's agenda, I force myself to answer the phone.

"Jason." It's my standard greeting. I do not know when we evolved to this, but it has been this way as long as I can remember.

"Were you planning on telling me you were moving in with your boy toy? Or let me correct myself. You were moving *our son* in with your boy toy."

"We haven't moved."

"Really? Then how did he invite Sierra over there to hang out?" My head hits the back of my desk chair. Ethan really does like Trevor's place. Just like I expected, he loves having the upstairs area to himself. And he invited his two closest friends over for dinner and to hang out tonight. It's unfortunate that one of his closest friends happens to be Jason's close friend's daughter.

"Terrell told you?"

"He asked me about it. And I knew nothing." Well, shit. It's on the tip of my tongue to feed Jason the plumbing story, but I hold back. He has a history of resorting to lawyers, and if he does so here, I don't want to be caught in a lie. It wouldn't look good in front of a judge, if it came to that.

"It's only for the next week."

"Well, I'm out of town next weekend. That's two weekends straight you'll have him." Technically, next weekend is when he was supposed to have him, and that's three weekends straight I'll have him, but who's counting? Clearly not Jason. He expects I'll bend to his scheduling needs, and I assume he wanted him this weekend. But this weekend isn't his weekend. Ethan wants to stay with me, and I want him to, so...

"You still there?"

"I am." The screensaver on my monitor has clicked on, and I focus on the multicolored lines dancing across the screen. He exhales, and then there's a blare of a horn. He cusses repeatedly. I hold the phone away from my ear and wait.

"Dumbass old drivers." I assume he's talking to himself, so remain silent. As a pharmaceutical rep, Jason spends a lot of time on the road. I used to think some of his anger stemmed from road rage. But now I know he's just an asshole. "You know, I never thought you'd be the type of mother who would move her son in with her boyfriend."

At least he didn't say boy toy.

A silence fills the line. I wait. The less I say, the better off we all are. Years ago, I began using text in only the most utilitarian and basic ways, as he pulled emotional texts and revealed them in court. My lawyer counseled me to remember that anything I put in writing could go in front of a judge. The same doesn't hold true for verbal communications, but there's no reason for verbosity.

"Are you going to say anything?"

"What would you like for me to say?" We're talking on the phone, but I can visualize his nostrils flaring and his forehead crinkling as his eyebrows arch.

"How did I get involved with such a fucking bitch?" A *ting* from my computer alerts me that my next meeting is about to start.

"I have a meeting in three minutes. What do you need, Jason?"

"I need you to stop whoring around our son." I close my eyes. Inhale. Exhale.

"Jason, this is the first boyfriend I have had since our divorce. He's a good person. Ethan likes him. He's helping us out—"

"Yeah, I'm sure he is."

"Jason." I pause, letting silence pack a punch. "I will hang up if you continue to berate me."

"You fuc—"

"You can text me if you need to contact me. Your son is safe, and he has chosen to spend this weekend with me. In our agreement, you have every other weekend, but we allow for flexibility and Ethan's preference. I have maintained a log of every single weekend you have canceled on your son. Should you choose to take this down a legal path, I will share that log with the judge."

"Yeah, I'm sure a judge will look kindly on a woman who is screwing around—"

"Seriously? How many women have you had over while he's stayed with you? Can you even count them?" I let out a sigh. I have ninety seconds to end this call and enter the conference room. "To be honest, I think you are angry because you no longer control me. I earn enough money that I can afford to split expenses with you without having to cut back on groceries. Or maybe it bothers you I have finally moved on." For once, I wish we were on FaceTime so I could see his facial expression. "I don't know exactly what your issue is, but you need to get over it. In less than three years, he'll be off at college, and you and I will never need to speak again. Did you need anything else?"

Silence is my answer. I check the screen, and yes, he ended the call. Fine by me.

With a rational mind, I leave my phone on my desk and head to my meeting.

* * *

"Here. I'll take those out to the recycling dumpster." Trevor lifts the stack of pizza boxes. Ethan has three friends upstairs on the roof deck. We ordered wings, breadsticks, pizzas, and a salad. I am always amazed at how much food a teenage boy can put away, but Trevor doesn't seem surprised at all. He's the one who placed the order for four large pizzas.

I am finishing wiping down the table when my phone vibrates. It's Jenn.

"Hey, there. You calling to check up on your daughter?" I'd known she was coming over, but I hadn't expected that Jenn allowed her to ride over with a seventeen-year-old. But I also know the day is coming when I will allow Ethan to ride with friends with driver's licenses. I just hadn't wanted that day to be so near.

"No. She texted the moment they parked. She said he's just a friend. Did it look like it to you?"

"I think so." I'm so glad I have a son. "She's up there with three guys hanging out. To me, they all look like friends. Ethan wouldn't let anything happen to her."

"I know. He's so good to her. He stands up for her, you know?" Yes, I do. Trevor returns, and I point to the phone so he can see it.

"She's like a sister to him. Of course he does." He raises an eyebrow, questioning. I mouth, "Ethan and Sierra." A strange half-cocked smile crosses his face. *Intriguing.*

"Anyway, I didn't call about that," Jenn says, pulling me back into the conversation with her.

"No? What's up?" Trevor and I plan to watch a movie while the kids are upstairs. He pulls out a popcorn bag and holds it up. I nod, although I don't plan on eating any of it. Like Ethan, Trevor continually eats. I do not.

"Terrell cut Jason down a notch."

"What do you mean?" Trevor is sitting on the sofa, but by the tilt of his head, it's clear he's listening to everything and wondering what Jenn is saying.

"Well, he was on the phone with him, so I could only hear Terrell's side. But apparently, he was going off about you. Based on Terrell's reaction, he overstepped."

"Hardly surprising." Terrell and Jason work together, and he's had to walk a tense line at times, being friends with Jason and also being married to my best friend.

"Yeah. But he laughed at him. Like full-on laughed. Told him not to be such a hypocritical ass. It was pretty awesome to hear. Terrell didn't tell me everything."

"And he shouldn't. You and Terrell don't need to be fighting over Jason." He told Jenn years ago he would not tell her things that would make her hate Jason even more, because he had to work with him.

"Well, this time, whatever he said, it got to Terrell. It got pretty tense before the call ended." I cross my arms over my chest. Trevor is watching my every move. "But after Terrell hung up, he asked if we could go out on a double date. Said he wanted to meet your new guy."

"I think that can be arranged." Trevor's brows come together. I smile.

When I hang up, he asks, "Who was that?"

"Jenn. She was just checking up on Sierra. And she wants us to go out with her and Terrell. Are you up for that?"

"After our double date with Wolf, I think I owe you." I fall back against him. He wraps one arm around me and uses his other arm to click the remote.

"Is he still seeing her?" I really didn't like that woman. And only a part of the dislike stemmed from her being so young and wrinkle-free.

"I think so. He mentioned us going out with them again, and I brushed it off."

"Thank you." I drape my arm across his chest. This feels good. Hanging out, my son upstairs and safe with his friends.

"Before I start this movie, is there anything else you want to share? You looked pretty serious over there."

"Jason was being an ass. Nothing new there." Trevor's muscles tense.

"What did he do?" There's an undercurrent to his question. My palm flattens against his chest.

"It's nothing to get upset about. I have it under control. He can be rude, but I told him earlier today that I won't allow him to berate me anymore. Now that I think about it, I bet he's fuming, and he vented to Terrell. But Terrell won't put up with his nonsense either. That's what Jenn was calling to report."

Trevor's thumb flicks back and forth over the curve of my chin. "I love you."

I lean back to get a better look at him. Did I hear him right?

"I want you to know that. I love your strength. I love what a great mom you are. Your work ethic. Your determination. Yes, you're gorgeous. Sexy. But there's a lot more to you on the inside. The way I feel about you, it's something I've never felt before. And I want you to know."

He brushes his lips across mine, and I feel his heat everywhere. We have four kids upstairs who could come crashing downstairs anytime. Nothing is happening on this couch. But yet, everything is happening.

"This wasn't supposed to be anything serious. It was supposed to be a one-night stand." One last hurrah before forty.

He takes my hand and presses a kiss to my knuckles. "How's that working out for you?"

"Good," I acknowledge. My stomach twirls. It's not exactly butterflies, but it's not a settled sensation. "Scary," I admit. "The last time things felt this right, they ended up being very wrong."

"Jason?" Trevor doesn't need to ask. It's pretty obvious, given that Trevor is my second serious relationship.

"Jason and I were good in college. But I don't think he was ready for kids. Ethan was unexpected. Instead of us growing together, we grew apart. And I think you scare me because once again the kid thing could tear us apart." He opens his mouth, and I press my finger against his lips to shush him. "You don't know how you'll feel in a couple of years, any more than I knew how Jason would react to having a kid when he wasn't ready. But I'm willing to give us a go. There are no guarantees in life. You were right. I've learned that the hard way. And besides, I've read that people are saying more people will live to a hundred, and that means multiple careers and husbands—"

His lips silence me. When he pulls back, his lips curl up and he says, "That's the advantage of a younger man. I'm your last."

"Well, then, I'm a lucky girl. Because I saved the best for last. I've fallen in love with you, too, you know." How could I not? He's perfection. We sit there on the sofa, kissing, making out like restrained teenagers, until our lips are sore. And when I cuddle into his side on the sofa, it really feels like this could be it for me.

Trevor's phone vibrates. He gets up, apologizes, and leaves the room. I end up falling asleep watching the movie all by myself.

# The One Where Someone Gets Blown

Stella

In the morning, Patel escorts Kairi and me into the Arrow building. Kairi and I have shared small talk, but Patel has had little to say. For the two blocks, she jockeyed for position behind us, no matter how many times I attempted to make room for her to walk with us.

She is tense. It took me an entire block before I recognized she wasn't being rude by avoiding eye contact. She was simply looking over my head and around me, off into the horizon, up across roof lines, down every street.

Why would someone make a threat to not just Arrow employees, but our family members? And why this wine festival? I've scoured the invitation list more than once. Yes, there are celebrities on it. We're close to Los Angeles, and plenty of celebs live right here in Santa Barbara. We expect both California senators for the black-tie ball Saturday night. That's the event everyone seems most keyed up by. There's a possibility one estranged British prince and his actress wife might make it up from LA, too. They have tickets, but they are in Canada right now, so their attendance is questionable. There are a lot of names that mean nothing to me, but merely by being in attendance there's a presumption of wealth and possibly power. In other words, all attractive targets.

The online auction starts at noon today, but it wraps up Saturday night at the ball.

Patel has a Special Forces background. Most of the employees we hire at Arrow are former military. She is highly trained. I don't doubt that Trevor laid into her about keeping me safe on this short walk to the office. For the last two weeks, he's left early to drop Ethan at school, insisting he do it. None of us leaves the condos without escorts.

I think they're all over the top with their worries. We're in Santa Barbara. It's the land of palm trees, blue skies, and seventy-two-degree temps. Nothing bad is going to happen. Or at least, bad here is an uncontrolled wildfire. Maybe mudslides after torrential rains.

But I can't deny that Trevor's concern for Ethan and me has made me fall deeper in love. I don't think Jason ever cared this much for me. Even when I was pregnant and about to pop any minute, he didn't seem to care. He made it to Ethan's birth, but only because his parents were in town, and they took over reaching him when he didn't return my calls. He'd been in business meetings and had turned off his phone.

Meanwhile, Trevor hasn't wanted Ethan or me to be alone at all this week. When I call him, he answers on the first ring. He has a tracker in Ethan's backpack, and he also attached one to a belt buckle he wears. It's really sweet that he's so concerned for my gawky teen son. He gave me a necklace with a gold pendant that doubles as a tracker.

More than once, I've had visions of Trevor as the father of a toddler. He'd be one of those guys who looked for sharp corners on furniture and bought the plugs for electrical outlets. He'd spend hundreds on safety products. He'd be a really good dad.

"What's that sad look for?" Kairi bumps into me. She says it low, but there's no way Patel didn't hear her. She's on heightened alert. But she doesn't look at me. She's scanning inside the glass door at Arrow and holding out an arm for us to be still.

Kairi and I both stop on the sidewalk. The tinted glass is difficult to see through at most times of day. With the harsh morning sun's glare, it's almost impossible to see from where I'm standing. Patel gives a hand signal to someone inside and pulls back the door. She catches the door with her foot.

Fiona, the woman Wolf has been dating, and a man I haven't seen before, exit. One of our agents, Hayes, stands in front of the reception desk. There's another Arrow employee behind the reception desk. He's wearing a headset and talking into it.

"Morning, ladies." Fiona beams at us and waves with a wiggle of fingers. A black sedan pulls up to the curb, and the driver opens the back door for her.

I check the time as I step inside the vestibule. It's early for Fiona to be here. But if she's been staying with Wolf, like I've been staying with Trevor, then maybe he had him drive her over to the office. But I thought I knew all of our employees.

Maybe I missed one of the existing security agents we reassigned for this weekend. Wolf must have him trailing her, like Patel is escorting Kairi and me.

Patel enters her back area. Through the reception glass, I can see she's conversing with the man who had been talking into the headset. The buzzer goes off, and Kairi and I enter the elevator bank.

When we arrive on the main floor, a surge of energy ricochets through the cubicles. Every desk holds a person intently focused on a monitor. The conference room door is open. Kairi takes off in a confident stride, and I follow.

"What're we drinking?" Kairi shouts, smiling.

It's not even nine in the morning. The day is going to be a manic one. These guys aren't heavy partiers. But sure enough, Trevor, Wolf, and Erik each hold a highball glass with a golden liquid.

"Are you guys celebrating?" I ask. There are untouched coffee cups in a compostable holder on the conference room table. I move for one of those, but Trevor waves me off. He squinches his nose.

"Don't touch those. I don't trust the source." There's a bag of doughnuts too, but Erik picks them up and drops them into a garbage can.

"What's going on?" I ask.

Wolf and Trevor exchange glances. They both look boyish and happy.

"Did you catch the bad guy?" I have a low-level comprehension of what's been going on here, but it seems like they are ready to proclaim victory. That's the only reason I can think they'd be drinking alcohol before I've had my second cup of coffee.

"We installed the code," Erik says. Erik and Kairi high five.

"Fiona was working for Kane. As I suspected," Wolf adds.

He's smiling, and I'm totally confused. *Holy shit balls.*

Trevor comes around, and his hand falls to my lower back. "Remember, I told you there had been threats made?" he asks.

"Against Arrow employees."

"Well, we did what Kane wanted. We installed the code. He will not be a problem anymore."

"You said you wouldn't do that." I'm floored. "What does the code do?"

"It provides a backdoor into the payment systems for those registered to partake in the auction." Erik says, leaning back in his chair, both hands behind his head, stretching. He looks happier than I've ever seen.

"But you guys are supposed to keep that auction secure. That's why they hired you." I sat in on some of the pitches. They promised the community, our neighbors, to keep it secure.

One of the surveillance agents calls out from the main room and announces, "We're in."

Everyone rushes out into the main cubicle area. Erik leans over the guy to get a closer look at the monitor. He snaps his fingers.

"Do you have a location?"

"Not yet. It's generating."

"She can't be far," Kairi says. "We just saw her get in a car. She can't be more than a few blocks, maybe miles, away."

Wolf taps the guy. "Put it up on the big screen."

The television monitor on the far wall blinks to life. The screen shows a man with dark hair and mirrored sunglasses, tapping on a keyboard. He's smiling.

"Can he hear us?" I whisper to Trevor.

"Nah. That code that Erik installed? It also allows us to hack into the camera on a monitor or computer."

"So, wouldn't you be able to do that for anyone using the auction?" I don't like this at all.

"Yeah, but it'll be hours before anyone else is logging on."

"But what about all of those innocent people? What are you scared of? Why would you cave to a man like that?"

"Trust," Trevor says, eyes locked on the giant television. I am so confused. They are going to watch this guy steal from people?

"What is he doing?" I thrust my chin in the man's direction on screen. As I do so, a woman in a tight dress comes into view. You can only see her back and her waist. She sits on the edge of the desk.

"He's trying to get into all the accounts before the auction. But he's not really in the accounts. Erik created false pathways."

"Back in the day, he wasn't a good enough programmer to do this on his own," Kairi says. "We could have easily gained only a view of a different coder doing this work. That's his modus operandi."

"But all he's expecting to do is transfer funds. He wouldn't want to trust that to anyone else. And he's always been overly confident. Coming stateside shows his ego is now gargantuan." Erik is glued to the screen, watching.

Wolf is tapping on his phone. Then he's speaking with one hand over his ear. He's talking to someone, and he backs away to do it.

"Do you have a lock on the location?" Wolf asks the room.

"They're in the empty warehouse on Freeman Street."

"Get drones over there," Trevor directs.

"Why wouldn't you just go over there and get him?" I ask. This is crazy. The guy on screen does not look scary. We've been hiding from a man who wears sunglasses with diamonds encrusted in the corners. He looks like he could be a two-bit Elvis impersonator on an LA street corner.

The man on screen smiles wide as someone in the room shouts, "He's in."

The woman falls before him, and his chair rolls backward. The back of her head fills the screen. Her hands go to his waist. Apparently, we're about to watch this guy get a blow job. This is not the kind of surveillance I thought Arrow did.

# Locked and Loaded

Trevor

"Teams are in place."

Wolf headed down to the warehouse. I am at Arrow's offices overseeing the operation. We have multiple teams on the ground and some on standby. We looped in Logan, the one NSA contact I would trust with our lives. He pulled together a small, elite team for this operation.

We don't have sound, but I've been around Kane while he got a blow job before. I have a pretty good mental visual of the guy's eyes rolling into the back of his head as he shoves her head down and she chokes on him. I used to suspect the thrill of getting off in front of others drew him to the Asian sex clubs, but right now, he should be unaware he has an audience. If everything is going according to plan.

I tap my headset. "Logan, you there?"

"Yep."

"Tell them to cover his mouth and handcuff his hands. First thing."

"Repeat?" Wolf asks for clarification.

"Block his ability to relay commands," I clarify.

In my peripheral vision, I see Stella's confusion. We'll explain later.

To my right, on the small video monitors, aerial footage from the drones reveals a one-block radius. Tactical teams line the side of the building. I'd like to be with them, but today I'm strategic. And this should be an easy op.

One of our drones is heat seeking. I check the screen. The FBI has access to the same view. Six bodies on the ground floor. Two on the second. One on the southwest corner on the third floor.

On screen, Fiona's head jerks up. She licks her lips. Kane zips his pants and rolls his chair forward. There's action on his screen. Fiona bows down closer to the monitor, and we get a closeup of her slightly smeared mascara.

Fiona smiles, pointing. Her lips form the words, "How much did we get?" She's gleeful.

My focus alternates between the SWAT team on the ground, the streets that are cordoned off, the aerial view with the heat map, and the computer camera view. My skin tingles. This is it.

But as always, it's not the guy who's about to be busted that I'm concerned about. It's his minions and who he has on speed dial.

The heat map shows the downstairs of the building merge into a row of bodies. Someone at the end announces, "All clear."

We're in the building. No shots fired. Kane either hasn't inspired loyalty, or our ground units took them by surprise. I'd give anything to have a full video of that hall. I'll have to check the footage later. I need to see their facial expressions.

Kane lifts his sunglasses. He leans forward into the screen. He's catching on that something isn't right. My guess is he's noticing a bank account balance, the one he attempted to transfer funds to, isn't receiving matching numerics. But he did just loop the feds into one of his offshore accounts.

His dark, beady eyes widen, and his head snaps up. He must hear noises. Damn, I wish we had audio. But the visual shows it all. The shock.

The room erupts in applause. I train my attention on my partial view of Kane. I can't see his hands. I push by others, searching. There's no way Kane didn't foresee this as a possibility. No way he's grown that cocky. He's got an ego the size of Mount Rushmore, but… I push past the cubes to get closer to the television screen at the front of the room.

An FBI agent pulls Kane's wrists behind his back. Good. His hands are out of commission. No hand signals. He's out of view.

Logan's voice comes over the line. "We've got him."

Stella tugs on my sleeve as Wolf grins. Erik lifts Vivi up and kisses her. I wasn't even aware his wife was here. David spins Kairi around, and she laughs.

"Did you plan this?" Stella is still at my side. "Giving him the code was a trap?"

Erik pulls Vivi into his side and scans the room. It's his double-check for all the participants.

"Tell her," Erik says.

Stella is the one who has been the most out of the loop. I wanted to keep her out of it as much as possible. Maybe it's a holdover from my military days, but I'd prefer for her to not be seen as worthy of capturing for information. I've done my best to keep her at arm's length and made a point of announcing whenever possible that she didn't have security clearance.

"Kane's known our whereabouts since some time before the blackout. He bought a CIA officer. She's the one who sold us out."

"It's how you got shot." Her fingers graze over the spot on my shoulder. The skin where the bullet punctured is still angry. I'm wearing a shirt, but Stella knows my scars.

"Yep." I nod to Erik, Wolf, and Kairi. "We decided we'd been playing defense too long. Our options were to run again or go on the offensive. When we got a download of Kane's phone, thanks to Phantom, we discovered his current passions. Among them, building up a collection of rare wines. Erik found out about this wine festival and the online auction. He got Vivi's granddad to give Arrow an intro, then we did a bit of a PR splash to make doubly sure word got to Kane we'd be handling the security."

"But how did you know he'd come to you asking to change the auction code?"

"We didn't, really. But we knew he loved wine. The guy's got a colossal ego. He's been working his way up in the cybercriminal world. NSA has suspected a few of the international crime outfits have been taking part in some of the higher-end wine auctions. Driving the prices up to astronomical levels. Hundreds of thousands of dollars for a bottle of wine. Egos at play. Erik thought he'd bid like he's done at other auctions. Maybe hack it, do something to discredit our services. I expected he'd come after us during the weekend when we were busy. But he proved me wrong when he showed up and offered to clear the slate in exchange for inserting code. That was an unexpected play."

"Code?" Stella's deep blue eyes lock on mine. She's still confused, but I've got her in my arms. We're good. I brush my lips over hers. Conversations are abuzz around us. No one else is listening, but I finish the explanation for my girl.

"It can work like a backdoor. The way we set the auction up, a person has to have an account and payment information entered before they can participate. This auction has hundreds of wealthy individuals, trusts, and investment funds registered to bid."

"So, it was all about money?"

"I doubt it. We'll have to get in to see exactly which accounts he initially plundered. My bet is getting into the accounts for money was a step one. Once he cleared the funds and he deemed it safe, he probably had a plan to dig deeper. Maybe for ransom. My bet is he has some hackers stashed who were ready to go into phase two, and his ego was just big enough he might have even tried to attend the ball Saturday night."

"He'd never do that. If it was a masked ball, maybe…" Erik says.

"He's been in the States for two weeks. Didn't seem too scared of being caught."

Stella squeezes my arm, pulling my attention back to her.

"So, is this it? It's all done?"

"That should be it. It should be over."

"Then Ethan and I, we can move back to my place this weekend. You're going to be busy with this festival."

Her palm flattens on my chest, and she moves to step away. No doubt she's got a full work slate. Her attention is directed to her office door, not to the buzz of people and the radio updates from the men in the field.

"I'd rather you still stayed with me. As a precaution. Let's get past this." It's what I say. But the truth is, I've had them with me for two weeks. The idea of them moving out doesn't sit well. Besides, we're still FPCON Alpha in my book. The FBI will be all over Kane, but he's never been one to work alone.

# The One With a
# Game of Solitaire

Stella

Everyone in the office is all smiles. Most of our employees are on the festival grounds, which covers an entire swath of downtown Santa Barbara. A map hangs on the whiteboard inside the conference room with detail duty outlined. There's a list of VIPs, and coordination with their own security teams is occurring from our mass of cubicles.

Trevor has been in and out. He stopped in at lunchtime, closed my office door, and pushed me up against the wall. Not that I minded at all. His kiss had been possessive and needy. I'd been practically panting when he backed up, chest heaving, and pushed away. His phone vibrated, and I could hear a voice in his earpiece. He mouthed "tonight" to me and pressed his index finger to my lips.

For me, today has been much slower. Given Friday marked the start of the three-day wine festival, I blocked out the day so I could be wherever Arrow needed me. Trevor insisted he wanted me secure in our offices or his condo. That meant no meetings outside. And they had instructed us for the last two weeks that we were not to schedule meetings with outside vendors, following Alpha protocol. Our founding partners left no doubt as to their former-military background.

When my cell rings, it breaks my attention from solitaire. I'm five cards away from winning. I haven't played in ages, but I found myself unable to tackle the paperwork on my desk. There is a frenetic energy outside my office door, and I can't take part. I helped with the prep and the scheduling, and now the festival has begun and it's all streamlined execution. Unless something goes wrong, we're following a project plan.

My boredom let my thoughts stray, and I can't help but wonder if I really should hang out in Trevor's place this weekend. It would be an extended bout of uselessness, with Ethan and me both trapped in someone else's home. It was one thing when we had this big, bad boogeyman out there, but now all the Alpha rigamarole can be dropped. They caught the guy.

Playing house with Trevor has been fun. It's been more than fun, to be honest. Even though he gets up far earlier than I can consciously open my eyes, I love spending evenings with him. Ethan typically pounds up the stairs the moment we finish eating, and it has been nice to have someone to clean up with and decompress from the day. We found a healthy rhythm. But it is time to shift back to normal mode. Given Trevor will work all weekend anyway, it seems to me like today will be as good a day as any to make the change. Besides, I don't think Smelly ever comes out from under that bed. I moved his food and water underneath the bed out of concern for him.

My phone vibrates, and Ethan's photo fills the screen.

"Hey, hun. What's up?" I check my watch. A call at this time of day typically means he wants to hang with someone after school. Can I allow that? Shouldn't someone be there right now to get him?

"Is Hayes going to pick me up?"

"He's not there?" I'm up, halfway out of my seat.

"Not yet. Maybe he's just running late." I scan the bullpen and don't see him. "Let me check."

In the conference room, I review the assignment board. Picking up Ethan from school isn't listed. Erik's office door is cracked, and I can see Wolf and Kairi inside. They appear to be on a conference call.

There's no need for me to interrupt them. On top of security for the festival, they've been nonstop on calls with both the NSA and FBI. For all I know, maybe the CIA and a few acronyms I'm not familiar with. I grab my keys and head out the door.

Patel is on the phone when I enter the vestibule. I wave at her and push out the door. She might object, but I don't wait. I'll be fine driving to my son's school.

Traffic is light, and I pull in front of Ethan's school within twenty minutes of his call. One student wearing a hoodie sits on a bench. She scrolls through her phone. She's clearly waiting to be picked up. There's a huddle of four students splayed out on the grass. The bus and student parking lots are empty, but the faculty parking lot is still mostly full.

I pull out my phone and call Ethan. I'd expect him to be seated on a bench, like the girl in the hoodie. The call goes to voicemail. The school is pretty spread out. Entering the school doesn't make sense, because the moment I do, Ethan will probably come out another door.

I approach the girl. She's not familiar. She's wearing black nail polish and a ton of rings on her fingers.

"Hello?"

She doesn't respond.

"Hello?" No response.

I touch her shoulder, and she jumps. Her hoodie falls back, and that's when I see she's got in those blasted EarPods. She pulls one out and squints, probably seeing me for the first time.

"Sorry. Do you know Ethan Johnson?"

She nods. I can hear the music blaring from the white piece she's holding in her hand. The girl is going to lose her hearing listening to music that loud.

"Do you know where he is? I'm a little late picking him up."

"He already left."

"With who?"

"Guy in a black SUV." Hayes picked him up after all.

"Okay. Are you all right? Do you have a ride?"

One side of her lips curves upward, and she looks back down at her phone. "Yeah. My mom's about five minutes out."

That's when I see her phone and the app on it. She's tracking her mom.

I head back to my car and call Ethan again. It goes to voicemail, so I send a quick text.


Me: *U with Hayes? I'm at the school.*


I slide into the driver's seat of Trevor's Tesla. For the millionth time, I remember that I really need to go car shopping. He said this was a company car, but I've known for a while this is his personal car. Maybe that's something Ethan and I can do this afternoon. I've never been car shopping. It's something I'm sure Ethan, at fifteen, will gladly do with me. It's a better way of spending my time than playing solitaire, pretending to be busy while the office is abuzz.

I expect an instant apologetic response from Ethan. But there's no response. Taking a cue from the girl tracking her mom, I pull up my app to double-check Ethan's location. Only the app doesn't locate him.

Something is very wrong. Ethan always charges his phone, and he never turns it off. I try the app again. I tap the steering wheel. My nerves ignite. I scan the front of the school. I hope to see the doors open. For him to ramble out. His backpack slung haphazardly over one shoulder. The flag lifts in the breeze. Nothing. He's not here. Like the girl said.

My finger trembles as I press Trevor's name.

"Hey." He answers on the first ring. He sounds calm and collected. Muffled background noises sound through the line. He's busy, but bless him, he always answers when I call. I take a deep breath, determined to remain calm.

"Hi. I'm at Ethan's school. Does Hayes have him?"

"Hold." Silence fills the line. A white sedan pulls up, and the girl with the hoodie gets in. A teacher I recognize exits the building and waves as she crosses the street into the front teacher parking lot.

"Hayes isn't picking up. Why are you at the school? That wasn't the plan." He's stern. Serious. It does nothing to calm my swirling insides.

"He called me."

"Who?"

"Ethan." Now frustration and anger mix. "He asked if Hayes was still picking him up. I checked the job board. Picking Ethan up wasn't listed. I figured it was an oversight."

"So, you drove out there with no one? You're not supposed to be alone."

"Well, I am." I stop myself. Close my eyes.

"Where are you, exactly?"

"I'm still parked in front of the school. I talked to a girl. She said Ethan had gotten into a black SUV. It sounds like a company vehicle, but Ethan hasn't returned my call or text. And I tried to track him, but he's not online."

"Who signed for him?"

"Signed? This is high school. We don't sign kids out." My voice rises with indignation. "You've been here. You know how it works."

He curses. There are other voices. My eyes burn. My fingers tremble.

"Stella. Are you there?"

"Yes."

Through the windshield, there's a cloudless blue sky and palm trees. Inside my car, full-on terror takes hold.

"Listen. Patel is on her way. You are not to get in the car with anyone except Patel. Do you understand me? I don't want you driving. Get in the car with her. Do you hear me?"

"Oh my god." Reality crashes around me. "You said you got the guy."

"Listen to me. Stay with me Stella. I love you. You know that, right?" I nod as a tear escapes. "I love you. I love your son. We'll find him."

# Operation Rescue

Trevor

When I disconnect the call, Logan, Wolf, and Erik stare at me. Waiting. Local cops stand back in the hallway while two FBI agents photograph the crime scene. I left Arrow to visit the room where we arrested Kane.

*Motherfucker.*

I grit out the words and a few others limited to former SEAL vernacular.

Kane is in a holding cell awaiting transfer back to the East Coast. There are a slew of feds chomping at the bit for time with Kane. After his successful west coast blackout scheme, they want him locked up. The US isn't the only country that has an interest in putting him on trial. He's aware of this. Which means he probably has no plans to get transferred anywhere, and snatching Ethan might play into some elaborate plan of his.

"Kane has Ethan. Where is he?" I direct my question to Logan.

Logan's lips purse. He's thinking, but we don't have time. He needs to answer me.

"Give me a minute."

Obviously, Kane doesn't personally have Ethan. Spectre has him. And fuck me for not seeing this potential play. We had every single other person on safe ground. Hayes should have picked Ethan up and delivered him back to my condo.

Kane had one phone call with his lawyer. Unfortunately, we couldn't monitor that call. It's the one piece of this entire plan that I've hated. If it had been up to me, we would have had a device in that room and heard everything discussed. But the powers that be wouldn't allow it. No one wanted to risk him finding out and the violation of his personal rights being used to get his case thrown out.

The office location Kane rented is a live-work location. The building swarms with feds taking photos and dusting for fingerprints. Kane's not a loner, and there's an interest in those working for him. Kairi and Erik are in front of the computer Kane used this morning. The one that allowed us a bird's-eye view of the arrest. Erik is itching to get his hands on it.

I step back from the fray, observing. Logan, Erik's brother-in-law, is speaking to another agent, apparently negotiating. Technically, we're all on the same team, but when you get all these different bodies with different bosses, it can be difficult for the multiple teams to remember that. It's one reason I loved the seamlessness of our SEAL team. We each had a role, and we all had the same mission.

I don't know what Kane has planned, but in the back of my mind, it always felt too fucking easy. Logan is now on the phone, one hand over his ear to better hear among the hum of activity around us. Energy surges through my skin, through my arms and out my fingers. I observe the chaos. *Think.*

I mouth the word "tracker" to Wolf. He pulls up our dashboard of devices and flashes me his phone screen. I finger the one labeled SURFEJbdy.

It's not until the red dot appears on the map that I breathe more easily. Whoever has him didn't make him strip. And he's not far. He's still in Goleta.

Logan hangs up.

"This is where he's holding Ethan."

"Are you sure about that?" he asks.

"It's a tracker on his belt. I doubt his men would think of that. His phone is disabled. Is it possible they discovered the belt tracker and this is a trap? Of course. But it's possible this is exactly where he is."

"Okay. We'll surround the place. Do a fly-by with a heat-seeking drone. See what we're dealing with." Logan's thumb roams the map. "This looks like a residential area. We'll have to follow protocol."

I nod, but when Wolf's scary-ass blue eyes meet mine, without a word being uttered, I know he and I are on the same page. We'll let the FBI stake the place, but once we're done with Kane, I'm going in. Ethan's not staying with those fuckers any longer than necessary.

Logan checks his device. "I've got the location. And clearance for you to meet with Kane. Let's go."

Logan tears out of the room with Wolf and me on his heels.

Erik and Kairi shout after us, "We're coming, too."

They each have their own beef with Kane, so as long as they don't slow us down, I'm down with it. My thing with Kane and Spectre wasn't personal. I'd been hired to keep Erik safe. But now… threatening my woman and her son, that dipshit made it personal.

A dumbass ransom plan is the best-case scenario. Worst case is that Kane's arrest triggered an automatic release of his threats. And Ethan was the only one accessible. All of his other targets are with us or in our condo secured by armed guards. Ethan was the easiest to reach. It's clear I'm not the only one running the scenarios when I overhear Logan on the phone with his wife barking commands to get into a safe room.

My phone vibrates, and Stella's face shows on screen. Her mascara is smeared. Her cheeks are wet.

"Babe?"

"I'm with Patel."

"Stay with her."

She nods, and her lips curl inward. Her eyes are glassy. My heart cinches. She's crumbling. This is my fuckup.

"Babe…" I don't know what to say.

"Find Ethan."

*Fuck those tears.* "I will." It's a promise.

* * *

Logan jumps behind the wheel, and I take shotgun. The others crowd into the back seat. Tires squeal.

"Where is he?"

"At the police station being processed. FBI was preparing transport. He either had eyes on him, or that damn lawyer triggered his plan."

"He has unlimited means. It's possible he has a team coming to free him before or during transport."

"That's the only reason he's not already in transit." Logan has a headset on, and he takes calls as he tears through traffic. The red bulb on his dash flashes. Most cars follow the fucking law and pull to the right to let him pass, but a few are oblivious, and he curses as he whips around them.

"Here's the plan," Logan announces as the police station comes into view. "They're going to let us go in and meet with him. Everything's going to be recorded. They don't want us beating the shit out of him because they want to prosecute. They don't need his case getting thrown out. My boss is worried that's his plan. To get you guys wound up."

"What are *you* worried about?" I ask.

"That there's an extraction team coming. Or that he's going after my family, who are all the way on the fucking East Coast." Logan is married to Erik's twin sister. His fears are not farfetched. "But here's the deal. I'm standing guard outside that room. You guys go in, do whatever you need. See what the fucker wants. Go in with the assumption he doesn't know we've located Ethan."

Erik, Kairi, and Wolf are silent. Logan pulls up to the curb at the station, and we all take off at a run to the entrance. An FBI agent is at the door, waiting for us. He leads the way.

"He said old friends are on the way. And we didn't tell him," the agent says.

Hearing that unsettles me.

They have him in a room without windows and one door. There's a crowd of federal agents in the hallway. Logan grabs my arm as we approach.

"We need to end this. Don't fuck up prosecution's case. They're saying it's a tenuous case at best. We caught him red-handed in that room, but the connections to nail him for the blackout are weak. If we're going to put him away, this needs to stick."

I nod.

Inside the room, there's a wooden table, and Kane is handcuffed to it. He smiles wide when we enter, like he's greeting old friends at the neighborhood bar.

"Took you guys a while to get here, considering this town is pretty fucking small." His chair grinds against the concrete floor, and the sound grates. "Eh. Accommodations here are lacking. Think you can convince them to uncuff me? Leaning over this desk is straining my lower back muscles."

They stripped him of all his clothes. He's in the standard orange, which means there shouldn't be any devices on him, but the glint of gold in a back molar is new. I wouldn't put it past him to have something in a tooth. That's what I care most about —how he can communicate back to his team.

Erik ignores his request and approaches the table first. I move to a corner and run through a risk assessment. Wolf takes the other corner. Kairi wraps her arms around herself and stares at Kane like he's the boogeyman. But he's not. He's an out-of-shape sociopath. His power comes from the ability to pull strings. We've got him chained down, but can he still give orders?

"What do you want?" Erik leans over the desk, standing, forcing Kane to tilt his head up at an awkward angle.

"If it isn't Mr. Phoenix. What a fucking gay avatar name."

"T.J." He says Kane's first name, a name he hasn't gone by since grad school, with great calm. "Tell us what you want."

"Isn't that obvious?" He leans back but can't quite reach the back, so he shifts his weight. He grimaces, then with a look of pure hatred, says, "Have them uncuff me or the kid dies." His facial muscles relax, and he smiles again. It's like watching an actor on stage run through personalities. "Do you really think I can hurt you when you've got your two muscle men here? Me against them?"

Erik steps back from the desk.

"Logan."

Kane's smile erupts into one of pure joy.

"Can you uncuff him?"

Logan nods to a police officer standing in the doorway, and he steps up to the desk and unclicks both cuffs. Kane rubs his wrists.

"Isn't this more civilized?"

Erik follows Logan out, and I overhear him in a hushed tone tell Logan we need a dentist. And he needs to verify all of the onsite officers. He's thinking the same thing I am. There are a limited number of ways a man trapped in a room can communicate with the outside world.

Erik closes the door and leans back against it, crossing his arms.

"What's your end game?" he asks.

"End game? That's so sophomoric."

Erik exhales, his facial muscles frozen.

"What's your winning scenario?"

"Well, you see, if you backstabbing motherfuckers had been true to your word, we could have all been winners. Unlike you sons of bitches, I keep my word. Now you've double crossed me not once, but twice. And you, Erik, are my oldest friend. That hurts." He places his palm over his heart, his expression sad. He's believable. But the sadness morphs into apathy. "So, here's how it's going to play out. One by one, your loved ones will die. I've got teams assigned to take each one of them out. As promised, I keep my word." His fingers tap the desk. I lean closer, confirming it is indeed a flat surface. "Teams." He smiles. "Detailed plans. Once I believe you've all suffered adequately, I'll take you out, one by one."

He has confidence. Could it be psychosis at play? Delusions of grandeur? Yes.

"You already killed someone I loved." Kairi's voice cracks, but there's more anger in her tone than fear.

"And we might have been even, dear. Except here I sit, detained." His eyes widen. "You just don't learn, do you?" He glares at Erik. There's emotion in that gaze. But then he flips to a teasing tone to address Kairi. "I must say, I far prefer David to Lara. Lara whined too much for my taste. And she refused to go to strip clubs. But your man David, he'll go. But of course, you know that, don't you? He's planning to go to a strip club with his buddies before you guys get hitched. His bachelor party. And he already told you." He chews on the corner of his lip. His eyes narrow. "It's gonna hurt to lose someone so honest. Not that you are honest, are you? When you interviewed with us, it was as a CIA informant. Fucking cunt. You'll get your due." He glances around the room. "All of you will."

I don't know his game plan, but I believe he has one. Negotiating for his freedom hasn't come up. If anything, he's taunting us. Confirming he has surveillance on us. And Ethan is locked up with his men. I'll be damned if he's going to be the first pawn down in this sick bastard's grand plan.

"Logan," I say, not particularly loud. The door opens, confirming there's a pack of people outside this room listening. "Is there a more civilized room we could move to? Maybe one with food?"

Kane stands and holds his arm out. He looks so fucking happy I suspect he's going to break out in song. The guy loves karaoke. I've seen him hold that stance at karaoke bars.

"I love this guy. Mr. Surfer." My neck muscles flinch at the word. It's far too similar to the tracking device names I've chosen. But the similarity doesn't mean anything. "He knows how to treat an old friend. Or maybe he's just worried about his boobalicious beauty. You think Agent Tabitha Patel is going to be enough to keep her safe?"

My fist aches with a need to slam into his face. The guy comes up to my pecs. I could end his life with my bare hands.

"Logan?" My tone remains remarkably calm, considering my insides are an inferno. *Charlie Mike.* "Anyplace?"

He disappears. We all stand around. Tense. Wolf crosses his arms, and his watch faces out to the room. That's when I see it. Kane squints. Checking the time.

He has something planned. I exit the room. Logan is talking to the chief of police and an FBI agent.

"We need to move him. There's an extraction plan."

"We'll prepare a path and secure the perimeter," the police chief says.

"Can I get some alone time?" My question is to Logan. He gets me. His right hand has been fisted since Kane began dispersing threats.

When we re-enter the room, there are four solemn faces and one lunatic grinning. There's nothing more to say. He's waiting. And as the saying goes, sane can't talk to crazy, so the sane are staring him down.

Logan directs everyone out of the room.

To me, he says, "You've got ten minutes."

"Can't wait to see you all again," Kane calls. I don't miss the glare that replaces the faux smile. After the door clicks closed, he gives me his full attention. "Are you going to beat me up? If yes, I'm a little into choking these days. If you do it right, you can stimulate an orgasm. My dick gets hard when muscles like yours come around. I've already got a stiffy. Do you wanna check it out?"

There's a sound outside. Helicopter blades whip the air, creating a familiar heavy whoosh.

"Oh, my," Kane says with a delighted grin.

Red lights flash, and the sprinkler in the middle of the room pops down, dispersing water. Fire.

I raise my gun and aim it at Kane.

"Get up. Let's get you out of here. To safety."

"You know, that's what I love about you SEALs. You'd love nothing more than to put a bullet in my head, but you're going to do the right thing. You're going to get me to safety. Protect my life. I suppose you believe you'll get to heaven for doing the right thing. God, I love religious people." He grins and shakes his head as he traverses the room.

I aim the gun at him and instruct him to open the door. He does so, and the hallway is empty. There's shouting about the fire alarm.

Logan appears. He gives me a hand signal, directing me to the stairwell.

"To the stairs. On your right," I direct Kane.

Logan closes the door behind us. The back of his head covers the small square glass pane in the center of the door.

Kane steps down the stairs, one after the other, descending to the ground floor.

"Should've never fallen in love."

My teeth grind. "Move it," I command.

"I would've had jack shit to hold against you. But a busty redhead."

I point the gun at his back.

"Didn't read that as your type. Fiona told me. Didn't believe it at first."

My grip tightens on the gun. My finger itches.

"I could've gotten that for you back in Asia, you know."

I raise the gun.

"I always knew this was a possibility."

Aim at his head.

"That you couldn't play along."

I freeze on the steps. He continues descending.

"I'd hoped we could come to an understanding. But now here we are."

Shouts sound outside and down the hall.

Eight steps to the ground floor.

I pull the trigger.

He tumbles down the remaining stairs.

It's done.

The exit door on the ground floor opens. An FBI agent glances up and comes running. He pauses at the body.

"Tried to escape," I say.

Logan rounds the corner.

I hold a finger to my lips for silence. Point at my open mouth. We still don't know if that molar is a listening device.

"What's going on outside?" I ask.

"Helicopter fly-by. Media. Someone pulled a fire alarm."

Logan grabs the FBI agent and types a note on his phone.

There's a video camera in the top corner of the stairwell. I saw it before I descended the stairs. I don't care if I go down for this. That fucker wasn't going to let this die, and I'd rather spend the rest of my life behind bars than have him hurt Stella.

"Keep the prisoner here until the fire drill is over and we've determined the area is safe," Logan says loudly.

The agent nods and uses his phone to text. Logan waves at me, directing me to follow him.

Once we're out the door, I ask, "What was that?"

"Getting you to Ethan. I told him to keep it quiet that he's dead. We don't know what Spectre's orders are in the case of death."

"I'm worried that gold molar is a listening device."

"He's getting word out somehow," Logan agrees, texting as he hurries to a black SUV. "Get in."

As Logan speeds through city streets, the light on his dashboard flashing, I say, "Thank you."

"Thank you," he says.

"You can arrest me after we get Ethan."

"He was trying to get away." I side-eye him. "You did what you had to do." He swallows and glances out the window. "If you hadn't done it, I would have."

Kane might have been full of shit. He might have had no way out. But given Spectre's strength, the opposite could be true. By threatening our loved ones, by threatening *my* loved ones, he signed his death warrant.

Logan pulls up three blocks away from the neighborhood home we suspect holds Ethan. An FBI agent exits a standard-issue sedan. He flashes his badge and introduces himself.

"Special Agent Davenport."

The man is familiar to me. "Have we met before?"

"I was on site at the arrest earlier. I was also present at one briefing."

Right. I'm good with faces, not always names. But some of our meetings held so many faces we didn't play round robin with names, anyway.

"We searched the address you sent us. It's a rental." Logan pops the trunk and passes me Kevlar. Wolf rounds the street corner. His gear is already strapped on.

"We're not ready to storm the house," the agent says. I continue checking chambers and prepping. Wolf comes around beside me and follows suit. "We have more agents on the way."

Wolf hands me an extra clip of ammo, and I add it to my vest.

"Are you authorized to approach the home?"

I study the guy, determining how to best manage him.

"We're black ops. Anything goes sideways, it's on us." That's actually true for international operations, and it's when we're typically used.

"Black ops?" he repeats.

Logan shakes his head with annoyance. He wishes I didn't say that. But he slaps a hand on the agent's back and begins smoothing things over.

"Let's go," I say to Wolf. He hands me a headset, and I tap it on.

Kairi's voice comes across the line.

"Drone is in place. Four bodies are in the house. One is off alone. Two are close together. Probably downstairs. One is on the move. My guess is the one off alone is Ethan. Approach from the front of the house."

A car passes us but doesn't give us a second glance. We're both wearing black vests over our shirts, and I have infrared goggles hanging around my neck. But I'm not carrying a rifle, and my firearms are discreetly tucked away on my side. One has bullets, and one is loaded with tranquilizers. To the naked eye, they look like simple handguns. Still, if someone pays attention to us, they'd notice something was up. This is California. People rarely walk around with their guns.

"The front door is solid wood, no peep hole. The front windows have shutters that are flattened. Doesn't look like there are any cracks. Back of the house is a lot of glass. Definitely not the way to approach. There's an attached garage." It figures there's an attached garage. He didn't have to worry about someone noticing Ethan as he got him out of the car. "There's a narrow stretch on each side of the house."

"We're one block away," I say, letting Kairi know she needs to wrap up her reconnaissance summary.

"Windows on the sides have drapes. Not a great approach. There's a side door on the garage. I'd bet that's the best way to enter. And the heat map shows all the bodies are on the other side of the house."

"Wait, guys," Davenport huffs as he approaches. He's out of breath from jogging less than a block. He's also wearing a navy jacket, and I'd bet money the back of it has the big FBI letters on it. "We need to wait. Headquarters is debating media communications. They've already got a shit storm back at the police station. If media gets wind of the FBI swarming a residential address, this place becomes another shit show."

"Is the station being attacked?"

"No. Current working theory is he paid someone on the inside to pull the fire alarm and tipped off media for the helicopter swarm with the goal of expediting the transport. Then they'd attack the transport. Right now, Spectre is probably wondering why he's not being moved."

"You stay here, on the corner," I tell Davenport. Working theories are low priority. "We're going to take one loop around the block, and we'll be back."

I need to check for other vehicles. Kairi would have picked up on a roof sniper. It's apparent three houses down that this is a standard cookie-cutter neighborhood, filled with stucco homes and about enough width on each side of the house to drag a garbage can down. This place is a temporary holding location. It's not remote enough to be anything more. Or it's my worst fear and this is a setup. They found the tracking device, and this is a setup.

"That house backs up to a house with a swing set," Kairi says.

"These back yards are big enough to fit a swing set?" Lots in this neighborhood have been sliced and diced.

"Affirmative. And there's a kid who is outside swinging with his mom."

*Grand.* I tap my tranq gun and hold Wolf's gaze. He understands.

As we approach the house, Wolf tugs at my elbow and points to the ground. Tripwire. Experience has taught me they can tie those wires to traps or bombs. This one is probably just for an alert. Unlikely it ties to a bomb. But possible.

The door opens, and a tango with a lit cigarette hanging out of his mouth steps over the wire and onto the grass.

I pull the trigger. His hand slaps his bicep. The whites of his eyes increase in size for a nanosecond as he registers two armed men are feet away. Then he falls knees first, onto the tripwire.

*Fuck.*

Gun raised, I charge. He looks up, dazed. I remove his gun from his holster. He sits, slumped. Awake. Conscious but not overly mobile. I check him for any other weapons and his phone while Wolf keeps lookout.

He falls forward, and I check his pulse. Still beating. I roll him onto his back and tie his wrists. His eyelids are half open. He presents no present danger. I signal to Wolf. We can proceed.

But we don't know what that tripwire did.

I pause at the side door to slip on my heat goggles. Two bodies are on this floor. On the move.

I step over the doorway, searching the ground for any more tripwires. We have no background on these guys. No intel on who Kane hired stateside, nothing to indicate what tactics they are likely to use.

I round a corner. A man's back is to me. I shoot. He goes down, knees first. His hand flails backward, reaching for his gun. After tying his wrists, I remove his guns. I don't bother checking his pulse.

I take the stairs, knowing Wolf has my back. As I approach the landing, I hear another body fall from behind us.

Upstairs, there's a long hall. Using the goggle vision, I follow the heat.

Gun raised, I snap open the door.

Ethan is tied up, duct tape over his lips. His eyes are clear. Wide, but clear.

I check the closet. We're alone.

Within seconds, I cut the bindings, and he's free.

He stretches his lips and rubs his wrists. There are no signs of injury.

"You okay?" I scan him for injury.

"I screwed up. I shouldn't have gotten in that car."

"It wasn't Hayes?" I'd been half expecting Kane had bought Hayes.

"No, but he knew Hayes' name. Said he was covering for him and sorry for being late."

He rubs his neck, right above the t-shirt line. There's a red welt. "He had a needle. Injected me with something. I woke up here."

Wolf ducks his head in. "FBI's inside. He okay? Need a medic?"

"I'll take him to the hospital, but I think he's good. They shot him with something. Hayes didn't pick him up. Spectre did."

"There's an FBI agent outside who wants to tear us new ones for entering."

My thumb presses against the red mark on Ethan's neck. He grimaces. The needle went straight into muscle. It's going to be sore.

"I told him you had family in here. I think he gets it."

I don't really care if he gets it or not. Wolf and I are both former SEALs. None of those agents arriving would have been better at this rescue than Wolf and me. And it could have been a setup.

I ruffle Ethan's hair. "Let's get you out of here. Your mom wants to see you."

# THE LAST ONE

STELLA

Patel ushers me into the emergency room entrance of the hospital. Down the hall, Trevor stands beside Ethan, talking to a nurse at admissions. The room blurs the second I see my son, and I break into a run.

"Mom. Hey. I'm okay. Really." He's so much taller than I am, and his arm drapes around my shoulder as my son comforts me. I pat him all over, checking his cheeks, his eyes, his arms, searching for any sign of injury. Trevor said he was okay, but…

"Where did they inject the tranquilizer?"

He points to his neck. Then he laughs. He actually laughs.

"Mom, chill. It's okay. I swear. Like, I don't even remember much. I wasn't awake for long at all before Trevor got there. It was freaky. But I'm fine."

Tears block my vision. I can't stop touching him. His arms. His cheeks.

"Mom. It's okay."

"Okay. Okay." I swipe at my face. He's clearly fine. But there's this bulge of emotion, and he's okay…he's really okay. He's laughing. That means he's okay.

"I am thirsty, though. Feel a little out of it."

I brush my hand over his cheek, over his forehead. He leans into my touch, and I wrap him in my arms, hugging him.

A man in a blue nylon coat steps up to Trevor. He's telling him something. He backs away as the nurse leads Ethan and me to a private section farther back with a hospital bed and a curtain separating us from others.

The nurse says a doctor will be with us shortly, and Trevor joins us.

"Is everything okay?" I ask him.

"We found Hayes. They shot him with a tranq gun. In his apartment."

"But he's okay?"

"Yeah. It's interesting they used a tranq gun."

"Why?"

"They could have killed him. They weren't out for blood." Trevor doesn't say this like it's good news. Somehow, this bothers him.

"Those guns they had were real," Ethan says.

Trevor nods, and I grab Ethan's hand and hold on. Trevor links his fingers with my other hand. Touching seems to help.

"Ethan Johnson. Where's my son?" The reception desk is far away, yet Jason's booming voice reaches us.

"You called Dad?" Ethan asks.

"I had to." Dread for the scene he's about to make pools in my stomach. He has every right to see his son. But once he's seen him, if he's screaming or acting out of line, I will pull him down the hall and tell him to get his shit together.

"What the fuck?" Jason flings back the curtain, and his gaze locks not on our son, but on my hand linked with Trevor's. "This guy endangered our son, and you're holding hands with the fucker?"

"Dad, I'm okay. It wasn't his fault. And he saved me."

"Saved you? What, like, he broke in and…" Jason trails off as he observes the gun holster on Trevor's waist. He removed the gun before entering the hospital, as he's not an official federal agent, but he left the holster on.

The FBI agent who spoke with Trevor earlier finds us.

"Hello," he says to all of us. "Logan wanted me to see if you could join us. He said if you're needed here, that's okay."

"We're okay," I reassure him.

Trevor brushes a kiss across my lips, nods at Ethan, and steps away with the FBI agent.

"What the fuck is going on, Stella?"

"Dad—"

"Don't fucking interrupt me."

"Jason." I am calm. I am strong. And there is absolutely no way I am letting him pull this shit. "Let's talk down the hall."

"We can talk right here. What the fuck is wrong with you? Our son is about to see a doctor, thanks to you and your choices."

"Jason. We need to talk down the hall because what I am going to say to you shouldn't be said in front of our son."

I step out into the hall and don't check to see if he's following me. I don't need to because I can hear his dress shoes clicking against the linoleum. Once we are out in the reception area, I stop near a security guard.

"I could totally take him away from you. After this shit, there isn't a judge who wouldn't give me custody."

"Jason, he's fifteen. There isn't a judge who wouldn't talk to him and ask him what he wants. But, aside from that, Trevor is a former SEAL who assisted the National Security Agency and the FBI in apprehending one of the FBI's most wanted. I don't think any judge is going to come down too harshly on my choice in dating him. But I've saved all of your texts to me for the last ten years. I took a photo of my damaged wall when you slung open the door. I could go on and on. Do you really want to take this to court? And after ten years, are we really still having this discussion? Yes, it used to scare me senseless. But now I can afford to pay a lawyer. Is this really what you want?"

Jason's skin turns an ugly beet color. His neck bulges. I really cannot believe I was ever married to this man.

"I'm glad you came out to check on your son." I share this for communication purposes and to calm him. I don't want him going back to see our son with rage-soaked skin. "As I texted you, he's okay. They did give him a tranquilizer. The doctor is going to check him out. They may take his blood and test it. You can join me when we meet the doctor, and we can ask our questions together."

His nostrils flare, but his skin color lightens. My calm combined with a nearby security guard are effective.

"I understand you were scared. I was terrified. But he's okay." It is on the tip of my tongue to apologize, but I won't.

He never apologizes; why should I? But more than that, the bastard might spin an apology in court. And I don't really know how this would fare in court. Ethan is at the hospital while under my care. My fingers trembled when I called Jason. I didn't know where he was, or how he would take it. When I called, he made it clear I was interrupting his time at the nearby Ojai spa. But to his credit, concern for his son did override his annoyance.

Jason glares. I hold my ground. Wait. Without a word, he leaves. I don't have any idea where he's going. I return to Ethan to await the doctor.

I am with Ethan for a good fifteen minutes before Jason joins us. I have no idea if he called his lawyer or what he did, but when joins us, he's back to his pasty normal.

Shortly after Jason returns, the doctor clears Ethan and says we can go home as long as we keep a close eye on him. As I'm reviewing the paperwork with all the potential side effects, Trevor joins us. He stands at the edge, away from us, and I step up to him, wrapping an arm around his waist.

"The doctor says we can go. Everything okay?" He pulls me tight up against his side, and I relax into him.

"Now it is." He presses his lips to my forehead.

Ethan hops off the bed. Jason strides over and holds out a hand.

"I hear you saved my son. Thank you."

Ethan and I watch as the two men stare each other down while conducting common civility. I don't know if Ethan is surprised by this mature side of his father, but I certainly am.

When we return to Trevor's condo, we discover Vivi, Erik's wife, stocked our refrigerator with dinner options and a note to let us know if she can do anything. Ethan claims a spot on the sofa, and Astra jumps up and lies beside him.

Trevor takes my hand and pulls me back into his bedroom.

"I'll be out late tonight. There are a lot of questions to answer about this case. I killed Kane earlier today."

"You did?" I search him for any indication of how he's taking it. Yes, the military trained him to kill, but it's not something he does lightly. He values life. I caress his jaw, and he takes my hand and places his lips in the center of my palm.

"He threatened you and Ethan. I'll do anything to keep you both safe. We don't know if he may have any retaliation instructions."

"What do you mean?"

"He threatened us all. It's conceivable he had instructions to carry out those threats in case of death. I doubt it. More than that, I doubt he would inspire the loyalty required to carry out postmortem instructions. But, just the same, stay here. Security is posted outside. Everyone else is next door."

"Of course. We'll stay as long as you need us to."

"I love you, Stella. Always." Those blue eyes fill with emotion, and my heart overflows. He would do anything for us, and he is everything to me.

"I love you, too." His forehead presses to mine, and we stand there, holding each other. Deep within, love circulates, warming me, binding me with the man holding on to me. There is no doubt. This is not a fling. He is my forever.

# Epilogue



Two months later

Trevor



The lights blink on, and the captain speaks overhead.

"We are approaching Los Angeles, current temperature seventy-two degrees and sunny. The seatbelt lights are on and will remain on until we land. Thank you for flying British Air."

I check the time. One of the issues with living in Santa Barbara is there are no direct international flights. You have to connect from either Los Angeles or San Francisco. Before, the fact registered as an annoyance. Now, impatience feeds a growing irritation.

Wolf said he'd charter a private jet, but I'd insisted it wasn't worth it. I spent the last two weeks in Syria on a protective detail for a CIA officer's family. One of our employees lost his leg on the exact same assignment, so I'd needed to fly out and fill in, plus ensure he had proper medical care. We'd flown him to Germany for his surgery. The whole ordeal had been emotional and exhausting, and now all I want is to get home and hold Stella.

Less than three hours. My connecting flight boards in an hour and half, which will leave me time to eat, stretch my legs, and call Stella. I close my eyes, and I not only see her, I feel her. My fingers itch to touch her, my arms ache to wrap around her. I want to breathe her in, hold her close, sink into her.

My married team members used to get all moody toward the end of a mission. They'd get these serious expressions and get pissed if something extended the duration of the assignment. I didn't get it. Thought they were pussies. Now I get it. My need is visceral.

The plane bounces on the runway and I, like the other passengers, switch my phone off airplane mode. Texts come through in a flurry.

Stella: *Have a safe flight! I love you.*

Me: *Landed. Can't wait to see you. Also, curious about a surprise Ethan mentioned?*

Stella: *That boy cannot keep a secret. What did he say?*

· · ·

Me: *Only that there is one. Don't worry. Your secret's safe. But the only welcome home gift I need is you.*

Three dots appear and disappear. I glance down. She's typing a long message.

Me: *Deboarding. I'll text when I'm down in customs.*

The plane I'm on is enormous, and every single one of us has to file through customs. I'm in first, so I have a jump on the others, but nevertheless, I charge off the plane and through customs like it's a race. By some miracle, there's no line, and I breeze right through.

I head straight to baggage so I can pick up my bag, then go through the whole process of checking it for the short leg remaining.

A woman by baggage has me doing a double take. I blink. My heart spurs forward in a rush, and my chest borders explosion.

*No fucking way!*

She squeals and runs forward, jumping into my open arms. I hold her close, her legs around my hips, my mouth to her ear, my hand wrapped up in her hair. A calm washes over me, and I pull back, so I can look into those deep blue eyes.

"Surprise! Figured I'd come down here and surprise you. We can drive you back in about the same time that connection would take."

My lips fall on hers and kiss her with everything I have. This is the welcome home I need. The welcome I've never had before, and the one I'll never give up.

The world blacks out. All I care about is the woman in my arms.

"God, I've missed you," I say against her lips.

She squirms against me, and I groan. She giggles.

"We're in the airport."

I glance around, and the place is packed with people. One or two are looking our way. I don't give a damn. But Stella does, and she scrambles down. She clutches my hand, and as we stand waiting for my luggage, I pull her back up against me and nibble her ear.

"Did you leave Ethan at home?"

"No, he's here. Back at the car." A mix of emotions comes with that, because I wouldn't mind having her to myself. Maybe find a hotel to check into, but I've missed Ethan too. It'll be good to see him.

"Any word from Wolf?" Wolf is off in Mexico, working a case that's unusual for Arrow.

"Kairi mentioned he's got the resources he needs. You'll have to get the full update from her. Tomorrow." She squeezes me. I get the message. We have other priorities.

"And Astra?"

"Oh, Astra has had some adjustments."

"Smelly making gains on her territory?"

We've been going back and forth between Stella's place and mine, but mostly we've stayed at my condo. While I've been out of the country, Stella and Ethan have stayed at my place.

We're through the woods with the Spectre situation. Spectre essentially disbanded. A subgroup has formed and rebranded themselves with a new name, Unavowed. The FBI and NSA are watching them, but with no greater emphasis than any other crime syndicate.

"Did you get to check out that listing I sent over?" Stella and I are looking at places for all of us to live that are closer to Ethan's school.

"I did. We have an appointment to see it together in the morning."

My bag arrives, and we charge out of the airport. Blinding bright sunshine and blue sky greet us. The road is packed with cars. Stella leads the way to the nearby lot with hourly parking.

Her auburn hair swishes as she glances back. Her fingers are linked through mine. She's smiling, and there's color in her cheeks. The blue strands along the base of her neck are no more. She's one hundred percent auburn. For now. She pulls on my fingers, encouraging me to speed up.

We round the corner on Stella's small SUV. It's one she purchased shortly after the Kane fiasco. Ethan rounds the side of the car, grinning from ear to ear. In his arms is a furry fluff ball.

"What is this?" I ask. Ethan has been volunteering with Sierra at the Santa Barbara animal shelter. He'd asked a week or so ago if I'd have a problem if he got a puppy. I didn't say yes or no. He's not my kid, but I reminded him he'd be heading off to college, and he probably couldn't bring a dog.

Stella's exuberant smile matches Ethan's. I stop and look back and forth between the two of them.

"You love Astra so much. And she's all alone, without a friend. This puppy is a husky. He's amazing. And she and Astra get along. And so... we thought she'd be the perfect welcome home gift."

"Did you, now?" I grin like a fool. I shouldn't be grinning. That dog is as impractical as they come. All that hair, and I'm not even sure it can run with me.

Ethan carries the squirming puppy over to me. It's damn cute. Long, soft hair, giant paws, bright blue eyes. Ethan hands her off to me, and I bend and set her on the ground. She immediately places her front paws on my thigh.

"You two." I grin and shake my head. They pulled a fast one on me is what they did. I hadn't actually agreed to another dog, but now this one is a gift. I pet the top of her head. Her fur is soft. Astra's is silky and thick. This puppy's fur is softer than anything I think I've ever felt. Her sharp teeth gnaw at my finger, and I pop her nose. It doesn't faze her. She goes right back for my finger.

"Well, this is a surprise," I say, standing, holding the leash. "What's her name?"

"It's your dog," Stella says, "so you get to name it."

"Sure, it's my dog," I say, still grinning. I can't even fake annoyance. I do love dogs. And as a kid, I begged for one. Now I have two. "What did they call her at the shelter?"

"I called her Charlie," Ethan says. The first phrase that comes to mind is Charlie Mike. *You gotta Charlie Mike. Continue Mission.* It's military lingo, but not a bad phrase to have in the back of your mind at all times.

"Charlie it is," I say. "She gonna be good for the drive back?"

"She rides in the back seat with me. She's great. I've got some rawhide bones for her. She's teething."

"Yeah, she's got some sharp ones."

Ethan and Charlie climb into the back seat. When I load my suitcase up and close the back hatch, Stella leans against me and scrunches her nose.

"You're not upset, are you? Ethan thought it would be a great gift for you."

I chuckle, kiss the tip of her nose, and squeeze her ass. The warmth coming out of me is like nothing I've ever experienced. I'm so fucking happy, it's unbelievable. It's one of those moments that in an out of body experience you recognize you never want to forget. You want to relish the moment and package it up in your lifetime memory bank. A blue-sky mental photograph.

These two, they're my family. And god, I've missed them. I hold her close, breathe her in, listen to a horn off in the distance, and snap that photo. Her soft body in my arms, the warm sunshine on my skin, the burning warmth pulsing from my center, and I savor all of it.

# Bonus Epilogue

A Twisted Path

Trevor

Three years later

The suitcases stacked in the middle of our living room rouse far too much emotion. Stella doesn't want me to load them in the car tonight, in case they discover more that needs to be packed. But I don't want to look at them, so I stack them in the mudroom right outside the garage. Stella calls it the mudroom because she says I track in mud. I'm fastidious and careful to leave all the mud outside the garage, but I won't argue with her about a name.

We moved into this house about two and a half years ago. We're close to the beach and close to the Arrow gym. We've continued to grow Arrow, and we currently have projects and teams around the globe. At some point, every single one of our agents goes through training at our facilities. Most of the field agents we hire are already well-trained, but staying on top of your game requires work and continual skill maintenance, no matter who you are or what kind of background you have. I love staying on top of my training and keeping our guys fit and ready.

Spectre officially no longer exists. Does that mean we arrested every member? Not by a long shot. Cybercrime organizations, like the mafia of old, are nimble. You cut off the head, they regroup and reassemble. We worried for a while that some disgruntled members might angle for revenge or follow some twisted orders to avenge Kane's death, but nothing ever happened. I suspect the men he hired weren't particularly loyal and if they spent time with him recognized him for the mentally unstable individual he was.

Ethan didn't suffer any fallout from the kidnapping. Nothing physical or emotional. If anything, he carried anger directed to himself for getting in the car until I told him to knock it off. He did what anyone else would have done. But the experience did impact his life trajectory.

Tomorrow, we'll be delivering Ethan to the airport for his departure to the Naval Academy. I didn't go to the Naval Academy, but given I'm a former SEAL, his father sure did blame me for his choice. I like to think I influenced his decision to some degree, but I think some of the long conversations he had with Wolf about his experiences at the institution had a greater influence. I can't imagine what this house will feel like without him lumbering about. Don't want to think about it.

He's out on the beach with Sierra, Jenn's daughter. Stella still swears they are like siblings, but I don't buy it. I'd bet money that the goodbye they have going on out on the beach isn't anything I want to walk in on, which means I'm inbound, walking through the house, searching for Stella.

She's not downstairs, so I head upstairs. The door to our bedroom is wide open. There's an unmistakable sound of vomiting that curls my stomach.

"Stella?"

The bathroom door is open, and farther down, the toilet room door is partially open. I charge to it, but a plastic pregnancy test on the counter with two straight blue lines halts my progress.

"Trevor, can you grab me that hand towel?" Stella points to my right. I get the towel in question and hand it to her.

"Are you—"

"Hey, Trevor." Wolf's wife is down on her knees, beside the toilet. Stella pats her head.

"We'll give you some privacy. I'll set the mouthwash out."

Stella pushes me out the bathroom and closes the door behind her.

"She hasn't told Wolf yet. You can't say anything."

"She came here to take the test?"

"I met her for lunch, remember? She got sick at the restaurant too. I bought the test, and we were closer to here. She thought she had a stomach bug."

"But you knew?"

"I suspected." She smiles and shrugs. "I feel for her. There's nothing worse than that nausea." She pauses, her hand on my forearm.

"Did you think?" She stares up at me. "Are you disappointed?"

I wrap an arm around my wife's back and pull her up against me.

"Did I think for a fleeting second you were pregnant? Maybe. I didn't really have time to register the scene. Am I disappointed? No. I told you a million times before, and I'll tell you again. There are plenty of ways to contribute to others' lives. You don't have to be the sperm donor."

She laughs, but I mean it. My next-door neighbor growing up, an old, retired vet, had more to do with who I am today than my biological father or any of the men my mom brought around. And I'm around young men all the time now, as a coach and a mentor. I don't need to be a father, but I need the woman in my arms.

She doesn't know it, but I bought a place for us on an island. It's for our next phase. We're nowhere close to retirement, but I have dreams of what life will be like for us in this next phase. Sure, we would've made a baby work. But I'm happy for us to be the aunt and uncle my friends' kids count on, and to find our own path forward.

Wolf's wife exits the room. Stella asks her if she'll be okay to drive, and she says she will.

When Stella returns, I ask her, "Are you packed?"

"Me?"

"Pack a suitcase," I tell her.

"But he's going—"

"And we are, too. You've got a bucket list. We've got buckets to fill."

"But what if he—"

I don't really want to ruin the surprise, but... "Our first stop is Annapolis. I hear they've got an amazing bed and breakfast for us to check out."

I manned up and offered for Jason to join us in Annapolis. But three months after Stella and I got married at the justice of the peace, he had a blowout wedding at the Ritz. He has a young daughter, and we haven't seen him around much, which is fine by me. Ethan stops by to visit them some, but he hasn't spent the night over there since Jason remarried. Needless to say, I wasn't surprised when Jason said he couldn't make it to see his son off.

Wolf assured me we wouldn't be the only parents dropping off kids or checking in on them. And I figure Stella's going to be emotional, so we'll hang in the area. Hell, I'll probably be emotional. I spend a lot of time with Ethan.

Annapolis is a gorgeous area, and we'll enjoy checking it out. Then I'm taking her to our new secret hideaway where we can snorkel, and maybe I'll talk her into learning to SCUBA dive.

"I thought Wolf said we didn't need to drop him off ourselves."

She presses her delicious body against me and gazes up at me with a love that warms me through and through.

"We don't need to. But I figured you'd want to. And I figured if I made it a surprise, it would be a good surprise. A happy surprise."

"You know I'm still going to cry, right?"

"Oh, I know. And Ethan made me promise not to get us seats near his on the plane."

"He did not. That bugger."

"It's okay. We're in first, and he's in coach. That'll teach him to ask for seats apart from us in the future." She laughs. It's a full-throated laugh. And yeah, we're both emotional as hell. But we're happy.

Life is full of chapters, and Stella and I are about to kick off a new one. For my part, I'm buzzed and excited.

When I look back over the years, my team and I, we've traveled a twisted path, but it led to a good place. We're happy. And happy is good. Like a fine wine, happy should be savored.

Thank you so much for reading *Savor*! If you enjoyed the story, I hope you'll take a moment to leave a review. Five-star reviews truly do sell books, bringing me closer to the day when I might be able to give up my "day job" and do this full time. So I'm deeply grateful for them.

This wraps up the Twisted Vines series, but the crew continues on in the Arrow Security Series.

Wolf's story, currently titled *Better to See You,* will release this fall as a spin-off from the Twisted Vines series. Keep an eye out for it in 4Q, 2022.

If you missed Erik's story, which kicks off the Twisted Vines series, it's available here Crushed.

# ALSO BY ISABEL JOLIE

**Coming this Fall 2022...**

Better to See You (Wolf and Alexandria)

How to Survive a Holiday Fling (Oliver and Kate)

**The Twisted Vines Series**

Crushed (Erik and Vivi)

Breathe (Kairi and David)

Savor (Trevor and Stella)

**Haven Island Series**

Rogue Wave (Tate and Luna)

Adrift (Gabe and Poppy)

First Light (Logan and Cali)

**The West Side Series**

When the Stars Align (Jackson and Anna)

Trust Me (Sam and Olivia)

Walk the Dog (Delilah and Mason)

Lost on the Way (Jason and Maggie)

Chasing Frost (Chase and Sadie)

Misplaced Mistletoe (Ashton aka Dr. Bobby and Nora)

# End of Book Gratitude & Wandering Thoughts

So, when I originally jotted down ideas for this book, it was tentatively titled *Screwed*. As Breathe evolved, so did this one.

By the time I got around to writing Savor, I needed something fun. And, for me, Savor is fun. Maybe I should have gone darker or more serious, but so far the feedback I've received is that other folks enjoyed this one. Maybe others need something a little lighter these days too.

If you see any of the social media posts or ads for Savor…you'll definitely see I had *fun* creating the marketing.

My husband told me that no one wants to read about a 40-year-old woman. I disagree. First, I'm not entirely buying there's a world of difference between 30 and 40, and second, *representation*! But he has given me cause for concern so I'll be crossing fingers and doing a nervous dance when this one goes out. Maybe I need to stop going down these iffy trails… we'll see.

Kelley R spent time with me sharing tales from the HR trenches, and we brainstormed some of the new company challenges. I truly appreciate her spending time with me and answering my questions. Amy Claire Major, Lori Whitwam and Jessica Meigs all played important roles in editing. By the time Jessica gets it, as proofreader, I'm always amazed when she finds the random extra spaces. I'm always like… "how can you see that space?"

For this cover, I found the stock image of the guy with the puppy. And sent it to Elizabeth Mackey (who did all the covers for this series and Haven Island) and asked if she could make that image work. And she did. I love it because of the puppy. (Remember…I needed *fun* when I wrote this). My husband, for the record, hates this cover. One person said it might be mistaken for Shape Shifter romance… I hope not. *shrug* If it bombs, I'll change it. But thanks go to Elizabeth for working with me on this one.

To all my readers — thank you so much for sticking with me and for reading *Savor*. I sincerely cross my fingers and look up to the stars in hopes you enjoy it.

# About the Author

Isabel Jolie, aka Izzy, lives on a lake, loves dogs of all stripes, and if she's not working, she can be found reading, often with a glass of wine. In prior lives, Izzy worked in marketing and advertising, in a variety of industries, such as financial services, entertainment, and technology. In this life, she loves daydreaming and writing contemporary romances with real, flawed characters and inner strength.

Sign-up for Izzy's newsletter to keep up-to-date on new releases, promotions and giveaways. Or stalk her on your favorite platform. And no, she's not on TikTok. Her teen daughters tell her to *Stay Away*…